SHE
MYSELF
AND I

For Jakob and Lucas

Cataloging-in-Publication Data has been applied for and may be obtained from the Library of Congress.

ISBN 978-1-4197-2570-8

Text copyright © 2017 Emma Young
Book design by Siobhán Gallagher

Printed and bound in the U.S.A.
10 9 8 7 6 5 4 3 2 1

Amulet Books are available at special discounts when purchased in quantity for premiums and promotions as well as fundraising or educational use. Special editions can also be created to specification. For details, contact specialsales@abramsbooks.com or the address below.

ABRAMS The Art of Books
115 West 18th Street, New York, NY 10011
abramsbooks.com

SHE
MYSELF
AND I

EMMA YOUNG

AMULET BOOKS
NEW YORK

1.

WHAT REALLY MATTERS is *who you are on the inside, not the outside*. If someone tells you this, you know it means one of two things. They don't think you're that good-looking, either. Or they're worried you might be falling for the fiction of fashion magazine cover girls and starting to believe that all that matters in life is the skinniness of your legs or the poutiness of your lips. My legs *are* pretty skinny, in fact. What I can see of them. Which isn't much, given that I can move little below the neck, and that I'm looking at myself not in a mirror but a window.

It's a plate glass window that reaches from the vinyl flooring to the ceiling, and it was the first significant thing that I noticed about this room—so different from my bedroom in my dark, terraced London home. The second thing: no British channels on the TV, apart from BBC America. Third: no mirrors. New health and safety guidelines, according to Jane, the sturdy, sweet-faced nurse who showed me around.

"Bollocks," I whispered, not that quietly, but quietly enough that she couldn't be absolutely certain of what I said. I knew exactly why they didn't want me to look at myself. What I didn't understand was why she didn't just tell me. It's not as though I'm unused to significantly harder truths.

"I'll be your mirror," Dad said. And I knew he would, in a way. Unlike Mum, he's never been much good at hiding his emotions. Every tiny deterioration in my physical condition has been reflected step-by-inevitable-step in his sad, brown eyes. As a metaphorical mirror, he's exceptional. As an actual mirror, not so much.

"I need to know," I told Dr. Leon Monzales, "that everything you tell me will be the truth—or what you honestly believe is the truth."

The first time the chief surgeon came to visit me here in my room was the afternoon I arrived in Boston. Monzales has a daytime-soap doctor's voice. Husky, with a Mexican accent. He has a daytime-soap doctor's face and body, too. I've seen enough daytime TV these past few years to be pretty damn sure of my judgment on this. Broad shouldered, square jawed, with wavy dark hair, brushed back.

I was in my voice-activated chair over by the chest of drawers, on which Mum had laid out a few things she seemed to think would make the place feel more like home—or at least a little less like a modified-five-star-hotel-room prelude to a slasher movie. A stuffed squirrel with a faded Minnie Mouse sticker on its tail—my first soft toy. A silver-plated candle in my favorite citrus-woody scent. And a photograph that used to be on the bookcase by my bed: a picture I took of Mum and Dad and my brother, Elliot, standing in spring sunshine by the Gothic ruins of Whitby Abbey.

Dr. Monzales was on an oatmeal-colored, regular-person's upholstered chair. His shirtsleeves were neatly rolled up, his muscular hands resting in his lap. Judging by his posture, we could have been discussing summer vacation plans or whether nuts make or break a chocolate brownie rather than the imminent end of my life as I know it.

"Why are there no mirrors in my room?"

"Oh," he said. "Yes, I can see how that might seem a little bit strange."

"It doesn't seem strange. You don't want me to look at myself."

"I—we—I don't have a policy on that. Our psychological team felt that perhaps it might help with the adjustment."

"The nurse—Jane—told me it's because of new health and safety guidelines."

Monzales successfully combined an expression of surprise with one that suggested *of course she did*. "There's more than *physical* health and safety to think about, Rosa."

"My mind is okay."

"I know that," he said.

"You can leave my mind to me."

He raised his hands in surrender. "Rosa. Do you *want* mirrors in your room?"

I was on the point of saying yes—mostly, I realized, because I was irritated by the nurse. But did I *really*? At home, I avoid mirrors. Sometimes when I close my eyes, I can still half remember myself as I used to be.

"The psychological healing process, as well as the physical, you know—perhaps it will be easier this way," Monzales said.

"Will I really be *healed*?" I asked him.

He hunched forward, palms spread, like a saint in a painting offering a blessing. "Of course, that is what we've all planned for so assiduously."

But is it possible? A broken bone can be *healed*. A gash can be *healed*. But *me*? Is the surgery he is planning something that could legitimately be described as an attempt to heal? Not exactly. *Try to be precise, Rosa.* (When I talk to myself, I often hear Mum's voice in there, too.)

Anyway, this is a deviation, but a little explanation, at least, for why, three full weeks after that conversation about mirrors and healing, I'm sitting as close as I can to the vast window that separates my brightly lit hospital room from the darkened sky.

Three weeks.

It's March 15. 5:48 P.M.

At 4:30 A.M. on March 16, I will be wheeled away for the presurgery meds, then obliterating anesthesia.

I have less than eleven hours left.

Focus.

I peer at the window, and I see . . .

My legs. Beneath the black cotton trousers, they're emaciated. My shapeless waist.

My acceptable bust. Though a lot of good *that* does me.

My face? It's hard. And I don't mean because I'm looking in a window.

I'll have to take this in steps.

Below my room, running the length of this wing and separating it from Boston Harbor, is a narrow park. A couple of kids are out there, straining against their puffer jackets as they put the finishing touches on a lopsided snowman with what looks to be the plastic sheath of a hypodermic for a nose.

A man is watching. Beside him is a woman, her long dark hair loose around her shoulders. Even from here, three stories up, I can see that she's looking not at the kids but at a boy about my age who's over on one of the benches near the statue of Pan. I can't tell if the benches are inscribed with the names of dead patients who *loved the view* or *felt at peace* in this park, but I expect they are. I've been in enough hospitals by now.

The boy's wearing a heavy coat, but his slim body is contracted from the cold—or something, anyway, because his arms are tight against his sides and his gaze is fixed on the ground. His breath comes in clouds. It merges with the mist that's drifting in from the harbor. He raises his head. I'm caught. My heart freezes. He's looking *right at me*. Then he jumps from the bench and strides away.

Beyond the park, the lights of tourist boats out on the harbor and the city skyscrapers are twinkling away. I see the flash of planes taking off from Logan International Airport, soaring up and right across my field of view. I try to resist the impulse to wish myself on board one of them.

At last, I rein in my focus. And I see *me*.

My pulse jerks. Leaps. Jerks, like a corrupted download.

The reflection is far from perfect. My sharp nose and small chin are captured quite clearly, but my gray-white skin blends with the sand-colored wall behind me. My brown eyes appear black, and my dark blond hair fades into a hazy nothingness. In this window reflection, I seem—I don't know how else to describe it—*spectral*. It's appropriate, I suppose. I—*me*—the only *me* I've ever known—already I look as insubstantial as a ghost.

Full-on panic shunts into my chest. I drop my gaze to the parts of me I can affirm to be real. My useless knees. My wasted thighs. My so-wasted breasts. My awkward hands. After a face, the part of the body a transplant recipient has the most trouble learning to live with is a hand.

I have chunky knuckles and flat nails. On the first knuckle of my right middle finger is a thin white scar, left by a splash of boiling caramel from when I made Halloween toffee apples with Mum when I was eight. My left hand is palm side up on my lap. I see the familiar wishbone pattern of veins around the base of my thumb and forefinger, and the pulse in my inner wrist. Here the skin is thin. So thin, in fact, it seems to be fading, as though somehow it knows what's about to happen. Tomorrow, it will be gone. That scar, too. My *pulse*, too.

Another thwack of panic rocks my chest.

Then another.

I can't look at myself anymore. *"Lights off!"* I instruct the room.

The bulbs dim and my reflection fractures.

My runaway heart loses pace, just a little.

Breathe, I tell myself. *Count to seven in. Eleven out. Seven in—*

The door to my room clicks open.

"Rosa?"

It's Mum. I don't respond. I'm not sure I can.

"Sweetheart?"

I still feel frozen. But I don't want to make her any more worried than she is already. So I force my right hand to nudge the controls, and my chair swivels around.

She's in a white doctor's coat. A few strands of poodle-curly black hair have escaped her bun and are loose around her face. As she comes into the room, she smiles. It's a creditable attempt. Somehow, she even manages to rope in her eyes. But behind the smile, I can see she's terrified. I don't blame her. I'm terrified myself. I want to tell her it's okay, she doesn't have to smile. But I've never been able to talk to her like that. To tell her my heartfelt truths.

"Why are the lights off? Were you sleeping?" she says. *Sleeping?* Is she *kidding*?

Before I can confirm that no, I was not sleeping—that sleep has never seemed more remote than it does at this moment—

Dad shuffles in behind her, his gray hair ruffled, his beard untidy, his habitual woolen V-neck sweater creased. "Rosa? You okay?" he asks. "Why are the lights off?"

"I thought I'd better let my eyes down gently," I tell him.

They asked the same question, but he isn't trying to smile, and it's easier to talk to someone who hasn't decided her daughter's life is in her hands. Highly skilled hands, perhaps, and Dr. Monzales, not Mum, will be leading the operation. But still.

Back when she was working to get me from London to Boston, to this hospital, and the only surgical unit she thought capable of what she'd decided was my last remaining option other than death (which, it turned out, was not an option as far as she was concerned), it probably all made sense to her.

Now D-day is upon us. Or judgment day. Or whatever you want to call it.

"You shouldn't say things like that," Mum says quietly.

She walks over to the bed a little unsteadily, despite a body toned by thirty laps in the pool each morning and sensible, dark brown shoes. She sits on the edge, close enough that she can touch me. She takes my hand. Her flat-nailed, chunky-knuckled thumb brushes the toffee-apple scar. I wonder if she remembers. "Dr. Monzales'll be here in a minute."

I nod. This is scheduled. Still, something about the confirmation sends another rush of stress hormones through my body. You'd think it would have given up by now, wouldn't you? No point gearing up for fight or flight when neither is remotely possible.

"One last formal run-through of the procedure, so you can complete your informed consent." Mum's voice is tight.

"Sign my life away, you mean."

"Sign *up* for life," she says, and obviously realizes how idiotic that sounds. She shakes her head. "Rosa—" She hesitates. In those arctic blue eyes, the polar opposite of mine, I read guilt. Uncertainty. Fear. And I feel bad.

"It *is* going to be okay," Dad says. He comes to sit on the other side of me, and he brings with him such a familiar scent: the cord of his dark gray trousers, and coffee. It confuses me for a moment. It's a smell from *home*, and this place—this new high-tech hospital room, with its invisible monitoring and control systems, its plastic floor and artificial orchids in a waterless vase on the desk—could not be more different.

"Remember all the times we've talked about this," Dad says. "Doctors are taught to be cautious, but they wouldn't attempt something like this if they weren't certain they could do it. They *will* save your life. You know that."

". . . Yeah." (*I don't.*)

"It'll take time," Mum says, "but you're going to make it through this, and ultimately, Rosa, that's all that matters."

Make it through. She means the surgery. But, really, will I? Dr. Monzales has put my chance of waking up from the operation at 90 percent. Not perfect odds, but a lot better than the absolute zero I'd be facing otherwise.

Dad shoots Mum a glance. She squeezes my hand. I watch the action, rather than feel it. "Rosa, I want to tell you—"

"Tell her what?"

Mum and Dad look around. It's Elliot, my brother. He pushes the door wide and walks in.

Elliot is two years older than me. He's tallish, darkish, and handsome—if you think handsome is gaunt, with narrow shoulders, oversize pale blue eyes, and patchy brown facial hair. Evidently some girls do, because despite being in America for only three weeks, he's already managed to hook up with an elfin-faced, hourglass-figured documentary filmmaker (I've seen her Instagram pictures) four years older than him, who lives in Brooklyn. Not only that, he's been to visit her. Twice. He's taken to walking about with the latest *New Yorker* sticking out of the pocket of his Belstaff jacket and tweeting obscene answers to the weekly cartoon caption competition to his inexplicably exploding band of followers.

Elliot is everything Dad routinely criticizes him for. Vain. Lazy. Overconfident. Hedonistic. But if I have to have a brother—and there *are* downsides—I'd rather it were him than anybody else on this planet.

Mum and Dad watch him uncertainly, afraid he's going to say something inappropriate. I don't know why they're uncertain. It's basically inevitable.

"Tell her what?" Elliot says again. He mimes sudden understanding. "Oh! She's *flat-chested*. Sorry, Rosa. Maybe they can transplant your tits. They can do that, can't they, Mum?"

Mum turns ash-white. Dad stares at Elliot in obvious disbelief that he—responsible, sincere, earnest Dad—could have spawned somebody like him. Frankly, I share it. But the completely moronic comment makes me smile. Which Elliot knew would happen. Which is why he said it. See? Downsides. Who wants their brother talking about their tits? But rather him than anybody else on this planet.

"I *wanted* to tell you something Dr. Monzales told me this morning," Mum says. "That the mood among the entire team is so positive. Everybody is perfectly ready, he says."

Elliot isn't listening. He pulls the *New Yorker* from his pocket, flicks to the back, and holds it up at the caption competition. A middle-aged naked man is climbing in through the window of an apartment. A middle-aged, frumpy-looking woman is on the sofa (fully clothed). She's staring up from her book in surprise. God, this cartoon was made for Elliot. He clears his throat—but there's a knock on my open door, and the next voice I hear is not his.

"Ah—Dr. Marchant. And Dr. Marchant."

Dr. Monzales strides into the room with a folder, nodding at Mum, then at Dad, who is not a medical doctor—he's a lecturer in botany. After shutting the door, Dr. Monzales shoots a cautious glance at Elliot, who has previously spoken in his presence. But his expression, his attitude, his *aura* is so serious, even Elliot is silenced.

After pulling the desk chair over to me, Dr. Monzales sits and fixes his intense gaze on my face. "Rosa, I need to go through the details one last time. Since you are eighteen now, we require your signature to proceed with the surgery. But more importantly, for me, I need to know that deep down, you are still in full agreement. That you haven't changed your mind? That you're positively sure you want to proceed?"

If I'm *positively sure*? The seconds scramble. Time is rushing. I force it to stop. Because after all the conversations, the logistical planning, the screening tests, the evaluations, the probing, the reports, the warnings, and the delays as Dr. Monzales asked for more time to perfect the surgical plans, this is *it*.

I glance at Mum. She rockets up the stiffness scale. If she's not careful, she'll shatter.

"I haven't changed my mind."

While Mum deflates with relief, Dr. Monzales seems to expand. He's always appeared confident and in control, but I've never been quite so aware of the *gravity* in *gravitas* before. He's like a human black hole. As he reads from a document in the folder, outlining one final time in graphic detail exactly what the surgery will entail—I know far more about the action of skull saws and silicon nanoknives than could ever be considered desirable—and what he plans to do to encourage the melding of the new me, I'm pulled closer, and closer, until I've passed the event horizon and there's no going back.

The morning after I arrived in Boston, I downloaded *Frankenstein* by Mary Shelley. I'd read it in paperback a couple of years before. Liked it. Given it an eye-level position on the bookshelf by my bed. Who knew then I'd have to *live* it? Now I know seven or eight long passages by heart. One, from chapter five, feels like it's burned into my brain.

The "creature" opens its eyes for the first time . . .

I had worked hard for nearly two years, for the sole purpose of infusing life into an inanimate body. For this I had deprived myself of rest and health. I had desired it with an ardour that far exceeded moderation; but now that I had finished, the beauty of the dream vanished, and breathless horror and disgust filled my heart.

At 4:30 A.M. tomorrow, two nurses will come for me. I will be wheeled to an anteroom to an operating theater, be injected with a sedative, and have an IV fitted to a vein in my right arm. Through the line, I'll be infused with propofol. Within a minute of this anesthetic entering my bloodstream, I will be out cold. My skull will then be broken open, and my brain will be transplanted into the skull of a girl whose own brain will very recently have been removed.

Right now, *she* is in a coma. Her body is intact, but her brain is dead.

I have essentially the opposite problem.

We're two halves of a person. But together, I wonder—and I can't get this thought out of my head; it's stuck there tighter than the catchiest tune—what will I be? *What will I become?* If I fall in love or strike a person, will she be doing the loving or hitting, or me? If I sleep with someone, without her consent, could it classify as abuse?

Philosophers have debated the nature of identity for centuries. If only all the eminent ancient minds who'd pondered these questions could be in Boston right now. Surely they'd never have dreamed their thought experiments could ever become real. And yet that's what's about to

2.

DR. MONZALES HAS left, and Elliot is talking.

There was a silence and he had to fill it.

He's slouched on the desk chair, his long body awkwardly arranged, telling us about his plans to meet Aula the documentary filmmaker at an illegal pop-up restaurant inside a condemned Manhattan water tower. "They bring in these top chefs," he's saying.

"Elliot. Seriously. Shut up."

He stares at me. Sits up a little. Rubs a hand across his face.

And I feel bad, because what do you talk about on a night like this?

Nine and a half hours to go. And there's nothing left that I want to discuss.

"Turn on TV," I instruct the room.

Mum tenses. She glances at Dad, as though expecting him to make some kind of reasoned objection. But maybe Dad is as exhausted and out of alternatives as I am, because he only pushes me into a better position for viewing the screen.

I watch as a tiny woman in a glittering pink leotard spins on the spot. She leaps and is caught by a vaguely familiar older man wearing what looks like a matador's cape.

"You had one like that," Elliot says.

"Not quite so many sequins," I point out.

I'd be surprised he remembers, but a photo of me wearing it, one satin-shoed foot up on a barre, did once hang above the radiator in the hall. (When I was ten, I took it down myself, because I knew no one else would. I didn't throw it away. I just put it in a kitchen drawer, where it became buried by the general detritus of life.) Yeah, I used to like dancing. No, it isn't something I want to watch.

"BBC America," I say.

The channel changes, and as I kind of hoped—not a wild hope, in all honesty, because BBC America is pretty reliable on this score—a *Top Gear* rerun is showing. An old one, from before Jeremy Clarkson hit that producer and everything changed.

Elliot turns to me. "You complete cock."

Reflexively, Mum says, "*Elliot!*"

But it's not an insult. Well, Elliot doesn't mean it as one. It's a term of abuse the presenter James May is particularly fond of. He's always calling one of the others a "complete cock." Now it's a kind of in-joke between Elliot and me.

The truth is, I have zero interest in the latest cars, or boyish escapades in cars. Dad loves *Top Gear*. Strange, maybe, for someone who loves trees, but there you go. I grew up with it. Next to being with my family, it's the closest I can get to home here in America.

Tonight, it's one of the specials. They're driving off on the hunt for the true source of the Nile. Hammond leaps about in kidlike excitement while Clarkson bellows melodramatic instructions, and I feel myself start to relax.

I have Mum, Dad, Elliot, and *Top Gear*. It will no doubt seem inexplicable to any normal eighteen-year-old girl, but I can't help thinking there could be far worse ways to spend what could be the last night of my life, and certainly the last night of my life as I've known it.

Next time I wake up, it'll be to go to surgery. The time after that, it will be in someone else's body . . .

Before any of us signed even the initial papers, Dr. Bailey, the hospital's chief psychologist, sent a report recommending that while it would be helpful for me to learn a few fundamental facts about the donor, the procedure should be essentially anonymous.

He wrote:

Experience with face transplantation in particular suggests that detailed knowledge about the donor is detrimental to recovery. Recipients tend to focus on the dead person's identity rather than their own.

This report arrived a couple of weeks after I first met Dr. Monzales, at our home in London.

The four of us (Elliot was at a lecture) were sitting around the table in our cluttered kitchen with mugs of tea. Dad, who doesn't notice this kind of thing, gave Dr. Monzales my favorite, which features a skateboarding cat, a parrot perched on its head. The incongruousness of *that* mug in *his* hand made everything seem even more surreal. Weirder than anything I could have dreamed up.

Mum is a brain surgeon. Her specialty is implanting electrodes to treat Parkinson's disease. Before Dr. Monzales arrived, Mum told me only that she'd met him many times at conferences, he was based in Boston, he was in London for a meeting, and he might have an idea of how to help me.

"It is a radical idea," she said, after a moment. "But I really think we should hear him out."

"So perhaps you have heard my name or you have looked me up?" Dr. Monzales said. He sipped over the parrot's head. "Maybe you heard about the first human head transplant, in China?"

I nodded in answer to the second question, not the first. Of course I'd heard about it. It had been all over the internet and TV. I glanced hard at Mum. Was *this* his "idea" of how to help me?

"I was joint lead surgeon on the procedure," he went on. "I have left my co-surgeon to the limelight. I don't care so much for attention. I prefer to focus on the work. And some work that has not yet been made public"—he lowered his voice a little—"is my development of an alternative with colleagues at Harvard Medical School."

His gaze intense, he said, "Rosa, the animal trials we have been obliged to perform show that *brain* transplantation can work spectacularly well. The recovery time is long—a few months, not weeks, as there are many new nerve pathways to be created. But the main advantage for a person, compared with a full head transplant, will be the absence of major neck scarring. A typical physical appearance—the scars hidden by hair, no obvious sign of major surgery. I believe this is the way to go, especially for people in your kind of circumstance, of your kind of age. When your mother approached me, and I heard about your case, I thought, 'Yes, perhaps you will be an excellent first candidate.'"

"Are you *serious*?" I asked him.

"About your suitability?"

"About putting my brain into someone else's body!"

"Look at the long evolution of transplantation," he said, his palms spread. "Consider what was once so controversial but now is routine, or close. The liver, the kidneys, the lungs, the eyes, the heart, the face—and so why not the brain? I am very, deeply serious."

I looked again at Mum. She nodded. "I believe it is achievable."

Dad was sitting next to me. He put his hand over mine.

"Not that this is the major concern in your mind," Dr. Monzales went on, "but you would not need to worry about the cost. The hospital has received some very large endowments. Everyone there is eager to pioneer new treatments to save children's lives. A treatment like this would be revolutionary."

Maybe Dad read my mind. "I know it sounds crazy, Rosa, and it'll take time for you to even get your head around the idea, but perhaps it's worth thinking about?"

Dr. Monzales nodded. "Of course, you will need plenty of time to think, to talk. Our chief psychologist can be in touch, to talk everything though, and if you would like, he has material he has prepared that he could send to you to read. If it is any reassurance, I have, I think, the same understanding of how outlandish the idea *sounds* but also the same certainty of success as when NASA sent astronauts to the Moon. It would be a giant leap for you into your own future, Rosa. And it would give hope to so many."

". . . You *are* serious," I said.

My head felt thick, my thoughts blurry. I'm not sure if I was disgusted or excited or afraid of hoping again.

Maybe all of the above.

After he left, Mum and Dad came back to sit on either side of me.

"In the end, it will be your choice," Mum said, and I think she was trying to believe she meant it. "If you eventually decide you don't want to do this, that's okay." But I could see in her eyes, as well as Dad's, that only something other than certain death would be "okay."

And so, after a *lot* of conversations with Mum and Dad, Dr. Bailey, and Elliot ("I'll take a year out of uni, Rosa; maybe I can even do a semester out there on American literature; I'll come to Boston, Mum and Dad'll have an apartment—*I'll be there with you*"), six weeks later, Dr. Monzales appeared on Mum's laptop screen with news of a potential donor.

This time, Elliot was there, too. We were all huddled at the table, watching him on Skype.

"Apologies that I cannot be there in person, Rosa. But I wanted to discuss this with you as quickly as possible. There is no easy way for you to hear this information. So, let me simply lay it out. This is what I can tell you: She is American. She is eighteen. She has loving parents. She was happy. Tragically for her and her family, an accident has left her in an irreversible coma."

"What kind of accident?" I asked him.

"All I can tell you is that it was a near-drowning, and there was no prolonged pain. And that her parents have undergone counseling. And they are willing to give their consent to the surgery. I know Dr. Bailey has recommended only a very limited exchange of personal detail, and the girl's parents agree— in fact, they have requested anonymity. So I'm afraid that is all I can tell you about her, except for her first name: Sylvia. And also, we have a picture. If you would like to see it. If it's all too much now, I can show you another time."

"I'd like to see it," I said, my throat tight.

He looked down, at his desk, I guess. A rustling sound came through the speakers. My heart like a ball of molten metal, I waited. Then he lifted a photograph up to the camera.

I stared at a girl with wide-set, deep brown eyes, olive skin, thick, wavy dark hair to her shoulders, and dimples in her cheeks. Pretty. Normal-pretty. Prettier than me. Nice—if that's something you can tell from a photograph. She was sitting on a sofa, in jeans and a black T-shirt. Around her neck was a heart-shaped amber pendant on a silver chain. Who gave her the necklace? I wondered. Her boyfriend? Her mum, on her last birthday? The last birthday she'd ever know.

Tears flooded my eyes. I had to sit there, helpless, while Mum jumped up to find a tissue.

Dad wrapped an arm around my shoulders. Elliot pulled his chair closer. The color had drained from his face.

From the screen, Dr. Monzales said quietly, "If you make the final decision to proceed, there will be many tears, Rosa. Of fear, I am sure. Uncertainty. Frustration, in the rehabilitation. But in the end, I believe, of joy. For Sylvia, unfortunately, there is no hope of recovery. But it need not be like that for you."

On the TV in my hospital room, the night before the surgery, Clarkson, Hammond, and May huddle over a battered map— they're still searching for the "true" source of the Nile—and Elliot drags his chair over to mine.

Eyes on the screen, he says to me, "Greggs vanilla slices."

A smile flickers on my mouth as I say, "Ginsters chicken and mushroom slices."

"Cheryl Cole's flowery bottom."

I think for a moment. "The stained bottom of a mug accustomed to Yorkshire Tea."

"The B&Q bank holiday bonanza!"

"The M&S ten-pound deal."

Mum says, "What are you talking about?"

Elliot looks at her. "Home."

"The Palace of Westminster," she says after a moment.

He shakes his head. "As usual, you're totally missing the point."

I shush them. Clarkson and May are scrambling across an arid landscape—I'm not sure what happened to Hammond—and Dad reaches for my hand. I can't consciously feel pain or pressure, heat or cold. But there's an unconscious part of me that feels Dad's hand. Suddenly, I'm more tired than I can ever remember.

My eyes close.

I jerk them open.

They close.

I never find out whether Clarkson or May finds the true source of the Nile, because here, now, in my hospital room, I fall asleep.

● ● ●

When I wake up, I'm on my back.

Panic hits. My heart pounds. Skips. Shudders.

The digital clock on the desk shows 4:16 A.M. The six flicks to a seven. The air is filled with an intense, sweet scent: lemons. Someone lit my candle.

Mum is gone. Dad and Elliot are asleep on their chairs. I can't reach them. The TV is off. *I have less than half an hour of consciousness left.* And then? The panic turns bitter.

Somehow, Elliot must sense this, because he stirs. He pulls himself up straight. "You awake?"

"Yeah," I breathe.

I hear the hum of the room, the hidden electronics, see the tiny green flash of the smoke alarm set into the ceiling. My senses strain, flailing desperately for something to hold on to.

And Elliot, who in so many ways is so different from me, says: "When people say what matters is what's on the inside, not the outside, they're right. You know that."

"I think that's probably officially the first time someone's ever said that to a person who's about to have no outside," I tell him.

"You'll have an outside. It'll be different. But *you* will still be *you*. *Irritatingly,* you still won't think my cartoon captions are funny."

"*Irritatingly,* you will still be a dick."

"And if I had the body of David Beckham—who, incidentally, I have a lot of respect for—I'd still be a dick. And I'd still love you. And I'd still be about to tell you my caption for that cartoon of that man climbing through the window—"

"Please don't."

"Point proved."

"What point is that?" I ask him.

"Switch off the lights and I'm still me, and you're still you. If you don't like what it's like afterward, we'll go and live somewhere dark and just be us, the same as we've always been. Except you'll be able to walk and you won't be about to die."

I'm going to cry.

I don't want to cry.

"Somewhere dark?"

"Yeah."

I swallow. "Like a crypt?"

"Like a house with the lights off, with very thick curtains." Believe it or not, he sounds serious.

"There are prison cells in China they call the dark cells," I tell him. "They're so small you have to crawl into them. After a few years, your hair turns white."

"I could live with white hair."

"Elliot—"

"No, *listen*. I mean it, Rosa."

"You'd live in the dark with me?"

"You don't change who someone is by turning off the lights."

There's a knock on the door. It opens. Elliot blinks.

Though I don't look at the two silhouettes, I sense their presence. I'm still focusing on Elliot. His T-shirt is crumpled, his hair is a mess, but his eyes tell me none of that matters.

"So that caption?" I breathe.

His gaze doesn't flicker. Not even now, as Dad jerks awake and two figures in green smocks and loose green pants bustle in. It's Jane—her brown hair clipped back, the tiny crucifix around her neck gleaming—and her plump colleague, Drema. They pad toward me, saying words I don't hear.

"I'll tell you when you wake up. Give you something to live for." He grins.

3.

APRIL 22.

Imagine being conscious but hearing nothing, seeing nothing, feeling nothing, tasting nothing, touching nothing, having the awareness of being awake but unable to move or sense a single thing—and then, every few seconds, or minutes or hours, because you have no sense of time, a wild explosion of light rocks your mind. The silence and the stillness are absolute. Then a grenade fires through what someone else might call my soul. Am I alive? Perhaps I'm on the point of death.

May 8.

A hum. It's all I'm aware of. I can't see anything. I can't touch, taste, or move anything. But I can detect that vibration, and somehow I know it's external to me. I can sense *something*. And I realize: I'm *thinking* about the hum. I'm thinking half-normal thoughts in undeniably normal words. I am alive. I *am* alive.

Dr. Monzales told me it would take time for my brain to connect with my new body, and my experiences during that process would be very difficult to predict.

Explanation A: That is what's happening right now, and gradually it'll get better.

Explanation B: I've survived the operation but my brain was injured. I have a degree of consciousness, but a permanent inability to move or communicate.

Either way, they'll know that something's going on in my head, because they had the world's most sophisticated brain scanners all lined up to use on me. They'll see activity in parts of the brain used for thinking, not just breathing and sleeping.

Which means Dad will be crying. Mum probably will be crying. Elliot? I have no idea what Elliot will be doing. I wish I could see him. *Right now.* I really wish I could see his face.

May 25.

A whining. It sounds like an insect, only it's higher-pitched, and it's . . . yes, it's changing. The pitch is changing. And I *feel* something. Pins and needles all along my left arm. *My arm.* I just thought: *my arm.* But can I read anything into that? Does my brain know what it's sensing? Did I really just feel something in *my arm*? High up. Near my shoulder. The exact spot where they were going to attach one of the electrodes for the brain-stimulating therapy. Am I dreaming?

June 7.

A voice. Low. Slow. I can't make out words. Dad's? No. I feel a trembling where my body should be. I can't pinpoint it. Could be legs, or torso. Could be purely imaginary. The voice, though—I *know* that voice. Elliot? No. Dr. Monzales? No. It's British. No—*ha*! But I can't make out the words. What's he saying?

June 9.

There's a flare going on and then off in front of my eyes. Bright white, then black. Bright white, then black. If it's real. It could be my mind hallucinating to escape the darkness, my equivalent of a desert traveler's mirage. But if I'm sensing the position of *eyes*, does that mean something?

June 14.

A scent: sweet, fresh. Familiar. My candle?

A voice: "I don't know if you can . . . me, so I'm not going to
. . . yet. When . . . wake up, Rosa, I'll tell . . . Come on."
That was Elliot. That was *Elliot*.

June 22.

"You remember that time I took you swimming at the King
Edward baths? You must have been three. You'd only been in
pools on holiday before. It was the first time I ever took you
swimming in England. We got in there and you said, 'Swimming pools live outside!' And afterward all the mums had
bananas and healthy stuff for their kids, and I had nothing
and you were starving so we went to the closest place, which
was a fish and chip shop, and it was getting dark, and you
said, 'The streetlights are on; we're going down the road to
a café and I want sausages and chips and ice cream.' And I
knew you were thinking of that book—the one about the tiger
who came to tea. He drank all Daddy's beer and I changed the
words so Daddy wasn't watching a fight on TV; he was watching a documentary on giant redwoods—oh, but that was the
other book—the one about the cat—"

"*Da*—?"

"Rosa? Rosa! *Rosa!*"

4.

THE FIRST FACE I see with anything like clarity is Drema's—though only her suddenly crazily wide eyes, then Dad's after she runs off and calls him in. Then Mum's. She cries. Even Elliot cries. I watch the tears run down behind the fabric of their masks, worn, I know, to help protect my immunocompromised body from infection.

"Rosa," Elliot says, "you can *see* me?"

"Yeah . . ." Though it comes out more like "yuh."

He says something, but I don't hear him. The voice wasn't mine. *My voice wasn't mine.*

The first time I truly fear for my life is on June 29.

I'm in a different room, still hotel-like, beige with a window-wall, but bigger, so that everything I need can be brought to me.

I'm looking at that photo of Mum, Dad, and Elliot by Whitby Abbey and wondering what they'll do with old family photos that include me, when my vision clouds. The room starts bleeping and nurses burst in. Later—I have no idea how much later—Dr. Monzales is beside my bed. "We have changed your medication, Rosa. Please, try to rest now. I am convinced you will be fine."

The first time I move one of my new limbs is on July 16.

I'm dressed in new black leggings and a new loose blue top, chosen from a wardrobe full of presents from Elliot and Mum, as well as things that I've ordered online, ignoring Mum's advice, but listening to Elliot's. Well, some of it.

"No, no skinny jeans, Rosa!"

". . . Okay."

"That jersey jumpsuit!"

"You're joking, right?"

"I wouldn't joke with you about something this serious, Rosa."

"In whose life exactly is the question of a jersey jumpsuit serious?"

He shook his head mock sadly. "Rosa Marchant, you have some really tough priority-reassessment work ahead."

So—I'm in new black leggings and a loose blue top, and my physical therapist comes in. She's grinning an excited smile that I can properly see, now that the immediate high-risk infection period has passed, and the masks have been ditched.

She straps me into something they call the Exoskeleton. It's a robotic, battery-powered frame that walks for you. It moves my new limbs while I watch, helping my brain gradually remember what to do. Eventually she reduces the input from the motors—and my right leg twitches.

The first meal I eat by myself—moving *my* hand, with a little help from Dad putting the spoon to my mouth—is tomato soup. Memories rush back. Being seven or eight, coming back chapped-lipped and starving from the park, asking Dad to open a can of Heinz. The taste is incredible.

Dad grins the way a dad might grin if his one-year-old just fed herself for the first time. I smile back. He says, "You still smile just like you. I'd know you anywhere, Rosa, just from that smile."

By now the muscles required to move my mouth have improved dramatically. I'm even getting used to hearing another voice speak my words. It's higher-pitched than mine. Sweeter. More melodic.

The first time I see myself in a mirror is on August 7.

I've seen that photograph of Sylvia, of course, and parts of my new self.

My legs. A little longer than my old legs. Slim feet. Longer toes than mine. My arms. Pale. Three moles on the right forearm, a wishbone of veins around the thumb and forefinger, strangely similar to mine. My hands. Long, slim fingers, with whorls on the tips that are proof of an identity that was hers and is now also mine.

But my face? They've been careful. Will I look *just* like her? I know I should. But will I?

Mum comes into my room as I'm struggling to get dressed. "Here, let me help you," she says.

"It's okay," I tell her. Awkwardly, I pull the end of a legging over my right heel. Then I shuffle forward to the edge of the bed and drag the waistband up.

"It's a big day, I know." She's trying to sound bright.

I nod and reach for a T-shirt that Elliot gave me with a block print of a girl curled in an armchair, a cat on her knee.

"You want to talk any more about what this could be like for you before we go through?" she asks.

"No."

Her turn to nod. I guess she's got the message that I'm nervous and I just want to get this done. But now that she's got it, I feel bad for forcing it on her. "Maybe you could help me up?"

So it's Mum I'm leaning against, her clean-skin scent that I'm inhaling, her arm that I'm gripping a little more tightly than maybe I need to, as I make my way unsteadily down the corridor to a door marked STAFF ONLY.

Dad and Dr. Monzales are waiting outside.

"It's a nurses' changing room," Dr. Monzales explains. "A full-length mirror is on the wall at the far end. No one is inside. We have it to ourselves."

He pushes the door open, and with Mum's help, I half walk and am half dragged past a wall of white lockers, chairs, and hooks—to the mirror.

I look at "myself"—my—her—body—properly for the first time.

I stare for a few wild, disorienting seconds. Then dizziness sweeps up through my brain. I might even pass out for a moment, because suddenly I'm in a chair, Mum crouched in front of me, Dr. Monzales's hand gripping my shoulder, his deep voice intense in my ear.

But I don't hear him, and Mum's face is overlaid with this image, burned into my reeling mind: a girl, average height, slender, with those wide-set eyes, a mass of dark chocolate hair, and a narrow-lipped mouth open in what *I* know is a kind of anguished amazement. A girl. Sylvia—me, half ghost and half alive.

Taking on this new appearance, leaving behind my old skin and emerging butterfly-like from my cocoon of sensory deprivation, is a thing of wonder, no doubt. But seeing myself in the mirror, another question hits me. I can only think I've been so concerned with the future that I've somehow neglected to process the fact that part of me will stay forever in the past.

That night, when the nurses are gone, the lights have been dimmed, and only Mum is left, looking tired, leaning over my narrow bed, stroking my forehead, murmuring "good night" like you might to a small child, I ask her: "What happened to my body?"

She stops mid-stroke. Pulls back. "*This* is your body."

"What happened to my dead body?"

"Your dead body?"

"What else would you call it?"

Mum doesn't answer.

"Did they bury it? Do I have a grave?"

"Rosa—"

"Has anyone brought me flowers?"

"Rosa—" Her forehead knots.

"Is there an inscription?"

Why didn't they raise the issue? Why didn't Dr. Monzales talk about what would happen to my body?

"*Mum?*"

She whispers, "It was cremated."

"... Cremated. What happened to the ashes?"

Mum shakes her head slightly. "They weren't kept."

They weren't kept?

"They belong to the past, Rosa. It's so important to focus on the future." She looks a little bewildered. Gently, she says, "What would you want them for?"

"I don't know—put them in an urn. Put them on the mantelpiece!"

They weren't kept.

In fact, someone threw them away. Somewhere in a biohazard landfill are the burned remains of my body.

Tears run from my eyes onto my cheeks. I taste the salt on my lips.

"Your body wasn't *you*, Rosa," Mum says, her voice breaking. She's losing her iron control . . . *She's* losing control.

It's like witnessing a skyscraper collapse or a bridge crumble. The crack inside me fractures right down to my core. I'm shaking from the shock of it.

"You're still here," she whispers. "And we're so lucky you are." A tear falls from each of her eyes.

I manage to reach up and use my hand to wipe Sylvia's— my—face. Then with her—my—thumb, I wipe away Mum's tears. This only makes them come faster, which obviously wasn't my intention.

For the first time in a very long time, I tell her a heartfelt truth: "I don't know if I'm crying or she is."

"*You are*, Rosa. *You're* crying. *You're* alive. *You* can walk, and with more therapy, you'll be running. You'll have your whole life to live, however you want to live it, with all the choices and all the future you should have at eighteen. This is *your* life. *Your* second chance."

And Sylvia's? I think. But I don't say it.

I want to believe Mum. I really do.

But when she finally goes, reassured that I'm calm and safe to leave, everything disintegrates. I start crying again. My chest is heaving. I'm not sure I can breathe.

5.

IT'S TWO DAYS later, and it's 2:44 A.M.

Since Mum left my room, I haven't gotten out of bed.

I know she and Dad are worried about me. Dr. Monzales, too: "It's totally to be expected that you'll have down days, Rosa, but let us help. You can talk to me. Let me call for Dr. Bailey."

But I don't want to talk to anyone. And I am okay. Or I will be. There's something I have to do, and I've been gearing up for it.

Now I'm pushing myself into a sitting position. I'm easing my legs onto the floor. I'm instructing the room, "Lights on."

2:44 A.M. Surely there's no one in the park.

Stumbling a little, the vinyl cold beneath my bare feet, I

make my way around the bed, to the keypad by the window, and press the up arrow. The gentle whirring as the blind retracts is almost drowned out by the rush of my pulse in my ears.

Awkwardly, because it takes effort to coordinate my arms, and I still have trouble closing the fingers of my right hand, I pull my T-shirt up over my head. Then I take off my underwear. And I look at myself in the window. Naked.

My reflection is trembling.

I look at myself and I think of *Frankenstein*: *The beauty of the dream vanished, and breathless horror and disgust filled my heart . . .*

I squeeze my eyes shut.

But I *have* to look.

Like the parent of a difficult child, I force them—my eyes—to do what they're told. To stare at that reflection. To get used to it. Because this is reality now.

And this is what my reality looks like, in full, in 3-D.

Her hips are slightly wider than mine. She has a round face with a neat nose, upturned at the tip. A low forehead, what with all that hair, which now reaches my shoulders. High cheekbones. Dimples in her cheeks when I pull a smile. A long neck, with a mole at the clavicle. Small, curved breasts. A flat stomach. I twist slightly. A skinny bottom. My heart races. *Shh,* I tell myself. *It's only you.*

And I don't feel horror. Or disgust.

She was American. Eighteen. Loved. Left by a near-drowning accident in a permanent vegetative state . . . The sum of my knowledge does not amount to much.

Now, as I look at myself in the window, I think about her parents. I guess I understand why they wanted their identities to be kept from me. And why, under the terms of the donation agreement:

The parents of the donor will receive full updates on medical progress until the recipient is discharged from hospital.

But as Mum and Dad wanted, too:

There will be no contact between the parents of the donor and the recipient.

I think:

Imagine knowing that your daughter's body is out there, and *seeing* her.

But imagine knowing your daughter body's is out there, and *not* being able to see her.

Which would be harder?

And:

Having another girl's body and knowing essentially *nothing* about her.

Having her body and knowing *everything*.

Which would be harder?

44

And what, exactly, in theory, would I want to know . . . ?

Right now, I need to focus on what I *can* know.

And so I scour what I can see of her—of myself.

Then I sit down, and I explore every inch. I touch my toes, my chest. I even part my pubic hair. Because if this is going to be my body, I have to know it.

When I decide I have been as thorough as possible, I get back into bed. I pull the duvet right up to my chin. I was scared. But I did it. And now I do feel more hopeful.

6.

My heart is pounding and I'm sweating badly, but it's from exercise, not panic.

"Elliot?"

I'm on a bike in the gym of the hospital's inpatient rehabilitation facility and Elliot is beside me, lounging on a stool. I just asked him a question. And he's frowning at the other kids, some on treadmills, others on bikes, a few spread-eagled on massage benches, framed by the glowing green of the floor-to-ceiling blinds.

"Elliot?"

This time, he catches my eye and nods. "If I were a geek, I would say, I *concur.*"

"You *concur?*" I breathe.

"Yeah: People are looking."

Elliot's on a two-week-long visit—to me, but also to Aula. Before he returns to London, and to his interrupted degree in English, I want his opinion. (And he owes me, what with his confession over dry croissants in Les Baguettes, the ground-floor cafe, this morning: "I was telling Aula's friends I *had* to fly back out because my sister's gone into rehab, and I haven't even seen where she's staying. They asked if it was drugs or alcohol . . . So I had to tell them you'd been communing with jaguar spirits in Guatemala and who knew *what* you'd been taking. Just remember the jaguars if you meet her.")

"He's looking at me again," I whisper to Elliot between snatched breaths.

". . . Yeah."

"You're doing great! Keep it up!" Vinnie, one of the nurse-trainers, pumps a fist at me on his way down the line of bikes. "Great work! Push it, now. *Push it!*"

"What if I get a seizure?" I ask him.

"The ER is thirty-eight seconds away, Rosa. *Move it.*"

"You utter *cock,*" Elliot says.

A couple of the other patients' relatives look around sharply. Vinnie, who was ecstatic when he discovered that we have a shared fondness for *Top Gear* and has fruitlessly tried to engage me in car-related chat on several occasions, only grins. The insult's become an in-joke that extends to him, as well.

Les Baguettes . . .

The rehab gym . . .

For three weeks now, I've been out among other people.

My progress, Dr. Monzales told me at a meeting in his office the day before I was transferred here—a wing at the other end of the hospital from my pre-op and isolation care rooms—has been "really, truly wonderful."

I do have weakness in my right arm and leg, which is "probably permanent," he says. Despite my daily meds, there remains a chance that my body will reject my brain—but that will always be a concern.

"So why can't I move to the apartment?" I asked, looking at Mum.

"This is still our plan," Dr. Monzales said. "It will be your halfway house, Rosa; nothing has changed. But not quite yet. Remember, you still have about a fifteen percent chance of suffering a dangerous epileptic-type seizure."

"So how low can the risk actually get?"

He said, "Realistically . . . maybe fifteen percent."

"So . . ."

"It's been a long time since you were around other people your age," Mum put in. "In the rehab wing, you can interact, but in a safe environment. Just a few more months, Rosa. That's all."

"A few more months?"

"And the ER will be close by, just on the off chance of a seizure," Dr. Monzales said. "But wait, Rosa, until you see the IRF! You will be in the section for patients aged fifteen to eighteen. There is a classroom for studies. But also bowling, music, video games. It is all possible *here* in the hospital."

So now I have a new room (good-bye, beige fantasy; hello, palette of greens) in this semi-self-contained wing for kids on a residential rehab program.

Jane was sent over with me, to keep a close eye. But none of the other nurses working here know about my surgery. As far as they're concerned, I'm just another traumatic brain injury patient.

None of them know about me.

Not Vinnie; not Dawn, my new educational specialist; not Dmitri, the Greek-American Manhattanite who skateboarded right into a Rolls-Royce on Fifth Avenue; or Jess, the tiny, big-eyed sixteen-year-old from Philadelphia, who dived into a pool, hit the bottom, and sucked in water for four minutes; or Jared, whose swept-up blond hair makes me think of one of the boys in One Direction—I can't remember his name—and who had a stroke at seventeen, and now spends half his life engaged in medically sanctioned gaming, because it strengthens the muscles in his left hand and arm.

Dmitri, Jess, and Jared all have rooms on my corridor.

My first encounter with Dmitri came as I was limping a little into my new room, and he was limping out of his. "Hey! Welcome. So, I'm off to a meeting on the value of graphic wall design in a pediatric inpatient setting. You have any strong opinions you'd like me to pass on?"

"On the value of graphic wall design?"

"In a pediatric inpatient setting."

"I don't think so."

"Yeah, me neither. If they do the place out in, like, black zigzags, I'll blame *you* . . . ?"

"Rosa."

"Dmitri." Before turning to go, he said, "It's on you, okay?"

He was smiling.

"Rosa?"

Another kid—skinny, in low-slung jeans—was heading along the corridor from the opposite direction, earbuds dangling.

"Hey," he said. "I'm Jared."

I was halfway into my room. He came to stand by me—a little too close—and leaned against the wall. "You just moving in? It's movie night tomorrow night. *Blade Runner.* You want to come?"

Was he just being inclusive with a new girl on the corridor? Was he asking me on a *date*? I know my cheeks flushed. I felt them get hot.

"Um, I'm not really into sci-fi," I told him. "But thanks."

He shrugged. "Dmitri was asking you about wall design?"

I nodded. "Yeah."

"There won't actually be a meeting—you should know that. It'll be his way of making you think he's important or something."

"Oh."

"You're new. It's only fair to warn you. At some point, he'll tell you about his cousin who's supposed to be, like, this top fashion designer in Milan. Only she works in a shop."

"So you and Dmitri have been here a while?"

"Both nearly two weeks into an eight-week program. You on that, too?"

". . . Yeah," I said.

"Okay, so you want to know anything, just ask me. I'm in room eight. Try me anytime."

"Thanks."

"Sure."

He was still standing there, watching me intently, as I

slipped inside my room, thinking, *Was that weird just because I'm not used to normal life?*

Right now, Jared's on the exercise bike three down from me, his scrawny calves pumping. Dmitri's just clambered down from one of the treadmills. (He hasn't mentioned the cousin yet.) Jess is being helped out of a gait-training harness by her mum. It's Jared who keeps glancing at me. But actually, Dmitri looks at me, too. So do some of the others. There must be ten patients in the gym right now and twenty in total in this section of the rehab wing, and I'm conscious of their eyes often on me.

"So?" I ask Elliot again.

He shrugs slightly. "Yeah. I told you: They're looking at you."

"More than normal?"

"Yeah."

"I've been here three weeks."

"Yeah."

"So you think . . . ?"

"Yeah," he says.

"Yeah?"

"Yeah, they're looking at you because—"

We finish the sentence together.

I say: *"They know."*

He says: *"You're cute."*

I stare at him.

He shrugs. "It's true. Aula tells me. I've shown her a few pictures."

I'm cute?

I glance back at Jared, then at Dmitri.

I know that after I'm discharged—at which point this "trial," as they call it, of brain transplantation will be deemed complete—the hospital is planning to tell the world what they've done. But my identity as *that patient* will not be revealed, Dr. Monzales has assured me.

Given all the looks, though, I'd been wondering if somehow the secret got out.

"You don't think they *know*?"

Elliot jerks his head toward Jared. "That boy down there—he's not looking at you with what I would term medical curiosity."

I'm cute?

A small white towel is draped over the handlebars of my bike. I grab it and throw it over my head so it hangs down either side, blocking out all the faces. I listen to the wheeze of my own breathing. It's stifling in here. Suddenly, my mind feels as overheated as my body. The blinds stop me from properly seeing the midday autumn sunshine, but I can *feel* it. I'm burning up.

At the back of the room is a glass door. It's not locked. I've seen people come and go. I'm supposed to stay inside. But now I'm gripped by a drive to escape from the rehab wing, to *get out.*

I pull off the towel and chuck it at Elliot. He fumbles the catch.

"Distract the nurses," I tell him.

He frowns.

"Ten minutes," I say. "That's all I want."

I walk away from the line of bikes, toward the door that leads to the spreading rectangle of parkland that's adjacent to this wing and the broad-branched trees that I've watched other rehab patients practicing their stretching and their Tai Chi and their yoga beneath.

"*Rosa,*" Elliot whispers hard.

I don't look back. Perhaps he's worried. But as I stride on toward that exit, there's a crash of something solid hitting the floor.

I walk faster, faster, my heart palpitating, until I get to the door, and I grip the cold bar handle in my sweating hand, and *I'm out.*

7.

OH. **IF I** were to believe in a god, now would be the moment. *Now* would be the moment.

Shivers race like scorpions under my skin. White-hot sparks erupt down the length of my body. I can't move. I'm stunned. Biologically mesmerized. I'm standing here on grass outside the hospital, and I'm effervescing from the light. Gorgeous gigawatts of peach-gold sunlight, hurtling through space, striking *me*.

I've never felt anything like this before. I doubt anybody has. My brain, so used to subdued, indoor signals—energy-saving lighting, a thermostatically controlled room, coolish washcloths, weakish tea—is in a state of something I think I have to call ecstasy. The heat receptors in my skin are going crazy, spiking signal after hysterical signal. I feel like a racecar that somebody has *finally* thought to take onto the highway.

The shivers strike deeper. They're in my muscles. They're catching at my veins. And then—*bam*—there's a shock to my heart. It skips. I gasp. A lightning strike of panic—and *whoompf*, the shamanic buzz is gone, and I see myself as somebody else might: a girl, standing in a park, blinking in bright sunlight.

I remain still, focused on the motions of my heart. While it's beating fast, it seems to be stable. *Thud. Thud. Thud.* No irregular gaps in the thuds. *Thud. Thud. Thud.* That's good. Well, it's something. I take a breath. Count to seven in . . . eleven out . . . seven in . . . At last, the strangeness evaporates entirely, and—part relieved, part devastated—I pay attention to the data streaming into my eyes.

I see trees. Four big ones, with generous, outstretched branches. Cedars, I think, the intense blues of the harbor and the sky shimmering behind them. And people. Everywhere. It's lunchtime, I realize. Yes, it's October, but it's warm in the sun. There's a group of nurses in green scrubs eating noodles out of boxes over near the harbor wall. A woman is pushing a stroller mounted with its own silver sun umbrella. A man in white sandals is chucking a ball at a young kid who's wielding a child-size tennis racket.

Through the gym window, I've noticed the kid with the racket before. And from my bedroom window I've seen the group of men over by the farthest patch of trees, a dense clustering that's more like woodland than park. They pile their doctors' coats and lunchboxes on a bench and hurl an American football inexpertly to one another. I've seen them before. But not like *this*. Not *directly*, unprotected by glass.

I've never been this close. Or this exposed. I notice details I never could have detected from inside. The kid with the racket is wearing Converse shoes decorated with felt-tip rainbows. The people aren't just mouthing words. They're talking. And it's mad, melodramatic conversation.

"That's crazy!" a woman shouts into her phone. Another says to her companion: "Yeah. Married four times before he knew." . . . "And then you told him you were *pregnant*?". . . "They still in New Orleans?" "Yeah. They were lucky with Katrina. It stopped at their doorstep." . . . "Hey, big man, everythin' goin' all right?" "Yeah, how 'bout you?" "Just chillin', baby." Everything sounds larger than life. *Everything.* English people don't talk like this. No one in this park says: *Tonight? A ready meal in front of* Bake Off. Or *Hmm, George, looks like rain.*

I notice something else. The bench piled with the doctors' belongings has a plaque. It's glinting. I find myself walking over, ignoring the background of shouts, squeals, conversation, someone singing a hymn.

I read the word *In* . . . but the rest is obscured by the raw cotton handle of a reusable bag. I reach out to push it away—

"Hey!"

I register the word but it belongs to the din I'm doing a pretty good job of ignoring.

"Hey!"

The voice is closer. I squint at the letters.

"Hey! What are you doing?"

It's *very close.*

I look around. It's one of the doctors, goateed, overweight, red-faced, panting.

"This is our stuff," he says, and I don't miss the accusation in his tone. "What are you doing?"

I'm about to tell him it's none of his business, but someone else answers for me.

"She was just reading the inscription."

It's an American voice. It belongs to a boy who's standing to my right, on the other side of the bench. Nineteen, maybe. Slim. Gray jeans. Tall. Black hair that falls over one eye. Black T-shirt. A gray canvas satchel over his shoulder. There's a tattoo on his inner right forearm, but I can't quite make it out. He's looking at the doctor, not me.

He says it again, matter-of-factly. "She was just reading."

The doctor swivels to face me. I say nothing. Don't move. So he's forced to nod uncertainly, shrug at his friends, then jog back to them.

The boy says, "In spite of everything, she loved this bench. Denise. Forever."

Surprised, I glance back at the plaque. He's on the other side of the bench. He can't read it from where he's standing. "You knew her?"

"Denise? No. I just—"

"*Rosa!*"

The voice cuts through to the bone.

"Rosa! Honey!"

Jane.

Jane. Jane. Jane.

Her heavily sprinting feet make their final approach.

"Honey, what are you doing out here?"

We're barely fifty feet from the hospital. But she's breathing hard.

"I—" I stop, unsure what to say.

The guy with the tattoo and satchel looks at me. "Wait, it's my line *again*? She was just reading."

Surprised—I think because this is the kind of interjection

I'd associate more with Elliot than a normal human being—I smile slightly. He smiles slightly back.

After an uncertain glance at him, Jane takes my arm. Her fingers feel red-hot. My sensory systems are confused. That peach-gold light tarnishes her face.

"Let's get you back," she says, "nice and safe."

Beyond her, I notice Elliot by the glass door. I see him shrug that he's sorry.

"Honey, what were you thinking?" Jane looks worried. But there's iron in her grip.

There's a phrase—I've heard it somewhere. It must be from a film, or something Elliot said, which perhaps still means it's from a film: *Resistance is futile.*

Option A: I meekly let Jane return me to the hospital. Option B: I convey in a single glance my not-unmitigated thanks to the guy with the tattoo (had I actually asked for a white knight?), tell Jane I still haven't forgiven her for the lie about the mirrors, but accept that, medically speaking, maybe it's better for me to stay inside. Option C: I punch her out and run away for cocktails and clam chowder or whatever normal people do in Boston.

Option C. Option C!

I turn only to find that the boy has vanished. I realize I feel disappointed. I tell Jane, "I just wanted some air."

I stomp toward Elliot, but halfway there, the doctors' football comes zinging toward me. I overreact, throwing myself backward, stumbling to my right, losing my balance. The world shoots sideways. Jane is behind me. She grabs me, but not before I've hit the ground. She hitches me back into a standing position. "Honey," she says, her mouth close to my ear, "we have air in the hospital. Nice, safe air."

I straighten myself, shrug her off. I try desperately to think of something smart to say in response. And I feel a hand on my arm. Elliot's.

"There, there, honey," he says, in a passable imitation of Jane's southern accent. "Let's get you back for a nice cup of hot sedative and some cozy wrist restraints."

Jane's expression says she can't quite believe what she just heard.

He winks at her. She shakes her head slightly, the corners of her mouth turning down.

As I let Elliot lead me back toward the hospital, he bends his head toward mine. I expect him to say something like *You happy now?* Or *Just humor them—you're almost done.*

But he says, "I pushed over this bench and they all came over. That boy Jared was right in there, and he wasted no time. 'Are you her boyfriend or what?' I was tempted to tell him I was your fart coach, what with you being England's number

8.

"IT WOULD BE normal to be feeling some anxiety. An upswing in anxiety, even. On a scale of one to ten . . ."

On a scale of one to ten, how tired am I of being asked to rate multiple factors—my pain, my level of effort, my sense of well-being, my ability to determine when I need to evacuate my bowels?

". . . how would you rate your current anxiety level? Now that you are in the final stages of your time here?"

There are three people who have to sign off on my discharge from the hospital. Dr. Monzales is one. Mum is the second. The third is, at this moment, sitting in the easy chair across from mine.

Dr. Bailey is bald-headed and gentle-eyed. Like Dr.

Monzales, he favors crisp, white shirts, open at the neck. The fact that I'll need his clearance to be discharged isn't my only reason for seeing him. Or at least, it didn't used to be. He *has* helped me.

I shrug. "Honestly, I don't feel that anxious at all."

Right now, it's true.

He frowns. "What's that on your arm? That mark?"

My gaze drops. It's a grass stain, I realize, from when I fell in the park. By the time I got back inside with Elliot, I had only five minutes before my meeting with Dr. Bailey, and I told Jane that if she had a problem, would she please speak to Dr. Monzales? (Yes, to my shame, I said "please.") So I'm still in my exercise gear, and I haven't had time to clean myself up.

"I don't know," I say, rubbing at it. "Maybe it's from the gym."

He looks unconvinced. But he doesn't press it.

"Well, Rosa, let's talk, then, about what's on your mind . . ."

But I'm not sure what to say. Because all I'm thinking about is what it felt like to be outside.

Dr. Bailey's office is bland. Neutral-colored and silent, apart from the bubbling of the aerator in a tank of tiny iridescent fish in the far corner.

I glance up at the high window, and at the light that's pouring in between the slats of the blinds. I realize I'm wondering if he's still out there, that guy who materialized, quoted the bench plaque, kind of defended my integrity, made me smile, and vanished.

Dr. Bailey clears his throat. "The life you left will not be the one you'll go back to, Rosa. But it's getting close now—that release. Into the unknown."

I force my mind into focus. "Not really the unknown," I say. "Mum's shown me all these pictures—"

"I'm not talking about your parents' apartment."

Oh, he's so literal, so oblivious to subtle sarcasm.

"Perhaps you'd like to talk more about how you'll manage interactions with friends that you had before the surgery?"

"There isn't actually that much to manage," I tell him. My illness and withdrawal from everything that was part of my life before it have seen to that.

Three days after my tenth birthday, two and a half years after my first symptoms, Mum and Dad got a letter from school saying that "with great regret" it could "no longer meet my needs." Mum hired a tutor, a retired headmistress with a dust mite allergy, who came to our home armed with textbooks and antihistamines four days a week.

It wasn't that long before my school friends dropped away. My fault, as well as theirs. Mum's fault, as well as mine.

I remember one afternoon—I must have been eleven—

Elliot walked Bea, my onetime best friend, home with him from school to our house.

"I saw Bea's mum," he told me, poking his head around my bedroom door, looking pleased with himself. "She'll pick her up at five."

But it was one of those days when the fatigue felt crushing.

Bea talked about how mean the new PE teacher was, and how they were going to the Algarve in summer, and how Bea had won an art competition with a picture of a horse that looked more like a dog, and she was going to have a kara-oke party, and did I want to come, because everyone would be there . . . And I said she could go.

Later, I heard Elliot and Mum in the kitchen.

Elliot was saying, in a kind of hushed shout: "She has to see her friends."

"It has to be her call, Elliot! You can't force it on her!"

"She's a kid. She doesn't know what's best. You have to help her see her old friends."

"What are *you*?" Mum half shouted back. "And why do I have to? So she can hear exactly what she's missing out on and they can watch her die, too?"

The few friends I have now, I found online.

The girl I exchange messages with most often lives in Tokyo. She has a Tumblr mostly about cats (it was her blog that introduced me to cat sushi—which does not involve any harm to a cat), and after we started swapping kitsch cat pictures with our own captions, I guess we kind of became friends. But if I ever meet her, AikaA, in real life, will she think, "Rosa doesn't look like how she writes"?

Hardly. I've never even mentioned the disease. As far as she knows, I'm just a regular girl who has a thing about cats and likes old epic movies (really old, like *Gone with the Wind* and *Lawrence of Arabia*) and macabre Victorian novels.

This is all true. But I've also told her other things . . .

Like, a couple of years ago, after a spell in the hospital for an experimental treatment had laid me up, I told her I'd fractured my wrist on a mountain biking trip in Majorca. Who knew they put the brakes on the other side in Europe? (Me, thanks to a Sussex cyclist's blog.) I also told her about all these bands I've allegedly seen in Berlin and Amsterdam, as well as in London. (I took all the details from Elliot's accounts.)

Yes, I've made up stories about myself. Don't we all, to some degree?

"If I remember rightly, you told your online friends that a car accident was the reason you were unable to communicate for months," Dr. Bailey says.

"Yeah."

"And so now?" he asks. "What do you tell them?"

"I'm making a really *amazing* recovery."

He nods. "You know, I wonder if, as part of your *amazing* recovery, you find yourself focusing on how it may feel to have a boyfriend."

First Elliot. Now my psychologist. What is with males? Dr. Bailey has broached this topic before, but not so explicitly. How it may *feel*? Surely he doesn't mean . . . "You mean . . . ?"

"Do you feel any remaining concern about having a relationship that would, naturally, to some extent, include an element of physical attraction?"

"You mean, will it bother me that someone will fancy the dead girl, not me?"

To Bailey's credit, he doesn't cringe. "That's not exactly what I meant. But it's close enough."

I think of how it was to feel that sunlight in the park. That light that touched the doctor and the bench and the guy with the tattoo, and touched me. I half hear myself saying, "I am her and she is me. We are indivisible, like the father, son, and holy ghost."

To his discredit, his expression hardens. I've just offended him.

And I feel . . . I do feel a little bad. I know Bailey's religious. There's a fish symbol magnet on his desk lamp. According to Jess, he met his wife on ChristianMingle.com.

The offense quickly fades from his face. But he says, "I wonder why you put it like that."

"It's not that I'm not grateful," I tell him. I sigh. "Maybe it's just that I've been a patient so long now . . ."

He nods. "You're *im*patient to get on with life in the wider world. It's understandable you would feel that way."

I think, not for the first time: *He's religious—and he accepts me.* At least, he's never looked at me as though I'm anything remotely resembling an unholy freak.

But that night, something happens to make me think maybe it's impossible to tell what someone's actually thinking unless they tell you.

And then when they do, it can come as a total shock.

9.

I'M IN THE park. The guy with the gray canvas satchel is there. There's a shiver in my flesh. We're standing by the bench, just looking at each other. I'm locked in on his expression. It's serious. Melancholy. He looks like someone who might read macabre Victorian novels. But who might feel that pictures of egg-wrapped sushi-kittens are just the sort of distraction that a mind that enjoys Edgar Allan Poe not only craves but requires.

Behind him, Dmitri is striding over from the hospital, calling to me. "Rosa, come back! I want to take you to Milan!"

I hear something else. A whispering. It's coarse. And it whips me up and out of the bewitchment of my dream into my forest-green room. The flash of the red dots between the numerals on my alarm clock is disorienting.

3:24.

My lips are parted—I think there's drool on my pillow. My body remains sunk in its own natural anesthesia. I feel sad, and irritated. *Why did I have to wake now?* It was a pretty good dream.

And I tense. Someone's behind me. They're standing or kneeling by my bed. I can *smell* her, her faint, individual body odor. She's whispering in a low voice:

"I take strength from you, Jesus Christ, our savior; your loving heart is everywhere. I humbly ask your pardon."

Jane. What is she doing?

"Forgive our negligence, our manifold offenses, the blasphemy of the disunion of the soul, of the ending of life, of the aberrant form."

The blasphemy of the disunion of the soul. *She's talking about them taking my brain from my skull.*

The ending of life. *She's talking about Sylvia.*

The aberrant form. *She's talking about me.*

I know what I *should* do. Jump up, hit the panic button, get the orderlies, have Jane removed from my room, insist on seeing Dr. Bailey, tell him she's set my recovery back months, have her disciplined and dismissed.

But I don't. For some reason that I don't really understand, I just lie there, listening. Tears well up. Gradually, they soak the pillow. The cheek that's pressed against it grows cold. I'm so rigid, and my breathing is so shallow, I think Jane must know I'm no longer asleep. But that doesn't stop her.

"Dear Lord, don't let her suffering be long. Bring peace to whatever she has, body or soul."

Don't let her suffering be long. What is she saying?

How long has she been there? Can this be the first night she's done this? For just how many weeks or months has Jane been taking care of me by day while by night she's been praying to her god for me to die?

10.

IT'S THE MORNING after that bizarre night I listened to Jane praying over my bed. The day after Elliot pushed over that bench, acting as prime accomplice in my escape.

I've completed my scan (I still have to wear an EEG cap for thirty minutes first thing each morning), I've just finished getting dressed, and there's a knock at my door. I open it and find Mum with a paper bag and take-out cup.

I think, *I should tell her about Jane.* But then she's smiling and kissing me. Her pink cheek is cold from the walk from the parking lot, I guess. "I have to rush to an appointment, but here. One latte. One cinnamon muffin." The warm, cozy scent drifts through the paper.

"Thank you," I tell her. I'm half waiting for her to mention the park, but she doesn't.

"I'll catch you later," she says. "Dad's going to bring pizzas over tonight from Figs. You want the one with the crispy eggplant?" I nod. "Six o'clock? Your room."

I'm still tense from what happened last night, but I manage a smile. "It's a date."

After she's gone, I think, *I should have told her about Jane. So why didn't I?*

I find myself remembering a conversation with Dr. Bailey that took place maybe a month ago. I'd just reread a short story by Poe about being buried alive. In it, Poe queries the location of the soul of a person who has no apparent vital signs but who isn't actually dead.

I remember thinking: *Is near-drowning like being buried alive?*

And: *At what point exactly did Sylvia die?*

I asked Dr. Bailey, "What do you think happened to Sylvia's soul and my soul?"

"Your *soul*?" he said.

"I guess you believe in souls."

He was silent for a few moments. "I have my beliefs, but they don't feed into my thoughts about you, or my work here with you."

"Why not? If they're what you believe?"

"I think it's important to have boundaries in life."

"But not in your thoughts?"

He sat up very straight in his chair. "There will always be people who try to categorize others and set them apart. I try very hard not to do that."

Maybe I should call Dr. Bailey and tell him about Jane.

I debate this with myself while drinking the coffee and eating the muffin—as close to a heavenly experience that I guess I can imagine—then I lie on my bed with my laptop, Googling "Christianity" and "souls." Then there's another knock on my door. And a voice calling: "It's me, Dr. Monzales. Are you there? Can we have a quick chat?"

After closing my laptop, I let him in. I sit on the edge of my bed. Maybe I should tell him about Jane. But again something stops me. He glances at the muffin wrapper and the take-out cup, which are on my desk.

"These are not from the hospital café." His voice isn't exactly suspicious, but there's an edge to it.

"No, Mum brought them. From the café by their apartment."

"Ah." He nods. "Rosa, I know you left the hospital yesterday. I know you were in the park."

My heart jumps and races. I feel unjustifiably guilty. I fold my arms across my chest. "It's just that I'm starting to feel kind of trapped and—"

He holds up his hands. "It's all right," he says, looking

a little awkward. "I'm sorry. I should have thought of this before. Of course, have some time in the park. Maybe after your morning study session?"

Academically, I'm quite a long way behind where I should be; but to give credit to Dawn, she's nothing if not dedicated.

"I just ask, for your own safety, that you stay close to the hospital. For now. And in case . . . We don't want anyone taking photographs of you—we don't want the media, when this comes out, scrutinizing any pictures of faces from around the hospital, looking for the patient. Is that okay?"

I'm relieved. I try to force myself to feel more rebellious. To tell him: *I don't even need to be here anymore!* But something inside me fails. Perhaps Jane has weakened me. ". . . Yeah."

"Okay, good. So I have this for you." He pulls a hinged silver bangle out of his pocket. "We issue these to many of our longer-term inpatients. It emits a radio frequency signal. It will allow you back in through the other doors, so you don't always have to be checked by security."

"A tracker?"

"Not a tracker! A bracelet of freedom, Rosa. Think of it like that." He smiles.

• • •

Just as Dr. Monzales promised back before I moved to the rehab wing, there is a classroom here, with space for up to ten laptops. But this morning's session is solo study. When I log in to my account, I find the modules that Dawn highlighted for me to complete. So I sit at the desk in my room, and I do my best to concentrate on quadratic equations and then alcohol group molecular bonding, aware that "my best" this morning is not likely to impress her.

As soon as I'm done, I tie my hair back, grab a *New Yorker* from a pile that Elliot left (given the condition of them, I'm not entirely sure he's actually read much, apart from the listings and cartoons), and take the elevator to the ground floor.

I brave the sentimentality of the ground-floor gift shop. I know—this from a girl with a weakness for pictures of kittens on rice, which I realize still sounds gruesome but honestly is just kitsch. I push my way past GET WELL! balloons and lurid cartons of rainbow-colored jelly beans and picture frames with pastel blue bears stuck to the sides, and find a pair of large black sunglasses, which I put on my hospital account. At last, I walk out, into the park . . .

Now I'm just a girl on a bench, taking in the fresh air and the sun, idly watching people going about their lives. Not thinking about Jane and what she said. Not wondering again why I haven't told Mum or Dr. Monzales, or if I should call

Dad. Not wondering if it's because I feel a kind of shame. Not thinking about Jane.

It's 12:14, and the park is filling up fast. Four nurses in scrubs just settled themselves with noodle boxes and chopsticks in the shade of one of the cedars. A couple of the ball-playing doctors are striding out from the ER, lanyards flying. And, I realize, he—Tattoo Guy—is sitting three benches down from me, holding what looks like an iPhone near the chin of a woman in a long pink fractal-pattern skirt and tan wedge boots.

She's doing most of the talking. Every so often, he nods or says something obviously encouraging, because she resumes her monologue. I'm too far away, and the background noise of people talking and a dog barking and a helicopter hovering out over the harbor is too loud for me to hear what they're saying. Eventually, he gets up. Says something inaudible. She nods. I hurriedly pretend to be focused on the *New Yorker*.

While to a passerby I probably appear to be engrossed in a piece about J.R.R. Tolkien's translation of *Beowulf*, my attention is on him. Out of the corner of my eye, I watch as he walks along the path, passes a bench, kicks a half-size soccer ball back to a toddler in a Spider-Man outfit, passes another bench . . .

"Matthew Radley. He loved life as much as we love him."

His voice is deep. Musical. My stomach clenches.

Is it weird to have this reaction to a guy I've barely ex-changed a word with? And to *dream* about him?

He sits down. Four inches of weathered gray-brown wood separate our legs. He's wearing jeans, a dark gray shirt, sleeves rolled to his elbows, and no sunglasses. How didn't I notice his eyes before? They're blue, but with an undertone of light. Of silver.

He squints in the bright sunshine. His face, neck, and arms are tanned. No distinguishing features, apart from that tattoo, which now I can see is of a constellation of stars surrounding two words in Latin: *Ad Astra*. I guess it means something to do with stars, but I'm not exactly sure what.

He's looking at me, and I find it hard to read his expression. Then I think: *A year ago, he'd have looked at you with pity, if he'd have looked at you at all.* The brute of a thought kicks me in the guts.

Seven-eleven, I tell myself.

I'm not even at the four of the seven-count inhalation when he says, "Could I interview you?"

What? "What?"

He waves the phone. "Joe Tyler, Bostonstream."

My words come in a rush, my lungs collapsing as I say, "You're a *journalist*?"

"I'm an intern."

"An intern *journalist*?"

He nods slowly. "Yeah."

A journalist. I scour his face. My heart is attempting to escape from my body. I'm searching for it—the sign that he knows. That he has *found out*.

"You know Bostonstream?"

It takes superhuman control, but I manage to shake my head.

"Bostonstream dot com. Interviews and reviews, mostly. I do this regular called The Bench."

When I don't respond—I can still barely breathe, never mind speak—he says, "So the idea is I go to a different bench every lunchtime. I sit next to whoever I happen to find there or I wait for someone to sit down, and I ask them to tell me about their life and their views on the issues of the day. I ask for their name and age." He misinterprets the horror that must be showing on my face right now. "I can change your name if you really want."

I glance over my shoulder, suddenly realizing there must be a film crew somewhere, capturing all of this. The approach. The enticement. The sting. He knows. I see only the wall of light from all the glass on this side of the hospital, the doctors jumping about, and the nurses talking over their noodles. But he must know, or why would he be coming out with all of this? Unless . . .

Unless what he's saying is the truth. And by chance he just sat down next to—without being immodest—the one person in this city who could most guarantee him international media stardom. How likely is that? I search his face for signs of deception. His serious silver-blue eyes meet mine. I have *no idea* what he's thinking.

"So—could I interview you?" he says.

"I—I . . ." My subconscious mind takes over. It weighs the options. If I say no, he'll leave to find somebody else. But how could I say yes? I'd have to concoct a story; it would have to be convincing; there's just no way—"Okay."

He nods. I don't know if he's pleased or relieved or even bored, because his serious expression does not change. "Do you mind if I record you?"

I hesitate. Is *this* the sting? He wants a sample of the donor's voice, so he can take it back as proof of life after death? Despite the sun, I suddenly feel cold.

"I can write it down," he says, "if you don't want to be recorded."

"I don't think I want to be recorded."

He opens up his bag and slips his phone inside. "Can I ask you not to talk too fast?"

"Okay."

"Okay." He pulls out a black notebook and a black pen. The

notebook's held closed with a red elastic band. He removes it and flicks to a fresh page, which flutters a little in the breeze. "Can I start with your name?"

"Is that how you know what all the plaques say?" I ask. "Because you do these interviews?"

"Denise and Matt?"

"Yeah."

He nods.

"There must be twenty benches in this park."

"Twenty-two."

"There must be hundreds of benches in this city. *Thousands* of benches."

His eyebrows furrow. "I guess."

"You know every inscription? If I gave you a park, I don't know, that one in town where all the revolutionaries are buried and said fourth bench in from the gate on the left, could you tell me what it says?" I'm babbling. I'm nervous. I don't want him to go. But I cannot be interviewed.

"I come to this park most lunchtimes. Not all the benches in Boston have inscriptions." His voice is low. He realizes he's under some kind of suspicion.

"Don't they? All the ones I see do."

"I guess you don't get out that much."

The way he says this isn't unpleasant exactly. But it's firm.

And something in me recoils. I get up. I register surprise in his eyes. To be honest, I'm surprised myself.

He blinks. "You don't want to do the interview?"

I'm so tense now I can hardly move. I think of Mum and how stiff she gets. Like mother, like Frankenstein's daughter. "I guess you could just make it up."

"Why would I do that?"

"I don't know. Don't journalists ever make up interviews?"

"Not any that I know. And why would I even want to when there's someone right in front of me I really want to interview?"

My nails dig into my palms enough to hurt. I'm out of my depth. A minute ago, he was insulting me. Now? Is he *flirting?* I glance at the next bench. A friendly-looking nurse is sitting there with a salad box and a *Redbook* magazine. "You could interview her."

"I don't want to interview her."

"I'm sure she'd have some really interesting things to say about the issues of the day."

"I think you have more interesting things to say."

"Unlikely if I *don't get out that much.*" I want to look anywhere but at him and this park, and the only place left is up.

A gull swoops past, and you know what I think? *Is it real? Is it remote-controlled? Is there a camera on its wing?*

But why bother with that? His phone is still recording, isn't it? There's a camera in his pocket, or his bag. Or in his notepad. Or in the tip of his pen. *I think you have more interesting things to say.* How unveiled can you get? What was I thinking? I just wanted some air. I just wanted to get out, to prove to myself that I wasn't a prisoner, and *what have I got myself into*?

I thought I was reasonably self-controlled, but my gaze searches for the security of the hospital, and I break into a lopsided jog, my weaker leg dragging.

Eyes swivel to me. I almost collide with a woman walking a dog. A shark-toothed terrier. It looks like it'd tear me apart if she let it. Her expression suggests she wouldn't be disinclined. A couple of nurses laughing over something on a phone stop to let me pass. As soon as I clear them, a woman in her fifties, wearing a tartan dress and sandals, steps out from under a tree and proffers a pamphlet. I don't look at it. She fixes her gaze on me. There's something in her storm-gray eyes, a kind of startled curiosity, that makes me want to *run*.

It takes all my remaining strength not to sprint inside. I keep the tears in check all the way to the elevator and up to my corridor. Jared's there, leaving his room. He pulls out his earbuds.

"Rosa?"

But I ignore him. I stumble into my room, fall on my bed, and let my chest heave.

Talking to a boy? Walking out in the world? Pretending to be normal? Thinking for one second my life could be just like anyone else's? What was I thinking? Does he—Joe Tyler—does he *know*? I have no idea. *What was I thinking?*

I stay like this, facedown on my bed, for more than an hour. When I finally get up, I go over to the wardrobe and open the door to reveal the full-length mirror on the inside. I make an inspection. My left cheek is creased from being pressed into crumpled bedding. My hair is damp. My cheeks are puffy. And, I notice, in the background of this depressing scene, something has been pushed under my door.

I retrieve it. It's a piece of paper, folded three times. While I was lost in self-pity, someone must have slipped it through. I expect it was Jared. Last week, he left a note inviting me to watch *The Matrix*—"I know what you said about sci-fi, but this could be actual *reality*"; I politely declined. But then I see this, in black scrawl on the front:

To the dark-haired girl who was wearing a white vest and blue jeans and who was in the park at 12:16, and who I think must be at this hospital and whose name might be Rosa but I'm not sure I heard properly. Other salient features: porcelain skin; kind of defensive, and

I don't blame her, because I was rude, and I would really appreciate it if you would get this to her.

My hands are trembling as I open the note. Inside, in what on reflection I decide is a neat counterpoint to the rambling message on the front, he's written:

I'm sorry. Joe.

11.

SOMETIMES I WONDER what it would have been like to be me thirty years ago, before the rise of the internet. Stuck in a chair, fitted with a colostomy bag, unable *ever* to escape other people's assumptions and judgments.

Online, I was free. Feeling equal to the people I messaged—knowing that they perceived me as an equal—was a revelation. My self-esteem soared. At least, while I was online.

Well, most of the time. There was one boy I used to message quite a lot, until I got the details of a concert by a Brighton band that Elliot had told me about all wrong, and the boy realized I hadn't gone to the concert and branded me a fake. (I cried into my pillow all that night. And the next. And the next . . .)

But real entanglement with real boys? I have to go back to elementary school, and Idris Hudson. He had huge brown eyes. I remember holding hands on the playground and scrawling him notes covered in hearts. This went on for two years. We were going to get married and have a baby called Ellie. Until he realized girls were disgusting. Then I went and developed a terminal nerve disease and we never saw each other again.

But this body? There must have been boys who had crushes on Sylvia. Her lips must have kissed theirs. Her hands must have touched their chests. They must have touched her. She was eighteen years old.

Joe sent me this note. Is he interested? Could he be? If he is, it's surely because of this body—not because of anything to do with me. But I guess this is the kind of problem that applies to regular people, too.

He said he often comes to the hospital park at lunchtime, and Dr. Monzales has already sanctioned it, so Jane can give me all the fake-concerned, critical looks she likes—I'm going back there tomorrow.

I wash my face, smooth on some moisturizer—which doesn't quite make the creases go away, but helps—and change into a fresh pair of jeans and my favorite top: a soft blue, with stars. I don't want to be here alone. The recreation room's rarely empty. Maybe I'll find Jess and tell her about Joe. Not the journalist part. The "is it weird to kind of like someone who was basically rude to me?" part. But perhaps it would be better to keep him to myself.

Just as I'm about to leave, there's a knock.

Mum. I hadn't expected to see her till six. She's in one of her white coats, and she looks pale. "Where are you going?"

"Hi," I say, a little surprised. "The rec room."

"No, you have to come." Her voice is taut.

"Where?"

She hesitates. "I don't want you to worry—it's nothing to worry about; it's just a precaution—"

"Mum."

"It's just the scan from this morning. It's nothing to worry about," she says. "It looks normal to me. But Dr. Joshi thinks the left prefrontal cortex, the—" She interrupts herself. "Look, it's okay. I just want you to come back, have another scan, in the suite."

I'm staring at her. The scans are always fine. "When?"

She raises an eyebrow. "Oh, next week. Whenever suits."

I don't miss the sarcasm in her tone.

As soon as we reach the scanning suite, they rush me in, and there are white-toothed smiles galore, which suggests to me that perhaps I should panic.

Dr. Monzales is there. He looks calm. But there's no small talk. As soon as I'm down on one of the black leather chairs, he slips an electrode cap on my head, and he, Mum, and Dr. Joshi, the chief neurologist, peer at the monitor on the desk.

Dr. Monzales's fingers flicker across a keyboard. Scientific sonatas. Or a death march? Is that what he's playing? He asks me questions: "What's your name?" "What's the quickest way to get from your room to the café?" "If you could change anything about your room, what would you change?" "How do you feel when you switch off the light at night?"

He views my multicolored brain from a variety of computer-generated angles. At last, he says, "Everything looks normal."

Dr. Joshi nods.

Mum releases a sigh that could fill a hot air balloon. She helps me remove the cap and kisses me on the cheek. Her lips are warm. "See you at six."

"Okay, Mum."

She smiles—a real smile. Dr. Monzales, too.

By now it's quarter to four. I'm hot. My hands are sweaty. There are dark smears of the gel that they use on the electrodes on my top. I don't want to go to the rec room like this. So I head back to my room and take a too-hot shower, hoping to wash out some of my bad mood.

The towel secured under my arms, I go to my laptop to message Elliot and find a picture from AikaA, my friend in

Tokyo, of a Persian kitten dressed as a Roman charioteer, a soft toy mouse harnessed to its cardboard chariot.

She's online right now. And she's in Japan. I can safely tell her about Joe.

I message her: *So I met this guy.*

Who??? What's he like? Send picture

I write: *Don't have a picture. He's—*

And I think—*what is he like? Why do I like him?*

Is it just that he's the first boy I've met outside the hospital, in this body?

He was rude. But I'm used to Elliot. I don't mind rude. In some ways, I even quite like it. (And he did apologize.) It's more interesting than nice. But there's something else: Unlike Dmitri, unlike Jared, unlike anyone I think I've ever met apart from Elliot, and maybe Dr. Monzales, he seems to have this kind of granite self-confidence. It's appealing. Well, it is to me.

I type: *Serious. Kind of intense.*

She replies: *Noooo!*

I smile. *What's wrong with intense?*

Everything!! Find warm funny genuine kind boy!

I write: *Oh no problem. Literally hundreds around to choose from.*

She replies: *Ha ha. Got to get to class.*

Now what? Actually, I don't want to talk to Elliot right

now. And I don't want to hang out in the rec room. There's an energy in my body. I need to *move.*

I ditch the towel, dig out some underwear, and pull on a pair of jeans and one of the T-shirts Elliot gave me (it says HOW THE HORSES FEARED—no idea what it means). My skin still damp with shower water and sweat, I take the stairs down, using the wall to help keep me steady. I detour through the near-empty gym and shove open that glass door.

I know: It's not right after my study session.

But I *want* to be outside.

For a few moments, I just stand there.

The breeze and the intensity of even the rapidly fading light reprise their roles as sources of near-spiritual wonder. I close my eyes and let that light burn away all thoughts of Mum and Dr. Monzales, Jane and Joe.

I listen to the chirrup of birds in the trees, the blood in my ears, the excited squeals of a kid in the dim, far distance. When I finally open my eyes, my retinas are scorched.

I blink. Gradually, pixel by glimmering pixel, I make out the trees and the benches, which are occupied only by two elderly men with metal canes. Then my brain registers motion to the far right of my visual field. I turn slightly to focus on it. It stops. *It* is a woman. She's over by the more densely planted region of the park, an area thick with bushes and reddening trees, fiddling with a wad of leaflets, turning from someone in the shadows who's walking away.

I recognize her: the woman from yesterday. The woman in the tartan dress. Only now she's wearing a baggy blouse and a long purple skirt. She has gray hair tied in a messy ponytail. A chunky silver necklace. She was watching me then. She's watching me now. I think: *Maybe she likes women and allegedly I'm cute*—and then all thoughts come to a train crash of a stop.

"Hey! Rosa?"

My heart hammering, I turn toward the voice. He says:

"It *is* you."

12.

JOE'S STILL WEARING the jeans, the gray shirt, the bag over his shoulder. I must be just taking him in, I guess, viewing him, like an exhibit, the way I've viewed boys for so long—not to interact with, Do Not Touch—rather than looking appropriately forgiving, because he says, "You got my note?"

He asked a question. It requires a response. "Yeah."

"The receptionist looked at me like I was trying to smuggle MDMA or something in the paper."

I nod, finally allowing myself to meet his gaze. There's so much light in the blue of his eyes. Like sun on sea. My heart racing, I say, "She has this crack-smuggling look for the people she really doesn't like."

"Okay." A pause. "Good."

He smiles, and with it, the rest of the world melts into action.

The park is a lot quieter than at lunchtimes, but a few people are around. As well as that woman, still fiddling with her wad of leaflets, there's a youngish couple in leather jackets intertwined on a stars-and-stripes picnic blanket under one of the trees. The breeze has dropped, and the air is thicker now with the scent of salt from the harbor, tinged with the odor of decaying leaves. Eau de Dixon-Dudley Park.

One of the elderly men heaves himself up from his bench. Joe notices him. He opens his mouth a little. Hesitates.

I say, "You were about to tell me what it says on the plaque."

"Then it occurred to me that knowing all the inscriptions on all the memorial plaques on all the benches in a park might not be on the all-time list of ways to impress a girl."

He wants to impress me? "There are *better* ways?"

"I guess I could give you my views on the issues of the day. Issue number one: As someone who has just spent close to four hours here, I can tell you there aren't anywhere near enough nurses eating noodles in this park. Or irritating doctors chucking footballs. The lack of irritating doctors chucking footballs in Dixon-Dudley Memorial Park is an issue I'll be raising in my next editorial meeting."

I smile slightly. "Four hours?"

"I sat down with this man. Then it was hard to get away. He wanted me to talk to his family. He brought them all out from the hospital, one by one. His mother, his sister, his brother-in-law, his son. I asked him to tell me about his life. He opened up. I didn't want to say, 'Actually, that's enough now.' They just went back inside. Then I saw you. About before, I am sorry."

I shrug in a way that's meant to suggest it's okay, not that I'm shrugging off the apology. And I think, *Someone who waits hours rather than offend someone who's baring his life is the opposite of rude.*

Then he says, "If you'll accept that, can I interview you?"

I glance back behind me. Someone's opening the gym blinds. I walk away from the door, into the park. Joe walks with me.

"To go on Bostonstream?" I ask.

"Maybe."

"*Maybe?*"

"I write stuff. They decide what they publish."

Hedging, delaying, and also because I'm curious, I ask, "Who's the most interesting person you've ever interviewed?"

"Most interesting?" We're by one of the cedars. He stops and seems to really think. Then he says, "Seven weeks ago, I sat down in this park next to a man who'd escaped North Korea with his mother over the mountains of Laos." He looks down at the grass around his feet. Takes a breath. "Actually. Interesting? I don't know what you'll think is interesting. I sat next to this girl. About our age."

He glances at me, then his gaze flicks back to the ground. For a long time, in conversational norms, he doesn't speak. I'm beginning to think he isn't going to, then he says: "Her mother was here, in critical care. She was in the last stages of leukemia and she'd gotten pneumonia. But she'd made it through the night, and she was doing better. The doctors said she was going to recover. From the pneumonia. The girl took fentanyl from the emergency drug tray. She injected it into a vein in the mother's neck. She killed her."

My brain reels. "The girl killed her mother?"

"She saw her chance."

"Did the mother want—"

"The mother had asked the girl's father to do it. He hadn't been able to."

"He hadn't been able to get drugs—"

"He hadn't been able to do it."

"What happened to the girl?" I ask.

"She was sitting here, waiting to be arrested."

"*Was* she arrested?"

"I guess so. Maybe not that day. Maybe what she'd done didn't come out till the autopsy."

"You don't know?" I say.

He shrugs. "I didn't read anything about it. She wasn't arrested that lunchtime. That's all I know."

"Maybe she got away with it."

"You don't get away with something like that."

"Maybe they didn't press charges," I say.

"Legally, they have to. Had to."

"You didn't write her story?"

"No . . . maybe I should have."

"No, you shouldn't."

He looks at me. "I know her story. I should have told it."

Unable to stop the fervor in my voice, I say, "I don't think all stories have to be told."

For a few moments, he just holds my gaze. I have no idea what he's thinking. He sighs. "They got frostbite on their feet."

". . . Who?"

"The man from North Korea and his mother. They got frostbite on their feet. But they made it to Vientiane. His sister had escaped to Seoul five years earlier. She flew to Vientiane, and there was this incredible reunion. They couldn't stop crying. They were all out and their nightmare was over. But the day they were set to fly to Seoul together, his mother developed a fever. The gangrene in her foot had infected her blood. She died in the taxi on the way to the airport."

I half whisper, "What was he doing *here*?"

"He married a woman who lived in Newton. She was in a car crash."

"Did she make it?"

"I don't know. One conversation. Thirty minutes on a bench. Then he had to go and visit his wife, and I had his story to write for the next day. Then my section editor ditched it for something on a woman who'd become a butt model after having cosmetic surgery on her ass. He'd overheard her talking about it on his train journey home."

For a few moments, neither of us speaks. Then I ask, "Do you like what you do?"

"I like what *I* do. Bostonstream's not exactly where I plan to be forever." He looks at me. "I thought I was supposed to be interviewing *you*."

I glance over at the nearest bench, which is facing the water. Beside it is a slim concrete lamppost, which I'm noticing because the bulb's flickering on. There's a line of them, I realize, all along the path, right to the wood.

The bench is vacant.

"How about this," I say. "You ask a question; I ask a question."

"That's not exactly the standard interview format."

"Then call it a . . . structured conversation."

"A structured conversation?" There's a glimmer of a smile in his eyes.

That smile cuts me deep. In the weeks leading up to the surgery, I listened to one particular song over and over. I focused on a single line. I'd obsess over it and what it meant for me and what I would become. It's about how if you look into someone's eyes, you can see their soul.

If the material eyes are a conduit to the immaterial soul, or mind, or whatever you want to call it, then I'm in deep trouble. Which was why I decided the lyric was all wrong. But now I'm looking into Joe's eyes, in the hospital park, this late afternoon, and I'm thinking: *Yeah, I'm in trouble. Now let me count the ways.*

13.

THERE IS A plaque. Of course there is.

In Loving Memory of Carol Anne Goodman, 1952–2016

I leave a space for it. It seems wrong, somehow, to blot out that loving memory with my still slightly sweaty back. Maybe Joe feels the same way because he sits on the other side of the plaque, angled toward me, satchel on his lap, pen and notebook resting on top. In the artificial white glow from the concrete lamppost, he might look a little more exhibit-like, a little less real, but there's an energy coming from him that lights me up from inside.

I have no idea what time it is. Mum said she and Dad would come by my room at six. If I'm not there, what then? They'll look for me in the gym, the rec room, maybe they'll knock on the other doors in my corridor, and then what? They'll alert security. Someone will find me. I have goose bumps, I realize. The breeze is coming off the harbor again and it's cool.

Joe says, "Are you cold?"

I might feel touched, I suppose, that he's noticed. But I'm not sure I'm ready to be touched. So I say, "As opening interview questions go, that is *a little bit lame.* The answer is yeah. My turn: Are you from Boston?"

He doesn't smile. I think, *You're too used to Elliot. Elliot is not like most boys. Lighten up with the playful insults.*

He says, "I'm from San Francisco. So you haven't been here long enough to lose your accent. How long have you been in the hospital?"

". . . About seven months."

"Seven *months?*"

"Why did you come to Boston?" I ask him.

"Family reasons," he says. "*Seven months?* When did you come to the States? What happened?"

I focus on the patch of mostly bare earth down by my feet and listen to the empty call of gulls out over the water.

After a few moments, he says, "In *this* park, if I ask someone what they're doing here, usually they can't wait to get it all out. I think everyone else they know has had enough of hearing about it, and here I am—"

"A shoulder to cry on."

"Someone who's interested when no one else is anymore. Maybe also because I'm not from around here, so I'm not the normal world, and we have that in common."

"What's the normal world?"

He shrugs. "Revere Beach. The Red Sox."

"I had to have this brain surgery," I tell him. "I was unconscious for a while. The rehab took a long time. I'm still under observation. Back to the format." My eyes jump again to his face, almost against my will. "Have you read *Frankenstein*?"

"I've seen the movie. One of the movies."

"So which is more scary: Dr. Frankenstein or his monster?"

"Dr. Frankenstein," he says. "Of course."

"Not the green flesh and the scars and the mismatched body parts?"

"Not the brilliant but irresponsible mind? The 'who cares what might result from my reckless actions' attitude?"

"Is that your question?"

He says, "What brain surgery?"

"Actually, it's not something I really want to talk about."

"Okay . . . then let me go again: Do you miss home?"

Eyes still on him, because now I can't take them away, I nod.

"What do you miss most?"

I think of saying the creamy stuff in Greggs vanilla slices or *Ski Sunday*, or women in their sixties in parkas sucking on cough drops. The types of things I say whenever Elliot asks me. Instead, I find myself telling him a heartfelt truth. "Belonging."

My body is not English. The cells in these hands, in these feet, in this heart, these lips, were generated by Hershey's bars and hickory-smoked bacon and Egg Beaters and T-bone steaks and whatever they drip-fed Sylvia while she was lying, suspended on the cusp of death, in her hospice. I fold my arms tight across my chest. The breeze swells the hair follicles in my arms. She was at home *here*, in America. Whoever she was.

"What do those words in your tattoo mean?" I ask him.

"*Ad astra*? To the stars."

"Is that your star sign?" I gesture at the tattoo.

"It's a constellation. Not mine."

I raise an eyebrow. Whoever's it is must mean something to him.

"Are your parents here?" he asks.

I nod. "Are yours?"

"Dad is," he says, frowning at the ground.

The tension level suddenly seems too high. I revert to an extraction technique of the sort perfected by Elliot. "So . . .

issues of the day. What's your opinion on croissants crossed with doughnuts?"

He looks up sharply. "What's your opinion of the Fox News coverage of Mexican immigration?"

I say, "Siamese kittens in flamenco dresses: freeing-occupied-France-right or invading-Iraq-wrong?"

He smiles. Oh, it goes right through me. And just for a moment, I completely forget about the strange way I came into this new life. Just for a moment, I'm sitting on a bench, awkwardly but to a degree successfully making my way through a not-very-relaxed conversation with a not-very-relaxed guy, and then I see something.

That woman. That woman with the leaflets.

She's over by the wooded area, the fall leaves engaged in what seems to me—as an English person used to life's grays and browns—an embarrassingly rampant display of color. The lampposts are lighting up the trees. She's looking up at the vulval reds and the jaundiced yellows, the surging oranges and the sickening greens, but I don't feel that she's genuinely appreciating the trees. I feel that she's there because she's watching me. My newly blooming happiness shrivels to a knot. Almost aggressively, I turn to Joe and say, "Do you think I'm pretty?"

He frowns.

"It's a simple question."

He says, "I don't know if pretty's the right word—"

Tears spark at my eyes. He's not sure if I'm pretty? It hurts more than I might have expected.

I get up from the bench and walk fast toward the trees. My right leg's dragging a little because of the ongoing weakness, and I know he'll notice, but I want one of the woman's leaflets. I need to know what she's doing out here. I'm covering the ground in uneven strides. She spots me. Lowers her gaze from the ludicrous kids' coloring set of a canopy. I hear feet in the grass behind me.

"Rosa!"

I glance around. Joe.

I turn back—and she's hurrying into the trees. The shadows suck her up. I'm shaking. She's stumbling away. She's gone.

Joe reaches me. Touches my arm. Needles pierce my skin.

"When I said—"

But I'm not listening. Who is she?

I notice something in the grass. My vision blurry, I bend, pick it up. I force my eyes to focus.

Shakespeare in the Park

As You Like It

The Savannah Company

Dixon-Dudley Memorial Park

September 23, 7 P.M.

$15

Shakespeare in the Park . . . What had I been expecting? Religious invective? A rant against doctors playing God? A photograph of me? *Shakespeare in the Park.* Paranoid. I'm paranoid.

The shaking gets worse.

Joe says, "Are you okay?"

I jerk my eyes to his face. I'm trying to keep my right hand together, but I'm failing. My thumb and forefinger separate. "I thought she was watching me." The leaflet flutters down to dead leaves. "I don't know."

"Do you know her?" he asks.

I shake my head. I can't look at him.

"When I said I don't know if pretty's the right word—"

"Yeah," I say quickly, "forget I said that."

"I can't forget it."

"I don't care." *I don't care?* My cheeks burn. Six-year-olds say *I don't care.* "Really."

He's watching me. My blurry gaze fixes on those words. Shakespeare. *Shakespeare.* The letters are swimming.

He doesn't give me any warning. He could say, *Who cares what might result from my reckless actions?* But he doesn't. He just puts his arm around me, and my body convulses. I feel—I feel . . .

I'm *freezing.* My flesh is gripped by cold. I'm *falling.* I'm *sinking,* and I'm *freezing,* so cold I can't feel temperature, only pain. And more pain. And terror. Then something very different: disappointment. It's overwhelming. A blackness descends, like the end of the world.

When I return to regular consciousness, I'm still standing in the park. Joe is holding my arms.

"Hey," he says urgently. "Rosa? *Are you okay?*"

I blink. My eyes won't reopen. Then they do.

He says, "I'll help you back to the hospital."

"I'm okay," I tell him. And I am. I think. I'm light-headed now. Just dizzy. I take a deep breath. *Normal,* I tell myself. I squeeze the fingers of my right hand together. They form a loose fist. Everything's normal. If I think it, it must be so.

"What happened to you?" he asks, searching my face. "Was it an accident?"

What can I say? In theory, though I'd never actually do it, I could explain my part in the story that culminates in the surgery, but what about Sylvia's?

Eighteen years old, in a coma, brain so badly damaged that she'd *never wake up.*

I cannot explain to Joe what happened for two irrefutable reasons: because he'd be so freaked out he'd run a million miles, and because I have no real idea about *her.*

I shake my head, say nothing.

14.

"MAMMARIES."

Dmitri grins. "Two points per letter. Eighteen points. And thank you very much."

I'm in the recreation room. It's like an oversize living room, with laminate flooring, six leather sofas, a selection of colorful canvas beanbags, and the contents of the Christmas wish lists of maybe twenty teens with Hollywood-high expectations.

There's an air hockey table (it helps repair damaged hand-eye coordination, Jane told me), a pool table, an electronic dartboard, a karaoke machine, an electric guitar with earphones, a half-size bowling alley, a cabinet full of board games, and ten gaming consoles.

Jared's on an Xbox with a new kid from Connecticut who got electrocuted in his dad's wheelchair repair workshop after a battery charger exploded. A couple of vehicle-accident girls are over on the air hockey table. Dmitri, Jess, and I are in one corner on beanbags, playing Super Big Boggle (The Biggest Boggle Game EVER!).

Somehow, I managed to get back to my room from the park just a few minutes before Mum and Dad turned up with pizzas.

They didn't stay too long. Mum looked tired. Dad really wanted to get back to finish up a chapter of the book on plant communication that he's working on while I'm here, and Mum's on her surgical contract with the hospital.

"How's progress?" I asked him.

"Think growth rate of a red oak rather than a sunflower," he told me, a little sadly.

After they left, I didn't feel like being alone. So I went to the rec room and found Jess pulling out all the board games from one of the cupboards. Super Big Boggle was her idea. When Dmitri asked to join us, I was suspicious. But not for long. So far, he's got *suck, tit, butt, ass,* and now *mammaries*.

I'd tell him to go and get off by himself, but I need a distraction, and Jess, who I thought would blush at all this, is smiling.

"Dmitri, you are such a *virgin.*"

"Oh, Jessica," he croons, "you could be the one. My special one. My first."

On her next turn, she gets *cock.*

"And funny!" he says. "I didn't know you were so funny."

She flashes me a smile. When she thinks *cock*, she thinks of Elliot, I realize (he's used that insult often enough around the gym). And I think of *Top Gear.* Jeremy Clarkson, I suspect, would play Super Big Boggle like Dmitri. I feel an urge to call Elliot. But it's 8:26. He's probably out with Aula, with his fake ID, in a trendy bar somewhere.

This floor is divided lengthwise by a corridor. The rec room's on the land side, rather than the harbor side, and has a strip of small high windows. Through them, I can just about glimpse the flashing lights of planes curving away toward the Atlantic. And I realize that I no longer have the wish to be on one.

"Rosa. Time's nearly up." Jess nudges my arm.

My flesh tingles. I remember Joe's touch.

Just a few hours ago, Joe's arm was around me. And I was *freezing* . . . and fainting. Should I have told Mum and Dad? Or Dr. Monzales? Was it a seizure? I don't know . . . maybe. No. Maybe.

I summon all the mental energy that isn't self-focused and manage to find *boat* and *play.*

I guess I don't have much to spare.

Dmitri grins. Triumphantly, he reads out, "*Gropes*. Not a nine, but yeah, not bad."

"What are you playing?"

I look around. Jared's turned from his screen. He's watching us.

"Go back to the zombies," Dmitri calls back. "This is a *word* game."

"I'm pretty good at words," Jared says.

"Dmitri is *amazing* at words," Jess says. "You want to hear his list from this round?"

"He's too busy killing dead guys," Dmitri says quickly.

"I've got time," Jared says.

Jess smiles at Dmitri. I guess he deserves payback for the lewd comments. "The way you got ma—"

Of course, she's going to say *mammaries*. But I'm pretty sure Jared would use this to embarrass Dmitri. "Yeah," I say, stopping her. "*Maximally* was an incredible score."

Dmitri looks at me, surprised, then beams. But I like him. And if Joe is a little intense but interesting, Jared's intense and a little off-putting. And there really was a meeting on graphic wall design, like he told me. I heard one of the nurses talking about it in the gym.

Jess shakes her head. She starts to list her words from the

round, but I don't hear them. I've noticed a streak of green and an aura of animosity over by the door. Jane. If I don't look at her, she can't see me. If I don't look at her . . . *If I don't look at her . . .*

Who do I think I'm bargaining with? Either way, she turns and vanishes. But there's something about the way she turns that triggers a vague memory. Of a shadow. Where—in the *park*? Someone vanishing into shadows.

Was Jane there for the surgery? I wonder. Did she shave Sylvia's head and disinfect her scalp? Did she wipe the debrider clean of damp, fresh fragments of Sylvia's skull? Did she help carry my de-brained body away to the incinerator? Did she read Sylvia's records? Does Jane know who she was . . . ?

I look at my slender hands. My mind floods with questions. Were these hands kind? Or cruel? Did they stroke, or hit? Did Sylvia have a sister or a brother? Did she help them with their homework? Did she ride bikes with them and make toffee apples? Did she like supernatural movies, or did she cover her eyes? Did her mother collapse when she heard what had happened? Did her father stand vigil over his daughter's stricken body? Was Sylvia unconscious from the outset, or did she gradually slip away? What happened to her?

What happened?

"And for my last word," Dmitri says, "*slut!*" He's gleeful. He looks at me. "Rosa, *lighten up*. It's just fun."

. . .

"Rosa? Were you *asleep*?"

Elliot.

I shift the phone a little away from my ear. "Almost."

"It's . . . nine twenty-seven," he says, half accusingly, a guitar loud in the background.

"I was off my face last night," I deadpan. "I needed an early one."

I hear his grin. "We're celebrating. Aula's sold her idea. It's about"—he adopts a spooky voice—"the creatures that come out at the crepuscule."

I roll over onto my stomach, wave my hand to turn on the bedside lamp, and prop myself up on my elbows. "Not even you can make *crepuscule* sound scary."

"As dusk falls, we witness the emergence of the moths, the bats, the"—dramatic pause—"anteaters."

"It sounds like some kind of organ," I tell him.

"The crepuscule of Langerhans!" he says, in the manner of a pompous doctor.

"The crepuscule of the corpus callosum!"

"What's the corpus callosum?" he asks.

"The part of the brain that connects the hemispheres. It used to be cut in cases of uncontrollable seizures."

Silence. Then he says, "Everything all right, or do I have to come and kick Jane in the crepuscule?"

I didn't even tell Elliot about the prayers.

"I would like to see that," I tell him.

"Or that boy? Jared. Does he need a kicking?"

"No . . ." I roll over again. "Elliot, I wish I knew about her."

"Who?" he asks.

But I know I don't need to explain.

After a few moments, during which the music gets quieter, which I assume means he's going outside, he says, "You remember all those reasons everyone decided an anonymous donation would be best for you as well as her parents?"

"I have her body," I say quietly. "She's part of me."

"*You* are you. If I had someone else's kidney, would that make me partly them?"

"It's different."

"If I had their kidneys and their liver? Their kidneys and their liver and their lungs. Their kidneys and liver and lungs and heart—"

"*Elliot—*"

"You remember that report that psychologist gave you? Before you even signed up for all this."

I don't answer. My elbows are beginning to hurt. I flop over onto my back.

"I remember entire pages. You remember the stats on heart transplants when recipients knew about the donors? *I* do. Forty-six percent had fantasies about the donor's physical strength, forty percent felt guilty the donor had died, thirty-four percent thought they'd taken on a part of the donor's identity with the heart. Just a *heart*. There was all that stuff from doctors arguing for totally anonymous organ donations, like they do in France, partly to stop all that from happening. You remember?"

"How many of those doctors actually had someone else's organs?" I ask him. "How many of them lived because someone else died?"

"You remember the case of Isabelle Dinoire?"

How could I forget?

Dr. Bailey's initial report included a section on her. She'd been mauled by her Labrador after overdosing on sleeping pills, and she was the first person to receive a face transplant. This was in France, so when the transplant took place, she knew nothing about the donor. But eventually, the donor's family approached her.

"So which do you think was better?" Elliot says. "Living with knowing nothing about the donor? Or finding out that this woman had hanged herself—and seeing her face in the mirror every day? I know with Sylvia it wasn't like that, but if you knew about her life, you'd look at yourself and you'd think about her. You wouldn't be able to help it. Why are you worrying about this so much now?"

Why am *I* worrying about this now? Perhaps it's because I'm close to leaving the hospital and *she* is who Joe—who everyone—sees.

Elliot says something else, but it's muffled. Not to me. "Rosa, I have to go. You know what I think: Maybe you should try to get to a point where you forget there even was a donor. *This is you.* I'll come and see you tomorrow or the weekend. Are you all right?"

"No need for us to go and live in a dark house," I tell him.

A pause. "Good."

The connection is cut.

I think, *Forget . . .* ?

Is he insane?

And if I did forget there was ever a donor, what else would I have to forget?

I remember trying to thump Elliot after he broke my new Shrek Slinky, and him, age eight, holding me at arm's length and saying calmly, "Rosa, you're a freak."

I remember dancing on my own in the kitchen to Rihanna's "Umbrella."

Feeling a glass of Coke slip out of my hand at Bea's eighth birthday party.

Losing my grip on the monkey bars in the playground, and Dad insisting, "Everything's all right, Rosa. *Everything's all right*."

I remember peering through the crack between the living room door and its frame and seeing Elliot kiss Catherine Smith, and feeling sad but not crying. Kissing someone . . . It would never happen. I was a different kind of person.

It was one thing to watch Elliot enjoying his life. Maybe Mum was right: It would have been unbearable to hear Bea and Lily talking about boys and parties and dancing. I shut myself in, Elliot and later my laptop my umbilical cord to life. And now . . . ?

Enough.

I couldn't ever forget.

15.

THE NEXT DAY, nothing happens until 4:42 P.M.

After a gym session, followed by two hours on an essay about the English Civil War, I go to the park and sit on the Denise bench, fully expecting to see Joe. But he doesn't show.

Dr. Bailey has given me lessons in avoiding what he calls catastrophizing. "If you find yourself with a bitterly negative thought about a situation"—*Joe has decided I'm completely unstable and the last thing he wants is to run into me again*—"try to think about the 'most likely' and the 'best case' scenarios."

Best case: He's utterly fallen for me and after a sleepless night of ardent obsession, he's so occupied in writing a detailed exposition of my many irresistible personality attributes that he hasn't noticed the time.

Most likely: Something came up at Bostonstream, and he's busy.

Still, my cheeks flush. Why did I ask him about Dr. Frankenstein? Why did I ask him if I'm *pretty*?

When I've finally accepted that for whatever reason he isn't coming to the park, I head back inside. I slump on my bed and I read. First, trashy websites:

THIS CELEBRITY LIED FOR SEVENTEEN YEARS

TWENTY MISSPELLED TATTOOS THAT WILL MAKE YOU DIE INSIDE

Then I download *The Facts in the Case of M. Valdemar* by Edgar Allan Poe.

I've read it before, but not recently. It's a short story about a man who is mesmerized—hypnotized—on the brink of death. His flesh lives on, though he, M. Valdemar, claims in a distinct, "gelatinous" voice to be dead.

The hypnosis has preserved him. It's incredible! It's horrible! It's also utterly outside his control. Once released from the trance, he instantly decays. Even the mesmerist is revolted: *Upon the bed, before that whole company, there lay a nearly liquid mass of loathsome—of detestable putridity.*

My flesh is dead. And I live on . . .

On a tray on the desk, my lunch is untouched. There's a skin across the vegetable soup. It's the color of detestable putridity.

I need air.

Something.

It'll have to be air.

After grabbing a sweater, I manage to slip back through the gym and out of the rehab wing unnoticed by anybody who might care. It's cool out here now. Dusk. The first stars are flickering between swathes of cloud. Beneath them, pale patches created by the park lights spread across the water.

There's no one else out here but me. I start to feel a little exposed. Perhaps because it's the only thing in the vicinity at least suggestive of protection, I head toward the wooded area beyond the last of the benches.

As I take the path in and walk among the trees, toward a clearing, I glance down at acorns so much bigger than those in England. I look up at the leaves. The fall isn't beautiful. It's a violent blood-spatter of death. Yet some of us—no not *some* of us. Just Sylvia and me. Like this tree, or at least its leaves, we are reborn.

My heart skips. Sudden nerves. I shouldn't have come out here.

I hear something. The flop of shoes on damp leaves. Someone behind me. There's a ripple in my heart. Another swish of leaves. Red alert through my nerves. Excitement. *Joe.*

It isn't Joe.

16.

HE'S LOOKING AT me. He isn't moving. *He isn't moving.*

A short man in black outdoor gear. Loose-fitting trousers and a fleece. Hollow cheeks. He's too far away, and in too many shadows, for me to see him clearly—but I don't *want* to. I want to turn and run out of the woods. But his gaze is fixed on me, and it's so intense it's reaching right into my muscles, holding them tight. He's looking directly at me, and his isn't the expression of a man on a casual walk through the woods. A wild thought occurs to me: *You can't kill me, because I'm already dead.* Still, I'm going to get a grip. I'm going to yell and I'm going to run.

Needles pierce my spine, releasing my legs. I'm about to run when I hear a scrappy noise off to my right. Footsteps. Someone moving fast.

Someone in a navy hoodie, hood up, making me think of a cobra, hands plunged in the baggy pockets. I can't see the face. The right hand, still in the pocket, angles up. Something *weapon-shaped* is aimed at the man in the fleece. A rough voice says: *"Wallet."*

Someone's mugging my would-be murderer in front of my eyes?

I'm trembling. My brain's moving like a slug.

The hand jerks again. *"Wallet."*

The man flinches and blinks. He looks wildly at me. His arm is shaking as he reaches for his pocket. He pulls out a wallet and throws it down on the yellowing leaves. He says quickly, "It's everything I have. Please, take it and go."

The person in the hoodie grabs the wallet. Then there's a shout from through the trees. A whoop.

The person in the hoodie seems startled. He twists, poised to run.

A girl giggles loudly: "Over here!" A boy's voice calls after her: "Wait!" Then another boy shouts: "Michael, where *are* you?"

Out of the corner of my eye, I see the gleam of what I guess is a phone flashlight. Then another. In a moment, they'll be here in this clearing.

The man in black looks hesitant, but he sees the lights

almost upon him, the person in the hoodie starting to stride away—and the man in black runs off, snapping twigs, quickly disappearing into darkness.

The person in the hoodie stops and turns to face me.

Joe.

Jesus.

Joe.

"I didn't think he'd actually *give* it to me."

Joe's holding the wallet, taking my hand, pulling me after him, away from the flashing beams. He whispers, "You know him?"

There's a giggle from somewhere among the trees. But it's fainter. They're heading in another direction.

He stops. In the darkness, I stare at Joe. I shake my head. "What's in your pocket?" I ask him.

"My phone. I thought—" He shakes his head. "Maybe that was stupid. But he was waiting for you. He was watching for you."

My body tingles and pinches, as if it's freezing around the edges.

"You said she was watching you—that woman with the leaflets. After I found out they don't really exist, I came looking for her. I didn't think she was coming. Then I found her around the back, where the ambulances pull in, and she was talking to him . . . I thought she was the one to follow." He frowns at the wallet. It's black leather. Worn. "Maybe he'll go to the police."

The world is swimming. I have no idea what's going on. "You did *mug* him. Even if it was only with a phone. What do you mean, he was waiting for me? *Who* doesn't exist?"

Joe nods, rubs a hand across his face. "I just wanted to know who he is. I'll send it right back to him." He glances down at the wallet. A beam flashes somewhere off to our right. "We should get out of here," he says. He jerks his head in the direction of the path I took in.

"What about the woman?" I whisper as I start to follow him through the trees. "*Who* doesn't exist?"

"The Shakespeare in the Park company."

As we emerge from the woods, he scans what we can see of the park—the benches, the path that splits, one fork leading around to the main hospital entrance at the front, the other toward the gym exit.

"What do you *mean*?"

He touches my back, urging me on. "Four companies are licensed to perform theatrical productions in this park. I checked. The Dalhousie Players. The Independence Company. Holt Street Productions. Southgrove Productions. There's no Savannah Company. Not that puts on plays."

I'm walking again, but I turn anxiously. "Why—"

"It's the perfect excuse to hang out in a public place, day after day, however long you like. You've got leaflets."

I can't quite work out what he's trying to tell me. "If people take them—"

"Why do you care? You're achieving your true purpose. If people turn up to see your fictional show and there's no show, *no one* cares apart from the people who turned up, and they're irrelevant. I don't know who she is. But *he* . . ." We step into the white glow of a lamppost. A hulking oak soars beside us. He flips open the wallet. "Is Daniel Johnson. You know the name?"

I shake my head.

"Fifteen Lake Drive, Hartford, Connecticut."

Hartford. I haven't heard of it. "What do you mean, true purpose?"

He looks at me. There's a metallic glint to his eyes.

"She *was* watching you. I saw her last time, and the time before. So today I followed her to a bus stop that takes you into the city. Then I realized he must have taken over. I didn't even see you go into the woods. But I saw him."

". . . Daniel Johnson."

"You're *sure* you don't know him?"

I wrap my arms tight around my waist and shake my head.

It may seem unlikely, but I don't think I've even met any Daniels. As far as I know, I've never heard of a Daniel Johnson. Never seen him before. Never seen *her* before, whoever she is, before she turned up in the park with the leaflets. But if they're watching me, they must know. One, or both, must know what I am.

Perhaps they're journalists, too, and someone's tipped them off. Suddenly, I remember the *shadow*. The woman was with someone who vanished into the woods. I *knew* that shadow. *Jane. Jane*, who believes I'm a blasphemy against her god. Has she told someone about me? Maybe they already have the photographs that Dr. Monzales was worried about.

Panic freezes my brain. But somehow it feels right to be on edge, out here, separated from everything I've known for seven long months. Then I'm struck by another thought. Joe noticed her. He was watching the park. Watching out for me. And I'm not paranoid. I should tell Dr. Monzales. Or Mum. Or both.

"I need to know who he is," I whisper. "If he's following me."

Joe's already pulling out his phone, to search the name, I guess. Mine is back in my room. He looks up. "No reception. Must be signal blockers in the ER." He eyes me uncertainly.

"You have any idea why people you don't know are watching you?"

I have no clue what to say. A flash in the sky grabs my attention. A plane is soaring way above us. Some trick of the distance or the harbor sucks up the noise. I watch it, that flashing, humanly vulnerable leap of faith. I want to tell Joe something true. But what?

"You think maybe you knew them but you've forgotten?" he asks.

"I . . . don't think so." *Be precise, Rosa.* At least, to the extent you can. "I had brain surgery. Maybe everything isn't normal. But it's not like I have memory loss. It's . . ."

"It's what?" he asks.

I look at him, and a heartfelt truth spills out. "Like I was . . . mesmerized. I feel like I still am."

It's an odd word to use in modern conversation, I know. Or an old-fashioned meaning of the word. It's also the closest I can get to an explanation fit for Joe's consumption.

A breeze suddenly gusts. The leaves of the oak beside us tremble in a death rattle. Droplets of old rain are spattered on our heads. The stale water moistens my lips. I want to spit it out.

"Mesmerized," Joe repeats, frowning now at the path. It's scattered with rotting leaves. They reek of bacterial decay, of vile putrefaction. "Yeah. I understand."

To my surprise, the expression in his eyes tells me he *does* understand. I don't know how. But it's like another loop of invisible thread has just been wound around us. Does he feel it, too?

17.

I SLINK FURTIVELY into the hospital through the gym entrance. At the last moment, I glance back, hoping to see Joe, but his image is blocked by my light and his darkness. I see only myself, reflected in the door.

I've never tried to get phone reception outside. But it makes sense that they'd have signal blockers in the ER, an enforcement of the signs requesting you to refrain from using cell phones in case you should interfere with the functioning of sensitive equipment.

I hurry out of the deserted gym, past the rec room, toward the elevators. There's good reception in my room. My plan is to get my phone. I'll search Daniel Johnson. Then I'll meet Joe in the café, Les Baguettes, which is open to visitors.

As I summon an elevator, I suddenly sense eyes on me.

Jared.

He's slouched against the moss-green wall, hands in his pockets.

He straightens a little. "You've been out?"

"Uh-huh."

"In the park?"

"Cocktails and clubbing," I say.

He frowns.

". . . Not really," I tell him.

"Yeah, you know, it's not like the stroke damaged my cognitive capacity."

I'd feel bad—if I had brain space to spare. "No, I'm sorry, I—"

The elevator arrives and the doors part. I'm half prepared for Jared to slip in, movie-style, with me just before they shut. He doesn't.

It's hot in here. As I pull off my sweater, I'm forced to close my eyes briefly, and it's not Jared's face I see in my mind but Daniel Johnson's. Hollow cheeks. Unnatural eyes. *Who am I to call someone unnatural?* I take a quick breath, then another. *Seven-eleven,* I tell myself. *One, two, three—*

Daniel Johnson. Who is he? A journalist?

Four . . . A nurse who cleared away the still-warm detritus from the operating theater? A mortuary attendant?

Five . . . An IT employee who decrypted Dr. Monzales's files? If he knows about me, does he know about Sylvia?

Six . . . Should I go to the police? Or to Mum?

Seven . . . Or to Dr. Monzales? Not yet. *Not yet.*

Before I can start my eleven-count exhalation, the bell pings. The elevator doors slide open. I walk fast along the softly lit corridor to my room. As I close the door, it locks automatically. It doesn't seem enough, somehow. If there was a chain, I'd hook it. If there were deadbolts, I'd shove them home.

Where's my phone? There, on the desk. I sit on my bed. My fingers tremble as I type "Daniel Johnson." Unsure whether it'll help to add anything else, I leave it at that.

I get 283,000,000 results.

He's a soccer player. A celebrity hairstylist. The Formula 1 correspondent for the BBC. A member of the Scottish Parliament. A photographer. Why did he have to have such a common name? I remember his address. So I add "Hartford." And I get . . . nothing. At least, nothing useful. I add "Dixon-Dudley Memorial" . . . nothing. I add "reporter" . . . nothing.

Perhaps this is a lot more straightforward than I'd suspected. He *is* a murderer. Or a rapist. Or a thief. He and that woman work together. She identifies vulnerable patients in the park, and he goes after them. Is that it?

It would be bad luck, on my part. But then, luck's not something that's always swung my way.

• • •

"So, it was, like, two years ago, and I was in Prague with my cousin and her band, and there are trams. She'd been drinking. Those big glasses. You know, like those German steins? She'd had four of them—*liter* glasses—maybe five. She stepped out. It hit her. The tram. Yeah. I heard the thud. She was in a coma for two months—"

I'm listening to the conversation at the café table behind me because it's something to pin myself to. I don't want to answer the question that Joe just asked me: "Do you remember *this*?" And I don't want to look at his phone again, because if I do I'm going to throw up. I'm steeling myself to answer.

Me, Rosa, the strong one, who does whatever she has to do and doesn't shrink from it.

Joe's just sitting there, forearms on the pale wood table, his phone between them, watching me with an expression that's excruciatingly close to suspicion.

At least no one else is watching me. Les Baguettes is not big. Eight tables, surrounded by a juice fridge, chiller cabinets, paper-wrapped meatball-and-cheese baguette sandwiches stacked by a microwave, and a hot drinks machine. The new kid and his visitor, a guy with a beard and a baseball cap, are occupied in their own conversation. The woman at the register is typing something on her phone with one hand while scratching at her paper cap with the other.

And then there's us.

As soon as I got here, I noticed Joe at a table by the juice fridge. His head was bent over his phone. It wasn't until, over the soft classical Muzak, he heard me scrape back a chair and looked up that I realized he knew something. I sat down on autopilot. Evidently, he'd gotten a signal. *Evidently*, he'd made some form of discovery. I wanted to ask, but my mouth was dry.

He put his phone down on the table. Said quietly, "Do you remember *this*?" He looked at the screen.

I looked, too.

At a photograph of my new body. Of Sylvia—of me.

In the photo, she was smiling. She was a few years younger, wearing denim shorts and a white short-sleeved top, her thick hair in a ponytail, a fishing rod, of all things, in her hands. It was a sunny day. She was squinting. She looked happy.

My mind is accosted with manufactured memories. They come rushing, my brain no doubt working to make sense of what I look like and what I just saw, because I feel like I can *remember* pancakes for breakfast, the crunch of a partially defrosted blueberry between my teeth, sunlight on a drive, the musty, plastic smell of a car in the warmth. A glimmer of water. Rocks. Shale. Minnows in the shallows.

"Rosa?" Joe clears his throat. "*Sylvia?*"

Sylvia.

I take the phone and I scroll up, above the picture, to a headline.

LEXINGTON TEEN IN COMA

And then down.

Sylvia Johnson, 18, of Courtyard Place, Lexington, is in a coma after falling through ice into the Old Reservoir on Marrett Road. The Lexington High School student is being treated at Massachusetts General Hospital, where doctors say there is a slim chance she will regain consciousness. Johnson's mother, Amy Johnson, 38, and her father, Daniel Johnson, 52, are at her bedside.

18.

I'M FREEZING. MY flesh is gripped by cold. I'm falling. I'm sinking, and I'm freezing, so cold I can't feel temperature, only pain. And more pain. And terror. Then something very different: disappointment. It's overwhelming. A blackness descends, like the end of the world . . .

The phone clatters to the table as though dropped from some other hand. I press my palms to my eyes.

Near-drowning . . . She slipped through ice, into freezing water. That's what happened. *Sylvia.*

And I felt . . . But it's impossible. *Impossible.* It was a hallucination. Or a seizure. This is her body, but it's *my* brain. *My* brain. Hers is gone. Her *life* is gone, left only in traces, in *other people's* memories.

Her father was in the woods here, outside the hospital. *Her father*, who—according to the legal document we all signed—agreed that there should be no contact between us. Who Dr. Monzales seemed so convinced did not *want* to see his dead daughter's body walk the earth.

Who's the woman? Her mother? *No.* We made eye contact that afternoon in the park. If she was Sylvia's mother, she couldn't have looked at me so unemotionally.

Whoever she is, she's been watching me. And the doctors didn't know. *Sylvia's* father nearly—did what? Kidnapped me? Was that her parents' intention? They gave consent to the procedure so that *she* could live, and they could take her back?

I think, *Imagine knowing that your daughter's body is walking around, and seeing her. But imagine knowing that your daughter's body is walking around—and not seeing her. Which would be harder?* Well, now I have my answer. Has her father been out there all these months, I wonder, just waiting for me to venture into the park alone?

"Rosa? Did you hear me? This is you, right?"

I glance over at the window and see only the fractured reflections of the café. Is her father out there now, hoping for another chance?

"No," I whisper.

As I push the phone back to Joe, another realization strikes. This one cuts me right through.

When I'm discharged, Dr. Monzales will tell the world about the surgery. When the news breaks, Joe *will know.*

He'll be—what, revolted? Disgusted? And he's a journalist. He won't be able to resist writing about me. It would make him famous. Reporters from all over the world will rush to find me. They'll hound me—and Mum and Dad and Elliot.

I *do not* want Joe to discover the truth. If I can buy time, perhaps I'll find a route to salvation. It's happened before.

I whisper, "This isn't me."

Joe's expression is disbelieving. I can't blame him.

"She looks like me. She *isn't* me. I'm *English.* I'm from *London.* I look like her. Her dad must have seen me. He must think I'm her."

"The photo—"

"Listen to me. Do I *sound* American? Ask me, I don't know, who's the member of Parliament for Glossop?"

"Who's the member of Parliament for Glossop?"

"I have no idea. But I've *heard* of Glossop." I hear my words tumbling out. "What eighteen-year-old girl from Lexington, Massachusetts, has heard of Glossop? Hartlepool. Grimsby. Northallerton. Herne Hill. Have you heard of Hartlepool? Lewisham. Rotherham. What eighteen-year-old American has heard of Rotherham? I. Am. Not. Her. Ask me how many weeks you wait to see a doctor on the NHS. Ask me who the judges on our *X Factor* are. Ask me what Jamie Oliver's kids are called. No, don't ask me, I don't know. Ask me—"

"Okay—what—"

"Poppy. One of his kids is called Poppy!" I realize I sound insanely triumphant.

The suspicion in his eyes fades a little.

"The Turing test for Englishness," he says, leaning back a little in his chair.

"And if I was this girl, when I saw my dad in the woods, I'd have said, 'Hey, good to see you—why are you skulking about out here? Come back to my room for some Hershey's bars and soda.' Wouldn't I?"

"Maybe you ran away. You think you haven't lost memories, but you have. That was a terrible accent, by the way."

"I would remember another life." I wrap my arms around myself and feel my pounding heart. Around her. Sylvia. I feel protective. Of us both. "You seriously think I'd run away and pretend to be some English girl, and persuade all the doctors and nurses, and even find people to pretend to be my parents and my brother? Ask anyone. Ask that woman at the register—she's seen me here with *my* family."

He shifts in his chair. Then he glances behind us, at the new kid and his friend who told the story about the Prague tram, and at the woman, who's yawning, still scratching at her cap.

"You should go to the police," he says quietly, "if her dad is here, and he thinks you're her."

I clasp my hands in my lap. Unclasp them. Clasp them. I feel . . . strange. Hot and numb.

She lived in Lexington. Her name was Sylvia Johnson. She fell through ice. And her father came to find me. What should I do? Suddenly, I feel overwhelmingly sad. *She fell through ice.*

I can't look at Joe, because I feel tears coming. And I'm ashamed. Confused. Sad. Ashamed. Tired. Sad, mostly—for her.

But I also know something for sure: I need to find out everything I can about her. To be able to live with her body, I need to know what kind of life she had. What kind of girl she was.

I glance back at the phone, which is on the table in front of Joe.

"Why did you look up that Shakespeare company?" I ask him. "Why did you come back and follow the woman?"

"I told you: I saw her watching you. I saw her just hanging out with those leaflets."

"So you left work and came all the way back here?"

"Why so suspicious?" he asks. "I wasn't even *at work*. Look, I started The Bench as a blog. It did okay. Bostonstream wanted to link to it but instead I talked them into carrying it and having me in the office three mornings a week, doing basic stuff, getting experience. So, Friday afternoons, no, I don't have to be in. Why did I help *you*? I guess you seem like someone who could maybe do with some help."

For a few moments, I just let all this sink in. I don't want to be someone who seems like she needs help. But I guess I do actually need it. I look up at him. "I'm sorry."

"Accepted. And in case you're wondering, I don't make a habit of mugging people. I'll send the wallet back tomorrow."

I nod. "I guess if the journalism thing doesn't really work out, though . . ."

"Yeah, professional mugger is now officially my plan B. *If* I don't get arrested."

Surely there's no chance, though, that Sylvia's father will go to the police. In coming near me, he's broken the terms of the legally binding donation agreement. All I can say to Joe is, "There were no witnesses, except me, and I only saw a hood." I frown down at his phone. "I'm not her. But I really want to know who she was."

"Was?"

"Before the accident . . . what she was like. What her life was like."

"Can you tell me why?"

"I—" I sigh. "Right now"—*right now? Not ever*—"I can't. I really appreciate what you've done. And I will totally understand if you'd like to just walk out of here."

The violins gently soar into a subdued crescendo.

At last, he says, "I guess that's not what I'd like to do."

I'm thinking about what to say—how to let him know that I'm glad, and I'm sorry—but he's talking again. "Look, I have some experience in finding out about people. If you don't want to talk to her parents—which I take it you don't—you can get a lot of information online. But if you really want to find out about her, and discover what's true, not just social media PR, you need to talk to people who knew her. So the best thing's probably to go to Lexington."

The room starts to spin. I don't respond. Of course there's no way I can go to Lexington.

"It isn't far away," he goes on. "Forty minutes, maybe. You could get a cab . . . or I could take you?"

The dizziness intensifies into a kind of mental tornado.

I feel like I have to fight against it to spell it out to myself:

Joe just asked if you want him to take you to Lexington.

Mum would go crazy. Dr. Bailey would downgrade me to unstable and order me interned for another six months. If I could ask Elliot right now, he would no doubt try to talk me out of it.

But I have free will, don't I? And Joe didn't ask what obstacles stand in the way of my leaving with him. He just asked if *I want* to.

I signed that legal document, too. I'm not supposed to ever meet her parents. And after what just happened—and that haunted look in her dad's eyes—I don't think I want to. This could be my chance to get closer to Sylvia.

"Would you really?" I ask Joe. "Take me, I mean?"

"If it would be medically safe for you to go, yes."

It would, surely. I'm in the final stage of my time here. Dr. Bailey himself said that. I could take my medication with me. I nod.

"How old are you?" he asks.

"Eighteen."

"So, it's your call. Look, it's Friday. I have to be at work Monday morning, but I could clear the weekend. You could think about it, and I'll give you my number. You can call when you've decided. Or we could go now . . ."

I don't answer right away.

His proposition hangs between us.

I feel on the verge of something, and I have to make the right leap. Like I'm out on the edge of a cliff. I'm swaying. I could fall either way if I'm not careful. Nervous tension is all that's holding me up.

19.

IT'S A FOUR-WHEEL drive. A hulking, shadowy silver car parked between other hulking, shadowy cars in the hospital's underground parking lot.

Joe presses a button on the keychain, and I hear the click of my future opening up. Perhaps I'm a little scared because fear for my own survival has long been the leitmotif of my life. But mostly, I can't believe that after all these months I'm finally leaving Dixon-Dudley Memorial. Not as I expected it to happen, but still.

After I throw a bomber jacket and my yellow overnighter —my cabin bag on the journey here to Boston, hastily packed with my medication, some clothes, and toiletries— in the back, climb in, and strain to pull the monumental door shut, that disbelief animates into something closer to excitement.

The engine kicks in. We pull out of the parking spot, angling toward the exit. Joe presents his pass to the scanner at the barrier. As the barrier rises, pent-up tension floods out of me. The release seems so substantial, and immediately afterward I feel so much *lighter*, that I can only compare it to an exorcism.

The discussions with Dr. Bailey, the case studies and the measured consideration of the attitudes of major organ recipients, conversations with Mum about life after the hospital—all that was theory. This is real. This is *me*.

The free world speeds past.

We're on a straight, dark road. Smart-looking warehouses to both sides. Dock buildings, I guess, converted into apartments. A corner café, shuttered. A thin woman in neon pink sneakers, swinging something heavy in a paper bag. A man in a suit shouldering a backpack.

A man heading home from work. A woman who's just popped out for a carton of milk. Normal people. And I'm among them.

I'm out, *I'm out*. The fact of it is spiking me over and over, shots of adrenaline to my heart.

I stare at a boy jogging past with an easy, loping stride. A woman in a window pulling up the blinds. Supersize traffic lights that make me think of *Sesame Street*. Uppercase road signs that make me think *I'm* on TV, watching myself.

Normal American people. In their normal world.

The road splits. We veer down to run parallel to the harbor.

The water's still, shiny black. The sky above it is speckled with stars and airplane lights. An SUV passes us, windows half down, pop music blaring, three young girls with braided hair in the back, shuffle-dancing in their seats, singing along.

I press a button in the door to lower my window, and I smell salt and rot. It's disgusting. It's *wonderful*.

Then I think, *How long will it be before someone at the hospital realizes I'm gone?*

I have to get a message to Mum, but I'll wait an hour or so before I text her. I want to give us time to get far enough away from the hospital.

Joe interrupts my thoughts: "I should make one stop. If I drop the wallet at the office, I can get it couriered back. That okay?"

I nod. "Yeah."

"And I know food probably isn't going to be uppermost in your mind right now. But I haven't eaten all day. Do you mind if I get something?"

I shake my head. "Of course I don't mind."

"The burger joint rated by Bostonstream as selling the best

burger under ten bucks is practically next door to the office. It'd be a crime for us to be so close and not to get some . . ."

I glance at him. "I couldn't let you add another crime to your tally for the day."

He shakes his head, pretending—I think—to be offended.

Then I realize a problem. I can't believe I didn't think of this before. "I—I don't actually have any money. Or a card. Everything at the hospital goes on my account—"

"I have money."

"I don't want to use your money."

"I guess you don't have any choice."

"I'm really sorry—"

"Rosa, seriously, it's totally fine."

"As soon as we're back, I can get money—"

"I told you," he interrupts, looking at me so long I start to worry about the road. "It's fine."

We turn a corner. A group of men and women in suits tumble out of a bar. Joe slows the car at a crosswalk.

I look up. Suddenly, we're hemmed in by tall buildings. I peer out at a grand old hotel, its windows of yellow light like pores in the brickwork, emitting human happiness, human warmth. The people in those rooms are hugging, celebrating, bathing, having sex. Not enduring physical therapy, not sweating in an Exoskeleton, not dreading test results.

We pass a sign for a college. And a theater. Blue-and-yellow banners run down a classical facade. They're rippling in the breeze, or maybe it's just the motion of the city—all the cars and the people, thronging the pavement, talking, eating out of paper bags, laughing, shrieking into phones.

Sylvia's father came after me. I have left the hospital. I'm out.

From the safety of Joe's car, I stare out at this world, unremarkable to anyone within a hundred-mile radius but me.

As we drive on, I notice parkland to the other side of the road. I can't avoid being drawn to the shadows. Tree after raggedy tree after tree and *gravestones?* Are those gravestones? Then this must be Boston Common.

The traffic slows again. Brake lights from the truck in front of us almost hurt my eyes. Joe says, "You still okay about all this?"

"This?" I repeat the word, because I'm not sure exactly what he's asking. *This*—us in a car. *This*—being alone together. *This*—with night coming.

"Leaving the hospital," he says.

"Oh. Making my escape in a strange car."

"With a strange guy you hardly know."

I look at him and let my eyes trace his profile, his shoulder, his arm, bent to hold the wheel. "Who, without me asking, followed this woman who's been watching me, pretended to be a mugger, and found out that a man who thinks he's my father is following me."

"Yeah, that guy sounds pretty strange."

He glances at me and smiles. Almost as quickly, his face falls.

I tense. "What's wrong?"

He's peering over at a narrow open doorway with a red awning above it and a line of people snaking from it, onto the pavement. The awning reads BART'S BURGERS.

"Nothing," he says. "Except that line."

We park on the street.

I grab my jacket, get out of the car, and as I feel the thud of my feet on free ground . . . Yeah, maybe *this* is my Neil Armstrong moment.

But I don't want to think too much about the momentousness of leaving the hospital, and I can't, because I'm being bombarded. Voices. Voices. Horns. Engines. A radio voice yelling from a cab window about someone being disgraced. A muffled loudspeaker somewhere blaring hip-hop. A dog yelping. I'm hit by sweet perfume from a woman untying a silk scarf from her neck, and then by the smell of fat from a Styrofoam box of french fries as a dreadlocked girl on a skateboard whizzes past.

Joe's at my side. He touches my arm. Points to the doorway. "I'll drop off the wallet and be right back. See if you can find somewhere to sit. I'll order. Burger and fries?"

I nod. "Thanks."

I have a mission now. I can focus.

I slip inside the burger joint, pressing myself to the doorframe to try to avoid knocking into anyone.

Perhaps my luck really is changing, because as I reach a window booth, the couple sitting there gets up. The guy is very tall and very blond. The girl's hair is cobalt blue. I know I'm staring. But I can't help it. And they don't look at me. As soon as they're gone, I sit down on the bench facing the window. The red leatherette's warm where the girl was sitting.

In here, it's still noisy. Louder, maybe. A couple of girls—maybe eleven or twelve years old—are giggling in the booth behind me. Customers are calling their orders at the register. I hear the rattle of ice cubes in glasses. Smell the hot dog on a plate carried by a woman with long scarlet nails. The red of those nails and her lips are visual sirens, screaming: *Remember, remember!* I lived in London. It wasn't that different. Almost every Thursday night, I used to go with Mum and Dad and Elliot to the restaurant maze of Brixton Market. But I've been cloistered in the hospital for so long. Being here—it's like that feeling you get when you've been sitting for ages, then you move, and blood gushes through your numbed limbs.

Movement outside catches my eye. A man striding past, yelling into his phone.

Beyond him, across the street, the trees are almost bare. Fragile brown oak leaves are still clinging to their branches, seemingly the last leaves left, the most reluctant to admit death and drop.

By natural law, I should be dead. But I'm in a burger restaurant in Boston. In *Sylvia Johnson's* body. In her country. Out in her world.

Did her dad see me leave? Has he followed us? I was careful on my way to the parking lot. I didn't see him. But perhaps he had somebody else watching out for me.

From a zip pocket of my jacket, I pull out my phone. I try to focus on what to text Mum. Forcing myself to block out my surroundings, including those giggling girls, I write, delete, write, delete, write.

However I phrase the text, it sounds just too bald or selfish or weird.

Then I think, *If I text, will she worry I've been abducted and it's not from me?*

I contemplate adding a line that'll confirm my identity.

Something only I'd know. The name of my first hamster: Cheeseball.

But that might come across as odd, too. So I delete my mess of a draft text and call Elliot instead. Then I end the call before he has a chance to pick up.

How long was Sylvia's father waiting to glimpse me? Who was that woman? Did I *really* see her with Jane?

I try writing another text to Mum.

In the end, I settle for:

I am totally fine so please don't worry. Just need a little time away. Am safe. Have drugs. Really, don't worry. I won't be gone long. Love you.

And I send another:

Tell Elliot there's no need for any dark house.

And a final one:

I'm going to turn my phone off for a few days. So don't worry if I don't reply.

And I am going to turn it off, because I've seen *The Wire* and *CSI* and even, once, when I just didn't have the energy to change the channel, *Hawaii Five-O*. I left my bangle back in my room, just in case it can function as a tracker, but I know the police can home in on mobile phone signals. And I wouldn't put it past Mum to call the police. But before I power off my cell, I half stand to search for Joe in the line that's still stretching out of the door. I make out what I think is his head. Before he comes over, I want to find the newspaper story he had up on his phone in Les Baguettes.

Now that I know what to look for, it doesn't take long.

I find five paragraphs. The photograph. And beneath the photograph, more detail.

Friends report attending a house party on Marrett Road on the night of the accident. Around midnight, a group that included Johnson left the party for the Old Reservoir. One teen, who was said to be upset over the breakup of a relationship, walked onto the ice. Johnson followed in an attempt to encourage her back. When the ice cracked, Johnson went under. The other girl made it to safety.

Emergency services were called, but by the time fire department officials located Johnson, she had been submerged for 42 minutes.

The cold temperatures had slowed her physiological processes almost to a state of hibernation, the article said. Her brain was dying. But her body was—just—still alive.

She went out on the ice to try to help a friend . . .

"Your order, ma'am." It's Joe; his voice breaks me from my reverie.

Quickly, I slip my phone back into my jacket pocket.

Joe puts a plate and a bottle of Diet Coke in front of me. Pale cheese oozes out from the burger. Salt glistens on the fries. He removes his jacket and sits down, back to the window, with another Coke, burger, and fries.

I take in, as though for the first time, the way his black hair falls over one eye. The tension of the muscle in his neck. The curve of his chest, down to his waist.

Medically speaking—yeah, maybe, *possibly*, I shouldn't be here. But all kinds of natural drugs are coursing through me right now, and I feel like they're awakening parts of me that were still anesthetized after the surgery. Parts that maybe never really woke up.

I let thoughts of what happened to Sylvia settle in my mind. I'm *out*, and I'm going to find her, and she and Joe—*this* is what I need.

"Brioche bun," he says. "Eighty-twenty beef and pork. Twice-cooked fries. Bostonstream gives your dining experience tonight a perfect ten."

My eyes reach for his. "Thank you."

He nods. Grabs a few napkins from a metal dispenser.

Deep breath. "I mean for the hoodie. And Daniel Johnson's driver's license. And for taking me away from the hospital . . . and the burger."

Now his level gaze meets mine. There's a soft smile on his lips when he says: "You're welcome."

It ejects me right out of the last of my worries.

I hit the ground in a very different place.

If I were another girl—if I were Sylvia Johnson, before she

half died in freezing water—maybe I might lean over this table and kiss him.

Would she want me to? *Would he?*

I pick up my burger and take a bite.

For so long, all I've eaten is hospital food, supplemented with the occasional pilfered treat. No wonder, then, that the burger tastes incredible. I take a fry next. It's crispy and golden on the outside, fluffy-soft on the inside. I remember reading in one of the online history tutorials that Americans renamed french fries "freedom fries" after France refused to join the war in Iraq.

"My freedom fries," I say.

Joe knocks the neck of his Diet Coke bottle against mine. "To your freedom."

"My *first* meal."

I take a napkin and wipe a little ketchup from my lips. "If you'd just got off death row and out of prison and you could have whatever you wanted, what would it be?"

He thinks for a moment, then he says, "When I was a little kid, my mom used to make me the solar system out of pancakes. Maple syrup for the sun. Strawberry jelly for Mercury. Honey for Venus. Raspberry jelly for Mars. Blueberry jelly and apple slices for Earth."

"That was dedicated," I say. "She went to a lot of effort."

"She had a thing about space," he says at last.

I glance at his tattoo. At the words *Ad Astra*—to the stars. "She isn't here in Boston? Your mum?"

He shakes his head.

I want to ask more about the tattoo, but I don't. "Do you miss San Francisco?"

". . . Some things."

Could he be more vague?

I search my memory for what I've read or heard about the city. "Like the people all being so relaxed and having shaman pool parties and drinking ayahuasca?"

He looks at me doubtfully. "Ayahuasca?"

"It's a hallucinogen."

"I know what it is. Where've you heard about it?"

"I don't know." But I do. "Probably the *New Yorker*."

"Really?" He nods, and I think it's a nod of approval.

He puts his burger down and wipes his fingers on a napkin.

"The people in the suburb where I'm from all work for Google and Facebook or venture capital groups or wish they did, or for one of the pharmas," he says. "The people all work at breakfast, work on their commute, work at the dinner table, want their kids to do the same. Except for when they're let out to do something recreational. Like going to a tutor to learn Mandarin."

"That's what your parents are like?"

He hesitates, and I can't help wondering why. "A little. So, Sylvia Johnson. What exactly do you want to know?"

I think about this.

"I want to see where she lived. I want to see the reservoir . . . I want to find a friend who really knew her. I want to know her heartfelt truths. What she loved. What she hated. Her dreams."

He says, "If you did tell me why, maybe I could help you more."

The lightness that has been spreading inside me since he sat down fades a little.

"Rosa, there's nothing you could tell me that would shock me."

I can't meet his gaze, so I look away, at an overweight woman in the line, cooling her face by fanning it with a folded *Boston Globe.* At a cashier, red-cheeked, counting out bills. I don't know them. They don't know me. Instability starts to rock me.

"Everyone has to talk to someone," Joe says.

I find my tongue. "Says the journalist."

"I'm not talking as a *reporter.* I'm not even a real reporter. I'm an intern for a mediocre—actually, a pretty shitty—website, and—" He stops. "Who is she to you? Who are *you*?"

I focus on my half-eaten burger. A skin has formed on the cheese. The droplets of fat on the plate have congealed.

"If I told you," I say quietly, "you'd get in your car and drive as far away from me as you could."

He leans over the table toward me. "I doubt it."

"You'd realize I'm the most horrific thing you've ever seen."

Everything around us goes still.

"Did you kill someone?" he asks.

I took Sylvia's living, breathing body. It's still breathing. Eyes on my hands, which are clasped in my lap, I shake my head.

"Have you ruined someone's life?"

". . . I don't think so."

"Have you committed a crime?"

"Not according to the laws of the United States of America."

"Then how can you be *horrific*?"

I can't possibly answer. And I'm so stiff now that if I don't do *something*, I swear I will fracture.

Grabbing my jacket, I get up from the table. I push my way to the door, making the woman with the *Globe* exclaim, "*Excuse me!*" and I head out, with no plan of where I'm going. I just need to move.

Now I'm out among a crowd of strangers. Their features disassociate and don't quite combine. I walk fast, glimpsing parts, but not wholes: a flash of gold hoop earrings, a piercing in a cheek, a waft of body odor, a pair of shiny black shoes.

"Rosa! *Rosa!*"

I stop.

Awkwardly, because I feel so rigid, I turn.

I realize I've gone quite a way down the street. Joe jogs to catch up. He's close now. I'm so intensely aware of how near he is, and how far away I know I should keep him.

"I just *can't* tell you," I say. "I signed something that's legally binding. I *can't* . . ."

Gently, he says, "Okay."

I guess the world keeps turning, but I'm not aware of it.

Then a siren whoops, and I realize we're outside a tobacconist's shop. An ornate board in the window advertises a Thanksgiving Day blend. As I spin away, I notice something else entirely: a statue on the pavement behind me.

It's bronze, of a man, shorter than me, striding along with old-fashioned coattails flying. He's gripping a case from which a giant bird springs. I take in the sweep of his coat, the gaping beak of the raven—

I jump. A hand is on the back of my upper right arm. Joe's. My arm burns where he's touching it. It feels like *life*—or the reverse.

Perhaps now that I've left the hospital, the mesmeric spell has been broken, and I'm decaying. I'm rotting from his touch, outside in. If I don't *do* something, I'll become a pool of detestable putridity, right here, on the street, in front of Edgar Allan Poe. I knew there was a statue of him near Boston Common. Well, here it is.

"Rosa?" Joe says. "I'll help you find people who knew her. We'll find out everything we can."

I stare at him.

I'm *not* decaying.

"Why are you doing all this?" I ask.

"I told you . . . to *help*."

"But why—"

He takes another step closer. "Because I'd like to help you. Because I hear all these stories and I can't ever do anything. Maybe this time I can *do something*."

I guess my emotions are running nuclear hot. My chest goes hard. I feel like I'm about to cry, and I do not want to. But even if he does help me, eventually—soon—he'll realize the truth. I'm not this pretty girl. Not Sylvia Johnson. *My* body was a ruin. Everything he sees is a lie. A route to salvation? Who was I kidding?

"I don't think you can give my story a happy ending," I tell him.

He fixes his unrealistically determined eyes on mine. "I can try."

20.

WE DRIVE THROUGH the darkness on I-95, four lanes in both directions, trees to either side. The radio's on. It's playing country. I peer through my window, trying to see beyond my reflection. Jagged shadows are all I make out, and advertisements on the sides of trucks. One screams at me to call 1-800-BAD-DRUG, another 888-HURT. Pain and near-death. They seem to follow me wherever I go.

Not just pain and near-death . . .

Joe's elbow is propped on the ledge of his window. He's driving with one hand. It's a casual approach to a journey that's so loaded for me.

Sylvia's ambulance must have made this trip, only in reverse. Her parents were at her bedside. She was smiling in that photo.

"And now, listeners, the lines are open. I have here in the studio none other than Ms. Connie Britton, and for the one in a million that don't know it, Ms. Britton plays country music queen Rayna Jaymes."

I turn off the radio. Music, I can handle right now. Chat, I cannot.

Black trees pass, and pass.

I'm grateful for the darkness. I can feel the rot around me, but at least I can't see it. And with every second, I do feel I'm getting closer to Sylvia.

The Happy Haven Motel is on the outskirts of Lexington.

Before we approached the city, Joe passed me his phone, and I searched our options. With an average of three stars out of five, this motel ranked last. But there were only five listings. And the others were ridiculously expensive.

"There are 287 reviews. Two stars: '*Yikes. A cigarette burn on our quilt.*' Five stars: '*The room was newly appointed; the bed was king-size.*' '*Nice breakfast. Of particular note were the two types of home fries . . .*'"

"Noteworthy home fries?" Joe said. "*That's* the place."

Now I'm reading a framed page of a magazine that's hanging by the reception desk. It's a travel piece about Lexington. Halfway through the second column, *Happy Haven Motel* is highlighted in pink. Joe is asking about rooms. Behind us there's a very grand but obviously fake dark wood fireplace set against the exposed brick wall. I guess I'm not the only thing around here pretending to be something other than it is.

I read:

Belonging to the Greater Boston area, Lexington is the sixth wealthiest small city in the United States, settled in 1642 . . . Famous for being the site of the first shot of the Revolutionary War.

I thought I'd vaguely heard of Lexington. I guess this must be why. I keep reading, or at least scanning, the text. Because it's something to pretend to be absorbed in while Joe talks to the receptionist, a woman in a tight black top, her wavy red hair loose around her shoulders.

She's saying, "A single room? Yeah . . . for how many nights?"

I feel Joe's eyes on me.

"Two?" I say.

"That'll be seventy a night plus taxes. Please fill out this form." She hands him a clipboard and a Happy Haven pen. "And I'll just need a card to put on file."

Out of the corner of my eye, I see him take a wallet from his pocket and extract a credit card. She does something with it behind the counter, then passes it back with two key cards.

"You're in room eleven. If you parked out front, just keep going—it's on your right. Breakfast is six thirty till nine thirty. You'll need a card to access the main door after midnight. All-night beverages and ice are available at the station over there." She gestures down the hall. "Enjoy your stay."

"Thanks," he says. "Do you sell toothbrushes?"

"We have a machine." She points in the direction of a nook beyond the fireplace. A minute later, he's back with a toothpaste and toothbrush set.

I don't know how he's feeling, but as we head back out, the shiver in my guts spreads to my flesh.

He left the car right outside. Beyond it, bright spotlights illuminate the drive that leads to the block of rooms. A covered concrete path runs alongside the drive.

"I'll walk down," I tell him.

He nods. If he thinks I'm strange for wanting to do this, he doesn't show it. He clicks the car open. "Okay."

Joe didn't look remotely nervous, but as I walk through the chill darkness toward our room, the web of nerves through my body tightens like a net. I can feel it—a skein of bioelectric skewers, squeezing with each step, until it punctures my lungs and my heart.

I've left the hospital without telling anyone and without a formal discharge. Now I'm at a *motel*. In a strange town.

I glance up at a desperate frenzy of moths around one of the blazing lights, and I think, *What have you done?*

But I tell myself, remembering a session with Dr. Bailey: *It's okay. Push yourself beyond your comfort zone, and you're going to feel that way. Fear shouldn't always be a signal to retreat.*

The doors to the cinder-block rooms are painted white, with steel numbers. TVs blare through some of the windows. A man in number five is dancing. Six is dark. So is seven. In eight, the lights are dim. They might just have a lamp on. Who's in there, I wonder? What are they doing?

As the door numbers rise, I try to take charge of my breathing.

Nine.

Ten.

Eleven.

Joe has already spun the car into an angled parking space. Suddenly, he's beside me, with his toothbrush kit, my bag, my jacket, and a key card. There's no hesitation as he slides it into the metal slot.

I shiver again. And I realize that shiver isn't entirely due to anxiety. More than anything, I think perhaps what I'm feeling is excitement.

Sickness, paralysis, more paralysis—then slow, hard work building up to this. Leaving the hospital. Walking, talking, eating a burger like anybody else. Standing outside a motel room with a guy I really like. Maybe even just for *this moment*, it's all been worth it.

The door swings inward.

Joe flicks a switch, and the bedside lamps light up. I try to focus not on the extreme conditions inside my body, but on what I can see.

The room is better than I expected from the internet pictures. There's a dark-wood unit with a TV, drawers, and a bar fridge, plus a desk. The beds have shiny, leaf-patterned ecru quilts. The air smells of roses—of freshener.

Joe puts my bag on the bed farthest from the window, closest to a door to what must be the bathroom.

He inspects a picture on the wall: a framed photograph of a collection of fall leaves. "*Massachusetts—the Spirit of the Country,*" he reads from a label on the plastic frame. "They got that from registration plates. The last motel I stayed in, the owner was really into Bob Marley. In the room, there was this poster of him with lions leaping out of his shoulders and ganja leaves sprouting from this ears."

I don't want to ask him whom he was with, but it's all I'm thinking. Except that I'm glad he's talking about nothing. Because I couldn't handle silence. But I can't think of anything to say in response.

I guess in some ways I should feel better in here. Quiet rooms are pretty much what I'm used to. But after my release into Boston, and the journey, free on the road, it seems claustrophobic. I'm in the world. And I want to be with Joe. But this is intense.

My right leg feeling especially slow and stiff, I edge around him and step outside again.

I stand with my back against the wall, my heart thumping.

Beyond the path and the parking spaces, there's nothing but trees. Because of lights from the town, I guess, and clouds, the sky is less the color of night than of a storm closing in. The mostly bare branches look like dead lightning strikes.

I take a cautious breath.

Was it weird to suddenly leave the room?

"Rosa? Okay?"

My head jerks around. Joe's in the doorway. I nod.

He comes to stand beside me. A few inches of weathered cinder block are all that separate us. I wish I didn't feel so tense.

"You want to drive around and find where she lived tonight or wait till the morning?" he asks.

"Maybe the morning," I say. "I guess I won't see much tonight."

My eyes are still fixed on the sky and the murky black trees.

"Not that much of a view," he says.

"It's okay." I wish my voice didn't sound so tight.

"If it wasn't so cloudy, you'd see the Big Dipper over there." He points just above one of the taller trees. "Then if you followed the two pointing stars on the right, you'd find the North Star."

I'm about to ask him if his mother taught him that, when he goes on:

"Which happens to be the name of a bar in the West End that Bostonstream recently awarded the title of best place to watch college football. Just in case you love college football and were wondering . . ."

Mention of a Bostonstream review makes me think of the burger place, and I don't need anything to remind me of the fact of the room behind us. "I'm sorry you paid for this as well," I say. "I'm keeping a mental note—"

"Are you?"

The way he says it, I suddenly feel small for caring. Which gives an edge to my voice when I say, "So, what, you don't you care about money?"

He shrugs, still looking up at the sky. "Yeah. Just not as much as I care about other things."

". . . Like?"

"You can probably guess. I'm not that original."

He's smiling a little. He's not disappointed in me.

I allow my spine to relax just a tiny bit against the wall. Forcing the sharpness out of my voice, because it's absolutely not his fault I'm on edge, I say, "Becoming a famous reporter?"

"Famous? Like TV famous? . . . No."

"For the world to love you?"

"That could possibly be expecting just a *little* too much."

"So, your girlfriend?" I say, barely able to believe that these words are coming from my mouth.

"If I had a girlfriend. Maybe," he says, his eyes now on mine.

I almost forget to breathe. But my body won't let me—and I don't blame it, after everything it's been through.

I guess in theory, I could ask him why he might not want a girlfriend to love him. But I sense that even if I did, he wouldn't tell me. *Extraction,* I think.

"How do you get by if you work only three mornings a week?"

He sighs. Returns his gaze to the sky. "Dad agreed to help fund this year. I need to accrue experience to stand a chance of getting into a good college next year." He says this in the tone of a teacher or career counselor.

"In San Francisco?"

"Probably in Boston."

"Because you like Boston?" I prompt him.

He frowns. "You can't really *like* a city, right? You love a city, or you'd virtually hack off your own hand to escape it— even if you knew that if you did escape, you'd only be pulled right back to go through the same thing again."

". . . To hack off the other hand?"

He smiles slightly. "Exactly. One thing about Boston: You can get out of it pretty quickly. I don't mind it around here." He gestures toward the skyline.

"Surrounded by nature," I say, in such a way that he says:

"What, you don't like nature?"

"Not so much."

"I thought everyone at least liked nature," he says. "It's what our brains were born to. Where we evolved."

But I'm not natural. And what has nature done for me, or Sylvia? It's human ingenuity that kept us alive long enough for this hybrid to exist. There's nothing natural about any of it. Not the good stuff, anyway.

"I don't think we evolved in forests," I say.

"I'm fairly certain we didn't evolve in cities."

He's smiling again. It might only be slight, but it's highly infectious. That, or I'm a particularly vulnerable recipient.

"I'd have been the most bored cavegirl ever," I tell him.

The attitude of his smile changes a little, in a way I find hard to read, until he says: "If I'd been the boy in the cave next door, maybe I could have kept you entertained."

Did he actually *say* that? My heart races. But I'm not going to retreat this time. "How exactly would you have done that?"

". . . I guess I'd have made this log bench and collected all the stories of everyone in the settlement. You'd have been the first to hear who was bitching about someone else's new fur outfit."

I shake my head. "I'm not sure I'd have been that entertained."

His smile deepens. He turns a little more toward me. "Okay . . . So maybe I'd have regaled you with tales about my fights with saber-toothed tigers and my mammoth-wrangling exploits."

I make a face. "Yeah, not enough."

"You'd have been an extremely high-maintenance cave-girl."

"Maybe just one who wouldn't have been satisfied only with stories."

"That's pretty much all I have to offer."

"Is it?"

His smile twists. "You're kind of an unexpected girl."

"*I'm* unexpected?"

He shifts around so he's facing me, his left shoulder against the wall.

"If I were telling your story," he says, "I wouldn't know where to start. Or what to put in the middle. Or anywhere, actually."

"I could say the same about you."

He seems to think about this. Then he says, "At least you know where to start."

"To the stars?" I ask him, glancing at the words *Ad Astra* on his arm. "What does that mean? You want to what, reach for the stars?"

He says, his voice very low, "That's not what it means to me."

He looks away. The clouds are parting a little. Cracks of blackness are appearing in the sky. Stars, too.

If he knows their names, he doesn't tell me.

I want to stay out here, with Joe. I *want* to take the conversation back to the caves. I also have Sylvia in my head, and the story from the newspaper. I do think it would be better to wait until daylight to see Lexington. But, in any case, there's something else I really have to do.

"I'm going to go back in," I say. "Could I borrow your phone?"

"I've got an iPhone charger—"

"It's not that . . . I don't want to use my phone in case—I don't want anyone to have any way of finding me. I don't want my parents coming after me."

He frowns. "You *have* told them you've left of your own volition, and you're okay?"

I nod.

Suddenly, I don't know what's in his mind—or rather, I have even less of an idea. The energy between us hasn't vanished but it's definitely faded.

I want to give him something. But I don't know what I can give. And now he's turning away, and he's pulling his phone from his jeans pocket and stepping back into our room.

After dropping Joe's phone on my bed, I grab a bottle of water and my canisters of meds from my bag. Quickly, I swallow one anti-epileptic and one anti-rejection pill.

Joe's over at the bar fridge. He opens it. "Empty."

I push the canisters back into my bag. There's a faint groan of springs contracting as I sit down on the bed. This mattress is softer, more yielding than the one I'm used to in the hospital. I pull two dense pillows out from under the tightly tucked sheet and stack them against the wall. It's a comfortable backrest. "All-night beverages available in the lobby," I say.

"Coffee and tea, probably. You want either?"

I shake my head. "If I drink coffee now, I won't sleep."

"You think you'll sleep?"

My heart catches.

"Being *here*," he says, apparently reading my mind. "Close to Sylvia Johnson. Or people who knew her. You know how to Sylvia Johnson. Or people who knew her. You know how you want to start?"

After we left Boston, before I went on TripAdvisor, I searched for social media accounts in her name but couldn't find her. I guess her accounts have been deleted. But there's no reason she shouldn't still be mentioned on friends' accounts.

"I don't know. Facebook. See if I can find girls in her class. Maybe ones who might have been with her at the party. Or the reservoir. Take it from there."

He nods. "I could provide moral support by lying around and watching TV while you work?"

I smile slightly. "Moral support would be great."

"Okay."

He kicks off his sneakers, finds the remote. While he settles himself on his bed, I try not to look at him, and I bring up a browser window on his phone.

And now, at last, after the sensory onslaught of Boston and the burger bar and the streets, then the stress of getting here, to this room, and even our conversation outside, I feel myself starting to relax.

Joe flicks through a couple of channels. Stops.

There's an Arabic logo in the corner. Al Jazeera.

I asked if he has a girlfriend.

Focus.

Rosa.

Focus.

While Joe concentrates on a report about an Iraqi business-man who's buying back female slaves from the so-called Islamic State—bullets rattling and voices screaming in the background—I search "Lexington High School" on his phone.

On the school's website, I find the names of a couple of student council reps. Then I go to Facebook and search "Dinah Kennedy," a rep who would have been in Sylvia's year.

I find her page. All that's publically available are three photos of her in a midnight-blue maxi dress, hair elaborately done. Beneath the photos, friends have left a few comments:

YOU LOOK GORGEOUS! LOVE YOU!
Gorgeous as usual!!!

I pick up a little Happy Haven notepad and pen from my bedside table. I write down the nine names of the friends who left comments on Dinah Kennedy's page. Then I start search-ing these names.

My progress isn't exactly fast. Like Dinah, they allow only

friends to view the majority of their content. But most display a few photos, and again, I write down the name of anybody who has left a comment, then I search them. And eventually, I find a girl named Althea Fernando.

She has 895 photos, and her privacy settings are entirely open.

The most recent set of shots shows a girl in a kitchen. The photos look professional. There's Althea, I assume—jet-black hair, caramel skin, huge eyes—looking a little tired, wearing white overalls. Then there's a set labeled GRADUATING GIRL SCOUT AMBASSADORS. Here's Althea again, a shiny sash emblazoned with badges draped over her shoulder, a blue-and-gold flag in her manicured hand.

Further back in time, I find pictures of a white fluffy dog with a diamanté-studded collar.

Althea in a silver gym leotard, a gold medal on a red, white, and blue ribbon around her neck.

A pink-frosted fairy-castle birthday cake and Althea's little sister, judging by the facial resemblance.

Some blurry pictures from what looks like a house party.

And then my heart stops.

It's her.

Althea and Sylvia.

Althea's arm is around Sylvia's shoulder. They're in a glade somewhere, both in denim shorts and sunglasses, gripping water bottles. The picture is dated thirteen months ago.

My chest tightening, I search on through the photos, and I find another: Sylvia, on her own this time, in a dark gray jersey dress and a lot of makeup, that little white dog in her arms. Then one of her back, with her reflection in a mirror. She's making a happy, silly face. Underneath this photo is a comment: *Thanks!!* And the name of the person who left the comment:

Sylvia Johnson.

Interspersed with irrelevant photos, I find even more: Sylvia and Althea in a battered blue kayak, Sylvia and Althea and another girl on a street holding cups of golden ice cream to their lips, tongues out. Sylvia and Althea in a kitchen in aprons, standing behind a plate of profiteroles. Sylvia being kissed by a long-haired blond boy in a green Starbucks server's apron, who's tagged as Adam Sagan. Sylvia at a party, tanned, pouting, in black jeans and a green tie-dyed vest, a luminescent red drink in her hand, the same boy holding her around the waist. In a place tagged as O'Neill's Bar & Restaurant, in that tight dark gray jersey dress, holding a microphone. *Awesome gig, Sylvia! So proud xxx,* Adam Sagan wrote at the top of a column of comments underneath.

And then, this:

A photograph of a page of a book. The text is handwritten. Evidently by different people. At first, I can't make out what this is. But as I scan the text, catching occasional words—*tragic, love, forever, heart, Sylvia, remember*—I realize it's a memorial book. There's a location tag: Cary Memorial Library. I read this: *So devastated, Sylvia—but so thankful I was lucky enough to know you. All my love. Adam.*

And, together with a few extracts from poems, these lines in slanting black:

Music, when soft voices die,

Vibrates in the memory—

Odours, when sweet violets sicken,

Live within the sense they quicken.

Rose leaves, when the rose is dead,

Are heaped for the beloved's bed;

And so thy thoughts, when thou art gone,

Love itself shall slumber on.

I know those lines. I've read them before. In an anthology belonging to Elliot. Mary Shelley invented Frankenstein's monster. Her husband described subtler ways to live on.

A woman screeches from the TV, and I realize I'm trembling.

"Rosa?"

I hear Joe but I can't respond.

"Rosa?"

He mutes the sound. Silenced jihadists continue waving rifles in the air. "What's wrong?"

Tears have rolled onto my cheeks. I rub them away. "I just found some photos of her."

"What kinds of photos?"

Deep breath. "Happy ones. Dressed up. At a party. Hugging this dog. With her boyfriend. Singing in a bar." I'm gripping the phone so tightly my fingers are throbbing.

I don't see Joe but I hear him get down from his bed. He sits beside me. I'm not moving. I can't. Gently, he takes the phone, and he backs up through the pictures.

"She's dead," he says quietly.

I nod.

He reaches out and when he lightly touches my shoulder, it's a collision. I jump. Instead of letting go, he edges his arm around me.

I squeeze my eyes shut. Slowly, he pulls me closer, and he turns toward me, so when I finally release my grip on myself, I slide against his chest.

My head on his chest, my arm on his chest. His body heat in my flesh. His arm around my shoulder. Maybe this was normal for Sylvia. For me, it must be like deep-sea diving, or rocketing into space. Suddenly, everything is different, in ways both terrifying and amazing, and I know I'll never look at my world in the same way again.

And if Joe's touch isn't enough, there's Sylvia.

In my mind, she's still there, smiling. I can't let the tears truly come, because I feel like if I do, they'll never stop. I want to speak, to say, *Don't let go,* but I can't, and he doesn't.

October 25: The first night I ever spend alone with a guy.

Yeah, we are fully clothed. And yes, his hands don't touch anything more sensitive than my back, my shoulder, and my arm . . . but my *back,* my *shoulder,* my *arm,* my *heart* are branded by that touch. I find myself thinking, *I'm so sorry, Sylvia.* She looked so happy in those pictures. Her body's here in this motel room in Lexington, beside Joe, but she will never again feel anything as vividly perfect as *this.*

I wake in the predawn. The curtains are thick and the window is screened, so without a clock or an internal sense of time, you'd never know if it was midday out there or the blackest apocalyptic night. I can't see a clock, but somehow I know I have a jump on the day. I can lie here, and if I don't move, Joe won't wake, so I can immerse myself in this—the bare skin of his arm against my face, the regular sound of his breathing, his smell. I feel transformed. Electrifyingly alert and elementally still. I have never felt as good as I do at this moment.

Then I remember the photos on Althea Fernando's Facebook page. Sylvia, posing and relaxed. Secure. Confident. But now she's dead. The moment dissolves into something bitter.

Slowly, so as not to wake Joe, I inch away from him and swing my feet down to the carpet. I take my bag into the bathroom. On a shelf beside the plain white sink are two tumblers with paper caps. I shuck the cap from one and fill the glass halfway with water. Then I find my toiletries bag, dig out my pills, and swallow my morning prescription: one little pink anti-epileptic followed by a big white anti-rejection tablet.

Dr. Monzales explained all the reported side effects of my various medications. If you've seen American TV, you'll know how they do it in the ads. There'll be a grinning silver-haired man in a pastel cashmere sweater helming a yacht or flying a kite with his laughing grandkids in a marigold-lit meadow, while a serious voice rattles through a list of hellish potential side effects of prostate medication or pills for high cholesterol— everything from a mild skin rash to death, or worse.

A noted side effect of my anti-seizure medication is the shedding of all your skin. Yep. People have survived this, apparently. Don't ask me how.

I had only Dr. Monzales's admittedly handsome face to focus on while he spelled out the risks associated with my medications. Footage of a girl lying on a bed next to a surreally good-looking boy might have been better . . . I guess advertising companies hope an appealing image will override a thousand ugly words. But aren't the words what lasts?

I forget what people look like—their features grow faint—but I remember certain things they told me with unfading clarity. Unkind words. Loving words. Gestures from their minds, not their bodies.

The mirror in this bathroom has its own built-in bulb. I peer at my bright reflection, and I think of those Facebook photos.

I put on a smile.

Then I lift my hand, hesitantly at first. I twist at the hips and imitate Sylvia's grin in that picture at the party.

I know exactly what I'm doing. I'm acting out her poses. But something strange happens. Suddenly, the expression in the eyes in the reflection no longer seems to be mine.

My pulse leaps.

Is this *me*?

"Rosa? You okay?"

Joe. His voice is so loud he must be right outside the bathroom. I recheck the mirror. The look that wasn't mine is gone.

I take a slow breath. Open the door.

It shouldn't be a shock, but it is: He's standing right there. Still in his T-shirt and jeans. Devastating. I smile, partly because it seems like the right thing to do. He gives me a slightly crooked smile back.

"Okay?" he repeats.

I can't really answer that in a single word or sentence, or in anything remotely appropriate in tone, fact, or duration. So I just nod.

"It's really early," he says.

"Yeah." I wish I didn't sound so nervous.

"An hour till breakfast."

Beyond him, I see the disheveled bed.

"Joe—" He waits. And yes, I was going to refer to last night. But it probably wouldn't be the best thing right now. I have to push, push before somebody—my parents, Sylvia's dad—finds me, before I'm caught. "Can we go and find where she lived?"

"Right now?"

I nod.

". . . Okay."

I dress quickly, pulling on my jeans, a T-shirt, and a pastel blue cardigan, a gift from Elliot, which is the reason, I think, that I fumble over the buttons. But I'm not going to think about my family right now.

Just before we leave the room, I borrow Joe's phone again. I should have messaged Althea Fernando last night, but I got diverted. It took *Joe* to do that.

I'm not sure exactly what to write, how much detail to include. In the end, I keep it simple:

Hi, I used to know Sylvia Johnson. It was a long time ago. I don't want to drag anything up but I'm really hoping to meet a friend, just to ask about her. Rosa.

21.

IT'S 6:04 A.M., according to the clock on Joe's dashboard.

I'm trying to distract myself from wondering whether Althea's replied yet—unlikely, I know—by reading, in the dome light, a month-old copy of *USA Today*, which I found on the backseat.

The lead story seems to be about a business scandal, which doesn't interest me. In a box on the bottom left of the front page, there's a simple graphic with accompanying text:

Did you know? About 35 million pounds of candy corn are produced annually. How adults eat it: 43 percent start with the narrow white end; 47 percent eat the whole piece at once; 10 percent start with the wider yellow end—

There's a click and a gust of cold. Joe's getting into the car with two oversize cups of coffee from the beverage station in the lobby. He passes one to me. Behind his head, beyond the parking lot, above the trees, the early clouds are separating, revealing glowing streaks of light.

Dawn, in Lexington. I'm in a car with Joe, in the town where Sylvia lived. It's hard to believe this is real.

"Thanks," I say as I take my coffee.

"So, I've been thinking," he says, and I have to try hard to stop myself from focusing on what it was like to have his arm around me, to sleep beside him. "What if Sylvia's parents are looking for you? Maybe you need a disguise. Do you think you need one?"

A *disguise*?

I had wondered how to avoid being recognized. I thought, maybe a hat. And my Jackie O sunglasses.

If Sylvia's dad didn't follow us from the hospital, though, I doubt there's much risk of him turning up now.

I take a sip of coffee. It's weak. But I'll take all the caffeine I can get. "That license address was in Connecticut."

"I guess maybe they moved after what happened to Sylvia. But her dad might assume you've found out where they used to live."

"If he's still looking for me around the hospital, and he

doesn't see me, won't he think I've gone into hiding? I don't know if he'd think I'd be back here."

"Back here?" His expression doesn't alter. Just his tone.

"Here."

"It's not just him," he says, apparently deciding to let my slip pass. "If someone sees you and thinks they recognize you, they might call her parents. A disguise would help."

I must look skeptical, because he frowns.

I know: There must be dozens, even hundreds, of people in Lexington who could recognize Sylvia. If a disguise makes sense—which it does—why am I so resistant to the idea? Because it smacks of pranks and silliness, I think. And the reasons I'm here are so very serious.

But if I'm serious about finding out about her—of course, he's right.

"Okay," I say. "Yeah, a disguise . . . What's candy corn?"

His frown deepens. I guess he's trying to work out why I'm asking.

I hold up the paper and point to the graphic. "Forty-three percent of adults start at the narrow white end. I don't even know what candy corn is."

"Really? I guess you can tell from the fact that it's on the front page that it is *extremely* important to Americans." There's sarcasm in his tone. He smiles. "So, candy corn—"

But I don't really pay attention. Because I find myself thinking:

What exactly *am I going to ask Althea?*

I have some ideas.

1. Was Sylvia kind or unkind? (*Kind*, I guess; though so far I have only one incident to go on—and what if she was out on the ice because she was the reason her friend's relationship broke up?)

2. Loves?

3. Hates?

4. Was she happy or unhappy?

5. What were her hopes and dreams?

But even with a disguise, how exactly am I not going to freak Althea out? My mind jumps back to the motel bathroom mirror. I freaked myself out.

Slow breath in.

Slower breath out.

Joe puts his coffee in a cup holder. He brings up the map app on his phone. Among the beige and yellow, I see a red pin on Courtyard Place. According to the newspaper story, this was where Sylvia lived. And I do want to see it. But to go there first . . . ?

I guess it seems weak.

Joe starts the engine.

"Can we go to the reservoir?" I ask.

"*Now?*"

I nod.

"You sure? Her street might be an easier place to start than the reservoir."

"Wide bit first," I tell him, thinking of the candy corn. "That's how I am."

I gaze out of my window at the passing homes and trees.

Now that the sun is up, I can properly make out all the oaks with the last of their enormous leaves, and the equally—to my London-accustomed eyes—oversize homes, all timber-framed and detached, painted in varying subdued colors, some with swing sets, some with basketball hoops, some with both. Almost every house I see is decorated for Halloween. There are fabric ghouls on stakes in the gardens, plastic skeletons dangling from branches, and pumpkins on front steps, arranged in order of ascending size.

It looks like the kind of America I've seen in horror movies. The "perfect" town, where people normally only act out being afraid.

As I peer out at all of this, I think: *Joe must have a theory to explain why I look like Sylvia, and why we're here.*

I guess he thinks we're estranged identical twins. It would

be the most likely explanation. Which only goes to show when "most likely" is wrong just how flat-Earth wrong it can be.

And I feel *bad*, because I am deceiving him deeply and utterly, while using him for my own benefit.

I think of Sylvia, and feel *bad*, because I'm using her for my own benefit.

How does anybody survive forty-two minutes under water?

I know Dr. Monzales cooled my brain to 16 degrees Celsius before and during the surgery, because low temperatures improve resistance to damage from oxygen deprivation. Evidently, the chill water of the reservoir protected Sylvia long enough not to save her, but, yes, to save me.

No prolonged pain.

Surely, though, she'd have been fully conscious—and conscious of everything—as she plunged into the reservoir. She'd have been terrified. Desperate to live.

She was pretty and kind; she had good friends who obviously loved her. I was . . . not that pretty. I'm honestly not sure if I was kind. Are online-only friends real friends? Well, which of them knows the truth about me—if the fact of my disease was an essential truth? The answer is: none.

In fact, when it comes to Sylvia and me, the only similarity I'm sure of is this: We were desperate to live.

So when I compare myself with the admittedly very little I've learned about her so far, the truth is: I'm worried.

The car slows. We're on a broad street. Electricity cables seem to run everywhere in bundled strands along and over the road. Joe hits the brake even harder, and we stop. We're at a red light. Beside us is a bagel shop, with a container truck parked outside. I notice an ad on the side of the container. It features a silver-haired man and an older woman cosmetically enhanced to within an inch of her life (yes, I know I'm on shaky ground). Just before the light changes, I make out the first of the possible side effects: *Exantra may cause insomnia—*

Joe must notice it, too, because he breaks the silence in the car by saying, "Side effects of silent introspection include but are not limited to debilitating rumination, angst, and regret."

I'm on my way to the place where Sylvia almost died while comparing myself with her and coming up short. Yet just like that, at Joe's words, my pool of toxic thoughts drains, as if he pulled the plug on my brain. I realize there are only two people in the world who can do that: Elliot and Joe.

"Silent introspection is normal," he says, eyes back on the road. "I just wanted to point out the side effects."

I clasp my fingers together in my lap.

"It's so unfair they're always bad," I say, focusing on my hands. "You never hear, 'Side effects include but are not limited to excessive happiness, improved energy, and a sudden passion for Byzantine art and poetry.' "

After just enough time has passed that I don't think he's going to respond, he says, "Side effects of hanging out with you include but are not limited to a reduction in debilitating rumination, a resurgent sense of positivity, and the reinstatement of a belief that life can involve meaningful action and even pleasure."

He doesn't take his eyes off the road. *My* heart spins. What should I say? What *can* I say?

"I—" My tongue dries.

"It's okay," he says.

I can't speak.

"It really is okay," he says.

But it isn't.

I want to make my mouth work, and to give him *something*, but now I see railings. Trees. A narrow road into a small parking lot. A glimmer of water.

We are here.

22.

"YOU WANT ME to come down with you?" Joe asks as the engine dies.

I take a deep breath. "I think maybe this is something I have to do on my own. But thanks. Will you wait here for me?"

"I'm not going anywhere," he says.

I guess there's only so much even the most reassuring words can do to a body in a situation like this. And now that we're here at the reservoir, mine is veering toward panic. If I get out and walk fast, at least there'll also be a physical reason for why my heart is pounding like this.

I grab my jacket from the backseat and get out.

After a couple of steps, I glance back, into the strengthening sun. It's pale gold, and it's bursting above the houses beyond the road.

There's no sign of anybody else. No other cars in the parking lot, and no one around. Not even an early dog walker. Only us and invisible birds sounding a high chirp.

Joe watches me through the windshield. I want him beside me, but going down to the reservoir really does feel like something I need to do alone, despite what he just told me about a resurgent sense of positivity, and meaningful action. Which I'm not going to think about right now. Partly because I'm not even sure *how* to think about it.

Focus.

What can I see?

At the other end of the parking lot, there's a wooden bulletin board on a pole, with a miniature pitched roof. Beside it, the beginning of a gravel path.

Dead leaves crunching beneath my feet, I walk over to the bulletin board. I pull the zipper of my jacket right up to my chin. The cold air smells faintly astringent. Pine trees grow here, I realize, as well as oaks.

When I get close to the board, I make out a yellow sign pinned to it:

THE OLD RESERVOIR IS CLOSED FOR THE SEASON. THANK YOU FOR COMING THROUGHOUT THE SUMMER.

And another, for a special screening of *The Orson Welles Show* at the Somerville Theatre, dated the previous month.

Closed? And yet Sylvia came here a little later in the year.

I glance back. Joe's still watching me. *A resurgent sense of positivity? From me?*

I set off along the gravel path.

Through light and shade, I follow it. Tree roots protrude in gnarly loops from the ground. I have to pick my way carefully over them, so I'm looking down as I walk, which is why I almost collide with the fence.

It's made of wire. There is a gate. It's padlocked. On the other side, scattered with decaying acorns and leaves and patchy brown grass, is a small beach. Past that, the water ripples, and I can see all the way to the other side . . .

Trees. And more trees. From here, it looks as though they stretch on forever.

I keep on the path, following it around to the left. The going gets more difficult, my way obstructed by tangles of branches and saplings. Still, I see no one, hear no one—only the invisible birds and the occasional engine back on the main road. As I push on, I try *not* to think that those bare gray branches resemble human bones. I try *not* to think: *That root looks like an arm rising from the grave to grab me.*

A bird shows itself, shooting up from the undergrowth.

Startled, I follow its flight path, and I realize that the fence ends a short distance ahead. A few more steps. A few more steps . . .

I round the fence.

Now I can get to the water.

Three strides over rough ground . . .

I crouch. I smell rot. The shallows here are thick with oak leaves and yellowing pine needles. Trees are reflected, brown and burnt-gold. I watch as a single oak leaf makes its one and only journey through the air, swinging from side to side, trembling, fluttering, all the way down to the water.

Farther out on the reservoir, ripples are forming, rolling toward me. If it was frozen solid, someone could walk across in, what—five minutes? Ten?

Sylvia can't have set off from the beach, because at that time of year, it would have been closed, the gate to it locked, as it is now. Did she stand *here* to call to her friend? Did she feel *this* wind? Was it from this spot that she stepped onto the ice?

My heart races.

When the ice cracked and Sylvia sank beneath it, every cell in her body would have been in revolt. Her heart would have been frantic; she'd have been scrabbling for the surface, desperate for an opening, fighting for her life, and losing.

I lift a hand to my forehead. A fizz—like an electrical

burn—seizes me between the temples. I jerk. There's a thwack in my skull. Suddenly, I can't see. Only blackness, then whiteness. I'm falling and freezing, and my arms flail. I realize I'm groping in rotting leaves. Gripping at tree roots. I know I'll have to fight to stay conscious.

I blink wildly to try to shake off the blankness. I'm sprawled on my back. I have to sit up. I *can't*. Still, I tense my muscles, determined to do everything I can to hold on to what I know to be real.

Dizziness billows through me in a wave. Then another.

I gasp.

. . . It's gone.

Very slowly, I haul myself up until I'm sitting, hunched over, my palms dirty with fragments of decomposed leaves. I try to rub them off on my jeans.

I hear a voice. "Rosa?"

Joe. He's emerging from the path, pushing saplings out of his way. "Hey!"

I do see him, and his voice registers—though not absolutely as belonging to him. I'm no longer dizzy, but I am floating. I *feel* as insubstantial as a ghost.

Joe squats beside me. He touches my arm, and my nerves explode. My heart pummels my rib cage. I'm not sure I can breathe, and I know that I'm alive.

"What are you doing?" he asks. "I was worried."

I manage to say, "What did you think would happen?"

"What did happen? Why are you on the ground?"

I don't answer.

He brushes leaves and pine needles, I guess, from my back. Rubs his hand on his jeans. "What happened?"

"Nothing."

"Did you fall?"

When I don't answer, his jaw clenches. He looks past me, at the reservoir. Then he stands up straight, his back to it.

"Here." He's reaching for my right hand. I don't give it. After a moment, he takes my left instead, helps me up. He must have noticed the weakness on my right side. Ashamed, I hide my hand inside my jacket. This body is not really mine, not yet.

For maybe a minute, we just stand there, listening to the empty rustle of wind in the trees and over the water. My head is aching. From the faint, I guess, if that's what it was. Very gradually, the brain clamp releases.

"You ready to go back?" he asks, and before I can answer, he says: "If you're not, it's okay. I can stay with you . . . or I can go wait somewhere."

"Where you can see me?" My voice sounds so small out here.

"Maybe this isn't the kind of place anyone should be on their own."

"It's just a reservoir," I say. "People must swim here in summer."

I close my eyes and I can hear them—people laughing, picnicking, opening bottles of beer, flirting. Then I feel the wind on my face. It's winter that's coming.

"We can go," I say.

"Sure?"

I nod.

"Okay."

Again, he holds out a hand. I hesitate, but not because I don't want to take it. At last, I close the gap between us. I let him wrap his fingers around mine. We walk back over the gnarled roots, around the bare limbs of trees. All the way to the parking lot. Holding his hand.

Now we're back near the car, close to houses and regular life, and what seemed natural somehow feels awkward. I pull my hand toward me to release it, but he doesn't let go.

He keeps his gaze on my face, forcing me to meet it.

There's a conflict in his eyes. I watch him consider something, reject it, then change his mind. "You look a lot alike," he says quietly. "But I could tell you apart."

I half hear myself whisper, "How?"

"She was pretty. You're one of the most beautiful things I've ever experienced. Not *one of*."

I swell and contract, swell and contract.

I float outside of myself, then shoot right back in. I have no idea what to say. Who says something like that? And to me. *To me.*

Maybe it's something about the early light, or what happened inside my brain by the reservoir, but he's glowing. He's so close I can feel the pulse in his neck and the tension in the muscle between his neck and his shoulder. His fingers touch my cheek. My body rings. I lift my face, and I kiss him.

If I were to believe in a god, *now* would be the moment. Every cell in my body fires. My lips are electric.

Then I think: *I was falling, I was freezing, and I saw someone in the mirror who wasn't me.*

23.

THAT KISS. I don't know how long it lasts, because time stops. All I'm aware of is the soft pressure of his mouth and the solidity of his body.

My familiar rush of self-doubt threatens to take the moment. But it doesn't steal all of it. As we climb back into the car, I feel the ecstatic tension of it still.

We sit side by side, in intimate contact in every sense except literally. Joe starts the car. I turn on the radio.

"No one's ever called me beautiful before," I tell him, my voice quiet. "At least, not including Mum or Dad."

Silence. Then he says, "I don't understand why not."

"She was beautiful," I half whisper.

"She was pretty," he says. "I guess it's hard to tell just from a photograph."

"Why?" I ask.

"Haven't you ever thought some guy was hot, then he opened his mouth and said something stupidly arrogant or stupidly childish or just really stupid? Still hot?"

I nod. He's right.

Then I find myself thinking of a documentary I watched in the rec room with Dmitri last week. It was about the high-end food industry that services London's multibillionaires. About the caviar tasting sessions, eighteen-carat-gold-bedecked desserts, *five-thousand-dollar* shots of antique liquor, and steak that some restaurateur exposes to Mozart, because, so he insists, it enhances the taste.

Dmitri was really into it. He wanted to *be* the guy paying five thousand dollars for a few sips of whiskey distilled when Abraham Lincoln was alive.

I felt sick. So many frauds. So much greed. I guess that's why I'm thinking of it now. I feel like a fraud. And I'm greedy for something that I—the old me—would not have had.

I want to wrap my heart around what Joe said. But it's a mirage. And so, at least for now, I can't.

I take a long breath and give him a small smile.

"Has Althea replied?" I ask.

The expression on his face tells me he's wondering why I'm changing the subject. But after a moment, he pulls his phone out of his jacket pocket. Checks it. "It's Saturday morning. She's probably still asleep . . . What now?"

"Maybe I should find someone else to ask to meet."

"Yeah. Maybe."

"Can we find where she used to live? And her memorial book? It was tagged—"

"Cary Memorial Library. I remember."

"But I should probably get a disguise."

He nods. Types something into his phone. A map appears. "There's a place not far away," he says.

We pull out of the parking lot, and my irregular life resumes, like vegetation sprouting after an earthquake.

We drive to a party superstore next to a dentist's office in a strip of shops just out of town. Past rubber bats, ghost-themed party-ware, plastic devil's forks, and jumbled racks of Halloween costumes—including one of Frankenstein's green-headed monster—I find a wig. It is blond and long.

Once the wig is in place, my own hair tucked up inside it, we drive off in the direction of Courtyard Place.

Now the town seems less deserted. There's a mom in gym gear with a couple of kids on scooters, a man in overalls with a leaf blower, a woman kneeling on her front step, chalking something onto a blackboard: *Enter if you dare* . . .

"This is it," he says.

And I see the street sign, in capital letters: COURTYARD PL.

So this is where Sylvia lived.

I have no idea which house was hers, but as we drive along, I realize they're all slight variations on one theme. Modern. Detached. Modeled on a colonial style, with integrated garages and glossy white-painted porches. Into their steeply pitched roofs are set half-moon windows to what real estate agents must surely describe as "cozy bedrooms packed with character." Was one of those rooms Sylvia's? Did she look down at the exact spot from where I'm looking up?

These houses are so different from the one I grew up in. I think of our redbrick Edwardian terrace, with its drafty front windows and rambling stepped garden. As time went on, a bungalow would have been easier, but Mum and Dad had the place modified to accommodate my chair, because I was determined that my disease wouldn't kick me out of my own home. My old house and hers are *so* different, except for this: From the outside, they look pretty much the same as all the others on the street.

As Joe crawls the car down around a curve in the road, we pass a garage that's open. The light's on, showing well-ordered racks of tools, kids' bikes and scooters, and a black car that seems to be plugged into an outlet.

To my eyes, this is all too good to be true. A world with everything anyone could wish for. Still like something from TV.

"Is it like this where you're from?" I ask Joe, trying to make my voice as normal as I can.

"I think they're pretty similar, Lexington and Burlingame," he says, peering out. "Our neighbor to one side had a Tesla. Our neighbor to the other side had a Prius."

"You had an electric car, too?"

"Actually, Dad had a mountain bike. Mom had a Honda VTX1300S."

"A motorbike?"

He nods.

"How did you get around?"

"I walked to school. They had this old Ford for when they really needed a car. Mom sometimes took me on her bike."

"I used to have a bike," I tell him.

Then I think, *Did I?*

I've made so much up.

But I did. I'm sure I did.

I dredge for memories, and I *do* remember hurtling along the path that ran beside the duck pond, Elliot yelling, "Just don't fall in!" And then—even more than I hated standing, dripping, thigh-deep in scummy water, my new bike half submerged—I remember hating the fact that I'd lost control. Five years old. I had a lot to unlearn.

Looking out at this neighborhood now, I know Sylvia would have had a bike. She'd have ridden it all over with her friends.

Every Halloween, she'd have put on a costume and trick-or-treated along Courtyard Place. Maybe she took her haul of candy back to her attic room. Perhaps, like me, she once stashed the lot under her pillow, and woke to find that, contrary to her mother's predictions, not a single piece had been squashed.

Tears fall down my cheeks.

I brush them away, hoping Joe doesn't see.

I'm *here*, where she lived. Where people loved her . . .

It strikes me: Maybe there *is* a way I could let Mum know I'm still okay without potentially giving my location away.

"End of the road," Joe says. "You want to drive back along for another look or go to the library?"

Deep breath. "Library, I think. Thank you. But can I borrow your phone? I guess I could email Mum."

"Sure," he says. Enters his passcode. Hands it over. As we pull away from Courtyard Place, I sign into my email account.

My inbox appears.

There's the usual stuff from mailing lists I haven't bothered to unsubscribe from—and then this:

From: Elliot Marchant

Time: 01:45 A.M.

Subject: READ NOW!!

It takes me a couple of attempts to successfully click on Elliot's email, but at last I get my finger to work properly. And I read:

FIRST, know this: Mum had security go through all the CCTV footage from the hospital and they talked to everyone in rehab. It shows you in the café with some guy that JARED says is a journalist who hangs out in the park. Are you with HIM?? Mum's talking to the police. They'll be after you, Rosa.

There's more, but I don't read it. I think the phone falls onto my knee.

"Rosa?"

I knew Mum would be worried. I didn't even think about CCTV.

How does Jared know who Joe is?

Then I remember seeing Jared in yoga sessions in the park. Joe's around there a lot. Maybe Joe has even interviewed him. Still, I can't believe Jared told Mum.

"Rosa?"

I make myself look at Joe. I cannot keep this from him. "Mum's had hospital security go through all the video footage. They know I was with you in the café."

He seems to think about this. Then he says, "Okay . . . and?"

"*And* she'll get the police to look up your license plate and the car park camera will show your car leaving. Maybe they can even track us all the way here with satellite images and—"

He interrupts: "You told me you told your parents you left, and you're eighteen?"

"Yeah."

"You know how many assaults there are in Boston every year? Nearly three thousand. Which is—what, like, eight every day. There are thirty thousand gangs in this country, Rosa. Three hundred million illegal guns. The police have a lot better things to do than go after an adult who was well enough to walk out of a hospital less than twenty-four hours ago. I wouldn't worry about satellites."

"Someone at the hospital recognized you. Mum might call Bostonstream—"

"Who would not give out any details about me. Not without police involvement. And like I said, they're not going to get involved. Not yet, anyway."

I lean back hard in my seat.

I didn't personally read all the fine print in the agreement that I signed before the surgery. I left Mum and Dad to do that. But there might have been something in there about me staying at the hospital until the doctors say I can go. The hospital must have spent a fortune on my treatment.

In the end, yes, I am eighteen and I went voluntarily with Joe. I can't see why he should get into trouble. But it could be different for me.

"If they do find me," I say to him, "I might have to go back."

He glances at me. "Then we'd better make the most of whatever time we've got." He hits the brake, pulls over to the side of the road.

"Maybe I should contact Sylvia's boyfriend."

"I don't know about the boyfriend," he says. "But send Althea another message."

"I could do that while we're driving."

He points through the window, at an ivy-clad stone building with narrow arched windows.

I lean forward, and I see the sign: CARY MEMORIAL LIBRARY.

I pick up Joe's phone from my lap. After he reactivates it, I message Althea:

Rosa again. It would mean so much to me to hear from you, I can't tell you. Please.

I know: I sound as needy as I am. But I'll have to take that risk.

Kind or unkind?

Loves and hates?

Happy or unhappy?

Hopes and dreams?

Better than me?

Only a close friend could answer those questions. And I *cannot* go back to Boston without answers.

24.

I GET OUT of Joe's car, my heart doing its best impression of a Ferrari on an autobahn.

I have to focus hard on what I'm doing so as not to stumble on the pavement.

My wig is in place. My sunglasses are weighing down my ears. I'm reasonably disguised. But if the police do put out an APB—I'm not sure what the letters stand for, but I've heard it on TV—on Joe's car, well, here it is, in full view.

Joe is peering past a cluster of wooden benches outside the library, down the street. It must be the main street, I realize. Both sides are lined with low-rise stores and banks, fronted with broad sidewalks dotted with trees. I see signs for a shoe shop, a restaurant, more than one or two shops selling homewares and craft supplies.

"What do you bet they all sell the exact same pewter jewelry?" Joe asks. "If your mom does find you, you could always try placating her with a gift of an artisanal cheese board."

I guess I give him a look, because he holds up his hands. "I just think you're probably worrying too much."

I'm about to head to the steps when I notice an inscription on one of the benches:

Francis Judd Cooke, 1910–1995. A life of music generously shared.

I think of that comment from Sylvia's boyfriend: *Awesome gig.*

She sang. Maybe she'd have had a life of music, if she'd had the chance.

"Rosa, come on."

I start for the steps. Then something—a whimpering—enters my consciousness.

It's so pained and insistent that it makes me stop.

Pulling its way along the sidewalk toward the library is a honey-colored poodle on a pink leash. Its claws are scrabbling at the concrete. The woman walking it tugs the leash. "Sadie, no!"

The dog pays no attention. As they get closer, it strains harder. The woman shoots me a curious glance. She allows Sadie to drag her over.

The dog jumps up, front paws on my knees, mouth gaping happily, tail wagging hard.

"I'm so sorry!" the woman says. "Sadie, *no!*"

I reach down to gently push it off, and the dog's slick pink tongue licks my hand over and over.

"It's like she knows you!" the woman says.

Yeah, I think. *It's like she knows me.*

I sense Joe's eyes on us and I don't look around. My heart is racing so fast I think I might pass out.

"Do you work at Doggy Day Care?" the woman asks.

I take her in: dark ponytail, fuchsia leggings, pink Nikes, aviator sunglasses, toned, thirties. I shake my head. The dog is still trying furiously to lick me. As I stroke its curly head, I hope the woman doesn't notice that my hands are shaking. I'm not sure what to say to her.

"Oh," she says, "Monday night training class in the park?"

I shake my head.

"Wait . . . *oh.*"

I doubt an "oh" has ever before carried so much weight for me.

She removes her sunglasses and scours what she can see of my face. "You do look a *lot* like her."

My heart is racing so fast; I'm *definitely* going to pass out. Joe comes to stand beside me. I grab his arm for support, struggling to maintain a neutral expression.

"Mom!"

A girl, perhaps twelve, long-legged in white jeans and

213

sneakers, is jogging toward us with another dog, also on a pink leash.

As this dog gets close, it, too, starts pulling to get to me. Only this approach is frenzied. Its tail is wagging a hundred times a second. It's white. Fluffy. Realization drop-kicks me.

It's the white dog from Althea Fernando's photographs.

The mom can't be older than thirty-three or thirty-four. Too young, surely, to be Althea's mother?

The girl, who's leaning backward against the pull of the dog, skids to a stop beside me. "Lexie, get down!"

"It's okay," I tell her.

Say it, I tell myself. *Say it*. "Who do I look like?" I ask the mom.

Her sunglasses are halfway back to her face. She hesitates before slipping them back on. "A friend of my niece. This is her dog—my niece's dog, Lexie. We walk each other's dogs sometimes."

"Lexie must love your niece's friend," I manage to say.

"Yeah. She's—she passed."

Another voice, a girl's, calls from farther down the street: "Hannah!"

The daughter waves to the girl, who's also in jeans and sneakers. She sets off again, dragging the dog. "*Come on*, Lexie!"

The whimpering gets louder, until distance softens it.

My brain screams, *Ask her, ask her!* "I'm sorry," I say. "Did you know her well?"

Eyes on her retreating daughter, the woman says, "I knew her mom, really. She was Althea's—my niece's—best friend. Seventeen, talented, smart, everything. Sang like Elle King." She sighs. Tucks a fallen lock of hair behind her ear. "You look a lot like her. Different coloring. I guess that doesn't bother the dogs."

The daughter calls, "Mom, we're going to Ranc's!"

The woman spirals the leash around her wrist. "I'm sorry about all that. Enjoy the rest of your day."

She walks away, dragging Sadie, who is only a little less reluctant than Lexie to go.

I stand there, unsure of how to face Joe. Identical twins *must* smell the same . . . I should have asked her more than two stilted questions. Yes, I was nervous. The encounter was a surprise. But perhaps I should go after her.

I realize I'm twisting my fingers together. They're glistening. Wet with Sylvia's best friend's dog's saliva. *Seventeen, talented, smart, everything.*

I can barely make out the woman—she's so far down the street—and what would she think if I ran after her now?

Swallowing back tears, I hurry over to the steps.

"Rosa?"

I don't acknowledge him. I don't even glance back. I don't want him asking me anything. Not right now.

Through a second set of doors, I find myself in the bright, light atrium of a public library. There are bookshelves and people with shopping bags, two kids with plastic lightsabers, a couple of girls with folders in their arms. I'm scanning for a sign for a bathroom.

There.

I shove open the bathroom door and practically fall against a sink.

There's no one else in here. So there's no one to see my tears. I left my jacket in the car, so after taking off my sunglasses, I slip them into the pocket of my jeans.

I hold my hands under a gushing stream of water. Then I pump soap into my palms and rub them and rub them as the water gets hotter. The mirror's steaming up. But when I look in it, there it is: that expression that isn't mine. My instinct is to turn away. But I don't.

Trembling, I hold my gaze.

And I have the strangely not-unnerving sensation that I'm looking at Sylvia. There's a confidence in her gaze that I never saw in my own reflection.

Seventeen. Talented. Smart. Everything. Sang like Elle King.

I was not talented. I helped no one. I certainly didn't save anyone's life. I gave nothing to anybody. I made up stories about myself. If I could ask the world, I know it would say: *It would be better if* you'd *died.*

I half slip, half drop to the floor. My back to the tiled wall, I feel crushed on all sides. I'm not sure I can take this . . . But I saw *her* reflection. And I have this strange, enveloping feeling that she is still somewhere here, in me.

"Rosa?"

The shell around us fractures but doesn't quite break.

Joe calls again: *"Rosa.* Are you in there?"

But I can't speak.

"Rosa?" he calls. "Althea Fernando replied."

25.

I HAUL MYSELF up and out of the bathroom.

Joe's there, right outside, holding his phone. "Okay?" he asks doubtfully.

I nod quickly, rubbing my eyes. "I'm sorry, I—" I take a breath. "What did she say?"

He hesitates. I experience a sensation I've had a hundred before, generally in the gap before a doctor gives me test results. In that gap, all kinds of possibilities could still be true.

He passes me the phone and I read: *I'll be at O'Neill's tonight. My shift ends at 9. Could talk then. The kitchen.*

The stress of what just happened on the street floods away. It leaves me feeling kind of unbalanced. But only for a second or two.

"O'Neill's?" It sounds familiar. And it doesn't take me long to remember why: The photo on Althea's Facebook page of Sylvia singing was location-tagged at O'Neill's Bar & Restaurant.

"Here." He holds out his hand to take the phone back. His fingers move quickly across the virtual keyboard. "It's an Irish bar and restaurant. On the outskirts of town. Near an air force base."

"We can go?"

"Of course we can go . . . Are you okay?"

I nod. "Just that woman . . ." My sentence trails. I take a deep breath. "She thought she recognized me."

He nods. "Yeah." He glances at my sunglasses, which are awkwardly stashed on my hip. "Maybe you'd better not wear those in here or you'll only get more attention. But you'll lose them like that." He holds out his hand.

I give them to him, and he slips them into his jacket pocket.

I'm worried he's going to ask me more about the woman, but he says, "I saw a sign back there saying the Lexington High School yearbooks have been moved to the Lexington Room. I guess the memorial book could be with them, wherever that is . . ."

He glances behind him, at the atrium and the anterooms and a desk where an ash-blond librarian is sitting.

"It might be better to ask," he says.

It's Joe who does the talking. I stay close behind him, my wig pulled forward around my face, hoping no one looks at me too closely.

The librarian informs us that two memorial books for students who attended Lexington High School are indeed held here.

"It's unusual, isn't it?" Joe asks. "To have memorial books in a public library. And the school yearbooks. Is the Cary name to do with the high school?"

"No," she says kindly. "It's to honor the original patron of the library, Mrs. Maria Hastings Cary, who first offered funds in 1867. But the library and the school do have a close relationship. Students like to study here. You'll find all sorts of school-related resources over by the young adult section." She hesitates. "I know the parents of the girl you're asking about wanted her memorial book to be available to all students, past or present, at any time. That way, they can continue to add to it if they want to. They can come and choose a chair and take comfort from it, if they want to. It can be different, can't it, holding something physical in your hands, rather than looking at a screen?" She points. "Over there. The far side. You'll find it with a few other folders on a shelf by the windows."

"Thank you," Joe says.

"You are very welcome." She glances at me, but I'm already turning away.

We head in the direction she indicated. Beyond a series of bookcases, we come to a couple of long, light wood tables, at which kids—high school students, I guess—seem to be doing homework. One girl whispers loudly to another, "It could be present active?"

I try not to stare—because I don't want any of them to look at me—but it's hard. Without a single exception, the girls all have long hair, held back from their faces in clips. The boys are mostly wearing chinos and T-shirts. Would Sylvia in her tie-dye and tight dresses have fit in?

"Rosa."

I look around. Joe's at a bookcase by one of the narrow arched windows. Next to every window, I notice, is an easy chair.

These must be the chairs the librarian was talking about.

This must be the shelf.

Joe's picking up a deep maroon leather-bound book. He holds it out to me.

I take it. On the front is *Sylvia Johnson* in gold-embossed letters. Beneath her name are the date of her birth and the date of my surgery—of her death.

Unaware now of anything besides this book, I take it to a

chair. I sit down. Open the cover. On the first page is a single paragraph:

In loving memory of our darling daughter, Sylvia Lauren Johnson. Please take a few moments to write down remembrances of her that you feel able to share. Share anything: your love, your anger, your sorrow, your grief, and any happinesses that you experienced together. Please also paste in anything you like—concert tickets, notes, anything that reflects time spent with Sylvia. Whenever we feel her loss most acutely, we can turn to these memories and know that so much of her will live on, as part of us.

I have no idea how long I sit there, with the book.

Each new entry hits my brain like an electric shock.

You'd have been New York's brightest star, Sylvia. Such a talent. And an even bigger heart. We've all lost so much. C.

Music, when soft voices die . . .

So devastated, Sylvia—but so thankful I was lucky enough to know you. All my love. Adam.

Of all the memories, this is one of so many that I'll always hold close: when Aidan B. was dating that girl from fencing club behind Sydnie's back, and you stood up in the cafeteria and went over to him and you sang your twist on that Alanis Morissette song . . . "He's a bitch, he's a liar, he's a sinner, he's a cheat." No one will EVER forget that . . . I will never forget you. Althea.

And more. So many more.

Page after page of comments, some distorted with what must be tearstains, and bits and pieces—wristbands, menus, certificates, theater programs—stuck in.

At some point, I get up from my chair. I might even put Sylvia's book on the shelf. Or maybe Joe does. Because the next time I'm properly conscious, I'm standing in the little vestibule by the main door to the library, feeling like I've just been hit a hundred times, all over.

Joe's there, too, right beside me. "You okay?"

". . . Yeah." My voice sounds strange. Not like me. Or her. Or what I'm used to.

"You sure you're ready to go?" Joe asks.

I lick my lips to loosen them. "Yeah."

"Okay. Look, before we go, I need the bathroom. Why don't you come back in with me and wait by the desk?"

"I can wait here," I tell him. It's cool and dark in here. And there's no one else. Just a wastebasket, an umbrella, and a table with some leaflets on it.

"If you come back inside—"

"I can wait here," I tell him.

"Maybe I should wait . . ."

"Seriously?" Deep breath. "You need to use the bathroom. I'm fine. I'll be here."

"Okay."

He doesn't look too certain about it, but he goes back into the library.

I stand there in the vestibule, my head swimming with everything I just read—all those memories of a person who is gone but is also standing here. Who, a few minutes ago, was reading her own memorial book.

I shiver. The little stone vestibule feels cold as a crypt. The door is ajar. I slip out, into sunshine.

As I stumble down the steps, I realize Joe still has my sunglasses, but I don't stop.

I lurch on, past the benches, onto the sidewalk. I'll wait here, in the warmth. The brightness hurts my eyes a little. I turn my head, and I see, on one of the shops down the street, a familiar sign.

Starbucks.

It catches at me. For a moment, I wonder why.

And then I remember.

Althea Fernando must have graduated from high school, but she's still here, in Lexington. What if Adam Sagan works *here*?

I have no way of telling Joe. But if he finds me gone, surely he'll wait. And I won't be long.

Sylvia's boyfriend. I've only seen a photo. He was good-looking, in a grungy kind of way. Did this body have sex with him? What would it feel like to see him?

26.

I WALK DOWN the main street, alone.

For the first time maybe ever, I'm out in the real world, by myself. Only, not quite by myself. Because I know I'm not really just me anymore.

The Starbucks is a small one. Narrow. Busy. By the window, a couple of women in heavy makeup and gym gear are deep in conversation. A casually dressed dad with a kid who looks about fourteen, textbooks open on the table between them, is shaking his head. "This would be easier," he says loudly to the kid, "if you didn't eat so much sugar."

The counter's over to the left. Five or six people are waiting in line. I make out one—no, two—servers in green aprons.

Both are women.

I'm about to walk around the line to get a better look when a male voice over my shoulder makes me turn sharply. "Turkeys are our friends. Don't you think?"

He's about my age. Maybe a little younger. I mostly notice white teeth, regular features, and biceps stretching the fabric of a tight-fitting T-shirt. I think I must have misheard, but then he smiles—the kind of confident smile that's accustomed to a positive reaction—and hands me a leaflet from a wad.

The cover reads: *Adopt-a-Turkey Project. Start a new Thanksgiving tradition and save a life!*

"Every year, three hundred million turkeys are slaughtered," he says. "They're crowded together in these nightmare conditions. They have their beaks cut off without anesthetic."

"I—I don't eat turkey," I say.

"You're vegetarian?"

"Actually, I just don't like turkey."

I hold out the leaflet for him to take it back.

His extremely green eyes narrow. "Are you on the Ultimate Frisbee team?"

I shake my head. "No."

"You're British. Obviously. You're at the high school?"

My pulse throbs a little harder. Again, I shake my head.

"So, what, are you new in town?"

"Visiting," I manage.

"What—family?"

"Kind of."

I know: A robot could do a better impersonation of a human than I'm accomplishing right now. I don't think I could be more off-putting. But he just smiles and says, "Mystery . . . I like it."

I glance past him, at the counter. Still, I can see only two women at work with the machines and the blenders.

"So, I don't want to get between a girl and her coffee. You're a guest in my town. Let me get it. I'm Brandon."

I blink at him. "Thanks, really, but—"

Only I don't get to finish my sentence because a hand's clamping my shoulder and Joe's voice is in my ear. "Rosa, let's go."

Brandon gives me a questioning look, which I think means, *Is everything okay, or do you want me to step in?*

I twist myself free.

"Let's go," Joe says quietly again.

I don't want a scene in this Starbucks. So I say to Brandon, "Good luck with the turkeys." And I walk around Joe and out, onto the sidewalk. I go a little farther down the street so Brandon and the women in the window can't see us.

Joe's holding my sunglasses. "Maybe you want these?" he says. "Or maybe you don't care anymore who might recognize you and call Sylvia's parents?"

"I guess that's up to me," I say, knowing how stiff I sound, but taking the glasses.

"You were supposed to wait for me. I had no idea where you'd gone."

"That's why you're mad?"

He frowns. "I'm not mad. I thought—what if her dad had found you? Or you were upset over something you'd read in the book, or you were still in a kind of shock after the woman with the dog, and you'd wandered off and fallen over, like you did at the reservoir."

I'm not sure what to say to this.

I take a step toward him. Then another. I'm close enough to touch him, but I don't.

If he was worried, I am touched. But perhaps there's another reason why he's not happy.

"I guess it feels like I'm always locking you out of my head," I say.

"It doesn't *feel* like that," he says, nodding a little. "That's how it is."

"I told you I signed a legal document," I say. "But it's not even the legal side I worry about." I look him in the eye. "Someone did something huge—beyond huge—for me, and in accepting it, I promised to keep it secret. I'm sorry I left the library. I'm sorry I can't tell you the truth. If you want to go back to Boston, you should, and if you can lend me some money, I can get it straight back from my brother. I'm really grateful for everything you've done." If I could stop my tears, I would. I wipe them away. "I'm also sorry I'm crying."

He says, "I guess if I go, if anyone is searching for my car, I'll lead them away from you."

"No! That's not even *vaguely* what I'm thinking."

"It's very hard to know what you're thinking most of the time."

". . . I know."

I reach out and wrap my arms under his. I press them tight around him. As I feel his arms close around me, the mess of emotions inside me resolves into relief.

We stand there, together. A huge part of me wishes I could stay like this, and never move.

He gently brushes hair from my ear and says quietly, "So do you want me to go?"

"*No.*"

After a moment, he says: "Why Starbucks? Did you want coffee?"

I shake my head. And I press my face harder against his shoulder.

"I don't think coffee would be good, anyway," he says. "You seem to be shaking."

I think of the dad and the boy with the textbooks. "Maybe I just need sugar," I mumble into him.

He holds me a little tighter. "At last," he says.

I realize we haven't eaten since last night. "Are you really hungry? Sorry—"

"No," he says. "I mean at last, you have a problem I can easily solve."

After I finally, reluctantly let go of Joe, I see a store across the road. It's not the name I notice first but the window boxes, which are planted with ornamental cabbages and purple parsley. I recognize them from a photograph on Althea Fernando's Facebook page. It was of Sylvia, Althea, and another girl smiling, tongues out over cups of ice cream.

This is Rancatore's.

It has the slightly mismatched feel of a non-chain place. The fridges and freezers are different sizes. On the wall is a bulletin board pinned with all kinds of community ads—for yoga classes and kids' math tutoring and guitar lessons.

My sunglasses in place, I join Joe, who's peering down at the glass-fronted counter. It's packed with tub after tub of chocolate chip, *kulfi*, pistachio, black raspberry, banana walnut, butter pecan, butterscotch ice cream . . . If there's a flavor that makes you think *delicious*, it's probably here.

"Can I get a small cup of chocolate mousse frozen yogurt?" I ask the aproned boy behind the counter.

Joe asks for a cup of butterscotch. "Sit down if you want," he says. "I'll bring them over."

Actually, I do want. Because I still feel pretty shaky.

I sit at a round wooden table. At the next table, a group of kids are fawning over a silky spaniel puppy.

"I want the dog!" a girl in a purple hoodie shrieks. "I want the dog!"

Another laughs so hard at her phone, ice-creamy saliva hits the screen. She grabs her friend's arm. "We are, like, the worst class ever!"

Hannah—Althea's cousin—isn't here. But it's a relief. I didn't come into Rancatore's to find her.

I have to balance the risk of someone thinking they recognize me and calling Sylvia's parents against the benefits of the entire reason I'm here: to find out about Sylvia.

I've seen where she lived, and where she went under the ice. I know she could sing like Elle King. Maybe when I'm feeling brave—and I'm alone—I'll properly try singing. Apart from singing along to music in my room, it's not really something I've tried since the surgery. What will matter most, I wonder— her vocal cords and lungs, or my brain?

Other achievements, if you can call them that, since being

here: I read so much in the memorial book. And my most important goal—to talk to a close friend of Sylvia's—is within reach.

Joe comes over. He puts my cup of frozen yogurt in front of me, with a little spoon.

"Thank you."

"You are welcome," he says.

"It's on my tab."

"If you like."

He sits down with a larger cup of glistening golden ice cream piled with miniature purple nuggets.

"What are those?" I ask him.

"Nerds. Don't tell me you don't know what they are."

"*Nerds?* . . . I wouldn't have guessed you'd go for an ice cream like that."

"Like what?"

"I'd have said vanilla, strawberry, or chocolate. No gimmicky flavors, no sauce, no topping."

He makes a face. "Butterscotch is not gimmicky. I don't like sauce."

"*Nerds?*"

"Don't you like candy?"

"Not really."

I dip my spoon into the slick, melting top layer of chocolate.

Slip the frozen yogurt into my mouth. It's not too cold as to be a shock. Not too sweet. Joe is watching.

I force myself to take a proper spoonful and swallow it. Then another.

When I've emptied half the cup, I put the spoon down. My heart's still racing. Perhaps partly from the sugar. But I'm thinking about Sylvia's memorial book.

A green wristband printed with GOVERNORS BALL was taped to one page, with this comment underneath: *Such good times, Sylvia. So much love.*

"Do you know what the Governors Ball would be like?" I ask Joe. "Like a proper ball? With long dresses?"

I watch him try to hide a smile. "It's a music festival in New York."

"Oh. Have you been to it?"

He shakes his head.

"What's Ultimate Frisbee?"

"Frisbee with teams that compete. A sport."

"A *sport*?"

"Why not?" he asks.

"I thought Frisbee's just something parents do on holiday with their kids. It seems like a strange thing to make into a sport."

"Says the girl from the island that invented hitting a tiny ball into holes."

"Is golf a sport?"

"So," he says, that smile still lingering, "sports really aren't your thing."

And he glances—I watch him—at my hand. My *right hand*. I take this as confirmation that he has noticed my weakness on that side. I can't help it; I drop my hand under the table, like it's burned.

"Sports aren't really my thing, either," he says quietly.

But they *were* Sylvia's.

At least they were three years ago, according to the Massachusetts Ultimate Frisbee girls' state championship silver medal certificate that I found in the memorial book.

I force myself to return my hand to the table. It's like lifting lead.

"What's wrong?" I ask him, because he's stopped eating. "Have you gone off Nerds?"

He looks a little relieved. "Now you've questioned them. Now you've said they mark me as a not-serious person. I'll only ever eat plain vanilla, strawberry, or chocolate."

Then he reaches out. Takes my hand. My right hand. Holds it in his.

His fingers are cold from holding the cup of ice cream. Maybe that's why chills start to unfurl through me. And he's looking at me so intently. But then the puppy squeals, and I glance over. It's wriggling, suddenly desperate to escape the hoodie girl's grasp. On the wall behind her, I notice a framed cover of a *New Yorker*.

The illustration is a simple drawing of an apple, an orange, and a pear. This triggers thoughts of Elliot, of course, and I do not want to think of Elliot.

The moment is gone. I looked away when I shouldn't have, and I saw something I didn't want to see.

I *want* to be the person who was standing on the street entwined with Joe, and who can still feel the tingle from his touch in her skin. I want to focus on being *that* person.

The most beautiful thing he has ever experienced.

The girl who Joe sees.

A sudden wail from the street halts my thoughts. A siren. It stops, then starts again. Louder. Closer.

Joe locks eyes with me. Shakes his head.

I whisper, "If they've found your car—"

Right outside the window now is a rapid-fire wail from what must be a police car.

"They're not after you," Joe says intently.

Maybe I should think "most likely."

But, as I know so well, most likely isn't always right.

27.

EITHER THAT POLICE CAR was looking for me and didn't find me, or it was after someone else.

I guess Joe was right. But just hearing that siren puts me even more on edge. Going into Starbucks without my glasses wasn't smart. Even being in Rancatore's, in disguise and with Joe, perhaps pushes me too far into "risks" and away from "benefits." I can't let anything jeopardize my meeting with Althea.

So, after we leave Rancatore's, I ask Joe to leave the car on a back street. Then we walk around places that would have meant something to Sylvia.

Like her school.

It's Saturday, so it's deserted.

It's windy, too, and dead leaves are blowing across the central courtyard, between the buildings.

"Empty schools make me feel kind of the same way as empty swimming pools," I say.

"Peaceful?" Joe asks.

"Not exactly."

When I notice the little loudspeakers mounted on the walls, the sinister vibe only intensifies. I imagine they must be used for announcements, but to me they give the place an abandoned-prison-camp feel.

After the high school, we stop by the playing field outside the nearby Bridge Elementary School, because, according to Joe's web search, this is where the Ultimate Frisbee team trains.

Another empty school. This one even has a silent playground, which doesn't exactly lessen the post-apocalyptic atmosphere.

After that, we drive to a mall in nearby Burlington. Lexington itself doesn't have much in the way of clothing stores. I guess Sylvia would have come here to shop. Joe buys a plain black T-shirt and maybe some underwear. I don't keep too close an eye—I'm too busy watching the girls out shopping with friends, or their mums, or their boyfriends. I'm one of them—a part of this world.

Then we head back to the motel.

I don't know what counts as going-out clothing in Lexington, Massachusetts, but I do at least have a fresh pair of skinny jeans and a loose, low-cut, chalk-colored top I can change into after showering. While I get ready, I listen to Elle King on Joe's phone. "America's Sweetheart." "Ex's & Oh's." Over and over.

And now we're driving.

It's 8:12 P.M.

Joe spins the wheel, sending us across four lanes, off the highway. Ahead, a green glow lights up the trees.

We pull into a parking lot. It's packed. At last, we find a space between an old sedan and a pickup truck, a bloody-mouthed ghoul tethered to the roll bar.

Joe looks at me. "Ready?"

I nod.

At the far side of the parking lot, backed by trees, is a colonial-style building. The emerald walls and the lighting, and *O'Neill's Bar & Restaurant* in Gaelic script above the porch, make it seem a little like something from a theme park.

Joe's heading for the steps that lead up to the entrance. I join him.

When I meet Althea, I'll tell her what Joe must be thinking: I'm Sylvia's estranged identical twin. By the time I leave O'Neill's, I'll have everything I need.

The thought of it starts to fill me with a kind of righteous elation.

I think:

We both *were buried alive—and now I'm digging us out.*

As we walk through a lobby, down into the bar and restaurant area, my senses kick in.

Music. That's what I notice first, and I recognize the song. It's by Mumford & Sons.

Then my sense of smell joins the party. I detect perfume. People. Beer. Pizza. Saturday-night release, if that's something you can smell.

O'Neill's is all dark wood and brass, and it's crowded. On a mezzanine level off to the left, men and a few women in military fatigues are spinning darts at a board. To my right, restaurant customers are tucking into burgers and salads, listening to the band. A cover band.

It's playing on the far side of the square-shaped bar. I can just about make out a small stage, and people dancing. Did everyone dance when Sylvia sang? Was Althea here, cheering her on?

Around the bar itself, mostly men are sitting, talking, drinking, and watching the TVs, which are showing sports. Men in chinos, in aged leather flying jackets, in faded T-shirts, with beards.

My attention's caught by a flash of green at one of the long tables. Every one of a group of ten or so girls is wearing a little green net veil pinned to her hair. A bachelorette party, I guess.

As I glance around, I'm cautious. I'm wearing the wig, of course, but sunglasses in here, at night, would only draw attention. If anyone who knew Sylvia really looks, they'll see her, and there's nothing much I can do—except keep my head down.

I let my eyes skip from face to face to face . . .

Everyone seems to be having a good time.

I feel a little like an alien, analyzing the room and making my estimations. But if you don't count going with my parents, which I don't, this is the first time I've ever been in a bar.

"Over there," Joe says.

He veers over to a high table with two bar chairs. These might just be the only unoccupied seats in the place.

Joe takes off his jacket, slings it over the back of his chair. I sit down opposite him, but so I'm half facing the wall, which is decorated with coats of arms of the counties of Ireland. A waitress in black spots us, comes over.

"Hi, folks, are you dining with us tonight?"

Joe says, "Sure."

"Okay, I'll bring menus right over. Can I get you some drinks?"

"A Diet Coke, thanks," he says.

"Yeah, the same, please," I say.

As she leaves us, she smiles.

"So what do you think?" he says, glancing around.

"I quite like it." It's true. From the outside, it looked a little cheesy. But it's full of all kinds of people. And the atmosphere's upbeat.

The waitress returns with heavy black menus.

"Here you go," she says. Another smile.

Joe opens his up. His eyes focus, I guess, on the appetizers and entrees. Mine are tracing the shallow-cut-marble muscle of his arms. I let my gaze trail up to his chest.

There's half an hour until I'm due to meet Althea.

"So, if I was going to tell my cavegirl friends about you, I'd like to have more to go on," I tell him.

He looks up. "What kind of more?"

"I'm wondering: What's the least cool thing about you?"

I've surprised him. I can see it.

"The *least* cool thing?"

I nod.

Looking thoughtful, he closes the menu. "I thought you weren't going to be satisfied with stories."

"Not *only* with stories."

". . . So you mean, apart from liking Nerds and knowing all these inscriptions on bench plaques?"

Which makes me smile. "Yeah, apart from that."

"Okay." He nods. "When I was six, I asked Santa for a metal detector. And I got one. That was the start of my metal period. I took it everywhere. Supermarket. Park. Bus stops."

"Your metal period."

"Yeah."

"Did you find anything?"

"If you call a handful of nickels and rusty nails anything."

But there was a hesitation before he answered that makes me say: "You *did* find something?"

"Here you go, guys." The waitress puts down two Guinness coasters and two tall glasses of Diet Coke, with ice and lemon.

Joe thanks her without looking at her.

"I never told anyone before," he says.

I wait.

"I didn't tell Mom because I knew she wouldn't let me keep it. I put it in my pocket and I took it home, then I put it in this little blue plastic treasure chest. Then I put that in my secret drawer and I didn't tell anyone."

"What was it?"

"A gold tooth."

I grimace. I know I do. I feel myself do it.

"I found it in the woods behind the park near our house."

"Someone's tooth?"

242

He takes a sip of his Coke. "Then that night I woke up thinking, what if it came from a skull? What if there was a murdered person buried out there and no one knew about it? But I didn't want anyone to take the tooth away, and I thought, if they're dead, it won't change anything now. So I kept quiet."

"You don't still have it?"

"When I was twelve, we had this lesson on ancient Rome and the teacher told us they used amulets. They thought they could provide protection from magic or disease. Archaeologists found some in Roman bath houses. The Romans must have thrown them into the water. I thought, if my tooth came from a dead person, maybe it could act as an amulet—as protection from death . . . So I took it to the bridge over the stream in the park near our house and I threw it in."

"And it's worked so far," I tell him, because I'm not sure what else to say.

Silence. Then he says, "It wasn't my life I was asking for."

My heart suddenly races. Why didn't I know right away? His mother. He must be talking about his mother.

I find myself cast into what feels like the far, distant past.

I'm in my chair, by the window in my pre-op room, trying to force myself to face my broken reflection. Outside, a couple of kids in puffer jackets are putting the finishing touches on a snowman. There's a man and a woman—

I screw my eyes shut. Quickly, I say, "You were there—at the hospital? In March. In the park, in the snow. Where the statue of Pan is. With a man and a woman with long dark hair."

I open my eyes. I expect Joe to look struck. Or stunned.

He doesn't. He shakes his head. "No."

"March fifteenth."

He frowns. "Why? What did you see?"

"She was beautiful . . . Was she your mother?"

"My mother was blond."

The last boy I saw with *my* eyes, apart from Elliot . . . ? It would have been too much of a coincidence. *His mother's dead.*

"What happened?" I ask him.

He doesn't answer.

"You ready for me to take your order, folks?"

Joe doesn't acknowledge the waitress.

I force myself to. "What's good?" I ask her.

"I love the shepherd's pie."

"Two of those, please."

When she's gone, Joe looks at me, and I swear I see a tornado in his soul. I can't look too long, or it'll suck me in. And I want to be sucked in, but I can't right now. I *can't.*

A new song starts up. There's a whoop from the bachelorette party girls. One is at the microphone now, I realize. The band's singer, an older woman in tight leather pants, is standing behind her and clapping. The guitars kick in, and the girl starts singing.

What should I say to Joe? What can I say?

I find myself defaulting to a method of dealing with panic that I learned back at the hospital.

Seven-eleven.

Five, six, seven . . .

"What are you doing?" Joe asks quietly.

In the gap before the in-breath, I quickly say, "Nothing."

"You're controlling your breathing. What's wrong? Is it what you said?"

I don't answer.

"Is it what you're going to ask Althea?"

Althea.

There's a clock by the bar: 8:42 P.M.

"Are you going to ask her what Sylvia liked?" he says. "Chocolate ice cream or butterscotch? Rom coms or horror?"

There's an edge to his tone. I don't like it. And I feel bad, but I won't retreat.

"If you were describing yourself, what would you say?" I ask him. "For someone to *know* you? Drives a big silver car? Hangs out in parks? Is that what you're *like*?"

"I'm not very deep."

"That is so ridiculously untrue."

He frowns at the table.

I want to tell him how sorry I am. I *want* to say I'm here to talk to, if he wants to talk. But the waitress returns yet again. She deposits cutlery and napkins and Worcestershire sauce.

Cutlery. Napkins. Worcestershire sauce. Such ordinary, everyday things.

He gets down from his chair. I guess I look worried, because he says, "Bathroom."

I watch him go, and everything feels wrong.

Why didn't I know right away? And Worcestershire sauce. Shepherd's pie. I should have ordered American food. Pizza. Burgers. Sliders. Or steak. Steak or sliders—what did Sylvia eat after an *awesome* gig?

"Hey! It's you!"

My head spins around.

He's standing right by my table. I recognize him. The *turkeys.* The guy from Starbucks. Brandon. He's wearing a blue sports jersey, tight across his chest. Heading rowdily for the bar behind him is a group of men, all a little older, also in blue jerseys.

He flashes me another of those confident smiles. He smells like he and everything about him has just been laundered. *This* is an exhibit. This boy.

"You aren't here on your own?" he asks.

He glances past me—at the two soda glasses, I guess.

I force my mind into focus. "No . . ."

"No," he says. "Obviously." He grins. "So, it's Rosa, right?"

I nod.

"How's the family visit going?"

"Yeah . . . okay."

"Where is home? I didn't ask."

I hesitate. "London."

"You're not in high school? Or college?"

What do I tell him? I find myself saying, "Actually, I sing in a band."

"Really?"

The way he says this, it isn't doubting. He's impressed. He believes me.

"You look like a singer," he says.

Yes, this strikes me as an odd thing to say. But, despite my personal inexperience, I think I understand that this conversation isn't about the words we are exchanging, but something else entirely. And this boy is not Joe. He is easier. More yielding. I find myself smiling a little, biting my lip.

"There you go. That's a singer's smile . . . You here with your boyfriend?"

"Not really," I say.

"He's not really your boyfriend, or he's not really here?"

Again, I smile. I get the sense I don't need to do anything else to keep this interaction going.

"That was your boyfriend in Starbucks, right? He seems intense. Though maybe I'd be protective, if you were standing there chatting to this interesting guy . . ."

"Having a meaningful conversation about turkeys."

"Right." He's smiling.

From the bar, a man shouts, "Brandon!"

He ignores it. "So how long are you in town? If you get tired of being around family, I could show you some of the sights."

"What," I say, "like a turkey farm?"

He pretends to flinch. "Like the belfry."

There's a wink in his expression. I have no idea what the belfry is, but I suspect I have the gist of what going there would entail.

"I could take you to Ranc's for ice cream," he says. "Take you on the bone cruise."

"Ranc's I like. The *bone cruise*?"

He grins, and it is kind of endearing. "I love the way you say that," he says. "Makes it sound like something totally more interesting."

Absolutely, I have the gist.

"Brandon!"

He holds up a hand to acknowledge the shout but doesn't take his eyes off me. "Why don't I take your number?" he asks.

"Yeah . . . Actually, I don't have a cell phone while I'm here."

"Really? Okay. Don't go anywhere."

He heads over to the bar, and after a moment he's slipping back between a couple of the old guys in flying jackets with a pen.

When he reaches my table, he says, "Where should I write this?" He's glancing at my chest. *My chest.*

I roll up the right sleeve of my top. On my inner forearm he writes a phone number. He takes his time, his hand gently brushing my skin. But I don't tremble. I hold it in.

When he's finished, I roll down my sleeve. He gives me a smile loaded with intent. Then he goes over to his friends.

I close my eyes, and I breathe.

Oh my God, I think. *What it is to be me.*

A couple of minutes pass between Brandon leaving and Joe returning, so I'm guessing—of course, I'm hoping—Joe didn't see what happened.

My sleeve's over my arm. But I can still feel exactly where the nib and Brandon's hand touched my skin. If I looked down now and the numbers were burning through the cotton of my top, I'm not sure I'd even be surprised.

I should feel . . . I *should* feel, I think, ashamed. Yet, I don't.

As Joe sits back down, he says something I don't quite catch.

"What's that?"

"I said, you okay?"

He shouldn't be the one asking that. I should be asking him.

The music's louder now, I'm sure of it, and the smell of pizza and grilled meat and perfume is more intense. Or maybe I'm just admitting more of everything deeper into my brain. Like Brandon. Like Joe. The way Joe's sitting now, his T-shirt has shifted, and I can see the tan line around his neck. I wonder what he would look like without the T-shirt.

He checks his phone and says, "8:54. You sure you don't want me to come with you?"

Deep breath. "No. But thanks."

I wish I could say something to ease the atmosphere between us, but I don't know what. Now is not the right moment to ask him more about his mother.

"I feel an element of responsibility for you," he says. And I realize he's justifying why he offered to come with me.

"You don't need to," I tell him. Gently, I think. Or at least that's how I meant it to sound.

He shrugs. But not in a dismissive way.

The instant I'm down from my chair, my nerves kick in. If this is another roller coaster, I'm strapped in the car and it's pulling away.

"Will you wait here for me?" I ask Joe.

"I'm not going anywhere," he says.

28.

IT ISN'T DIFFICULT to find the kitchen. I watch for a waitress with empty plates and follow her to a pair of swinging doors.

Before going in, I mentally rehearse one last time what I'm going to say. It's not the twin explanation part I'm worried about; I don't expect I'll need to go into much detail, and there's the fact of my face to support my claim. It's the rest: what I ask Althea. What did Sylvia love? What were her dreams? Can I be so bald about it? I guess I'll have to feel my way.

I walk into the kitchen and blink. It's so bright—and hot. I take in industrial ovens and a couple of steel tables. Heat lamps hang over one table, pizzas glistening underneath. At the other, a man with a shaved head, in a white T-shirt, his arms sleeved with tattoos, is chopping red peppers.

Another chef, in full whites, is frying something. He notices me. But it's a waitress, hurrying in and over to the pizzas, who spins and says, "I'm sorry, the kitchen is staff only."

"I'm looking for someone," I tell her. "Althea Fernando."

"Althea?"

"She said she works here."

The waitress lifts a plate to her forearm. "Her shift's about to finish. But you're not supposed to be in here. Let me go find her and bring her out. Just give me a minute, okay?" Another two plates of pizza clasped in her hands, she pushes through the doors and heads back into the bar.

I wait.

I don't have a watch or a phone, but it feels like a long time. Neither of the chefs seems bothered that I'm here. I've been waiting so long. *Months.* I can't wait any longer.

As I can't see Althea, I skirt the wall, heading past the ovens and a double fridge. I come to a door marked FIRE EXIT, with a bar handle. The whooshing sound of a dishwasher is soft in the background. Toward the back of the kitchen, there's another metal table laden with kitchen supplies—

And there she is.

Caramel skin. Hair up in a loose, high bun. Thinner than she looked in the photos. She's in whites, and she's wiping down the tabletop. It's only when I get close that she notices me.

The shock in her huge eyes freezes my tongue.

The cloth in her hand drops to the floor.

"You look—" She stops. "My aunt—"

"Sylvia was my sister." I whisper it so quietly that I have to say it again. "Sylvia was my sister. I'm her twin. I was brought up with another family."

Althea stares at me. I see everything in her eyes. *Every* emotion I can think of.

Abruptly, she makes for the fire exit. I follow, catching the door just as it's about to close, emerging onto a concrete area at the back of the building.

A spotlight illuminates four industrial plastic garbage bins and a metal bucket half-full of sand, scattered with cigarette butts. Beyond this little concrete oasis is blackness— trees. Bass booms from the windows around the side of the pub.

Althea pulls a pack of Marlboros and a lighter out of her pocket. With a trembling hand, she frees a cigarette. Holds the pack out to me. I shake my head. She lights the cigarette, takes a long drag. Returns the pack and lighter to her pocket.

I'm waiting, wondering what she'll say and whether I should offer more of my story.

At last, she looks at me again. "Sylvia didn't have a sister," she says.

I'm prepared for this. "She didn't know she did. She never knew about me. I only just found out about her."

Althea takes another drag. She shakes her head a little, to herself. "So you're telling me you're twins and your parents had you adopted."

"Yes."

She nods.

Now do I ask if she'll talk about Sylvia? Perhaps I should wait.

After blinking up at the sky, she presses the heel of her free hand first to one eye then the other. "I wasn't going to see you," she says, matter-of-factly. "Then my aunt called. She said, there's someone around who looks just like Sylvia. She wanted to warn me. In case I saw you and—" She knocks a column of ash to the ground, takes another drag. "So it's *not* that you're some girl who's seen pictures of Sylvia in the media and you think you look like her, so now you're here to—what—fuck with her family? Try to get their money? Her mother had a *stroke*."

Such sudden vehemence. It's my turn to be shocked. "I—"

She interrupts angrily: "I *know* that family. They wouldn't give a daughter up for adoption. So—what—they aren't Sylvia's biological parents? She looked just like her mom! Listen to you! Are you *British*? Some British family took you? Is that what you're saying?"

I try to keep my self-control. "They are her biological parents," I say.

"But then—"

I reach up and pull off the wig.

Sylvia's wavy, dark hair falls down around my shoulders.

Althea stares so hard her face jerks. She looks away. Looks right back. Takes a short, hard drag. "What do you want?"

"Just to find out about her. What kind of person she was."

"So you've seen her dad, right? *Your* dad? He knows you're here?"

Now what do I say?

"He *doesn't* know? But they know you've found out about her?"

"I thought I'd find out about Sylvia first," I tell her.

"You did?"

"I didn't expect—" And I find I can't finish my sentence.

"What?" she says bitterly. "Her to be *dead*? People to be upset by you turning up like this? I mean—you didn't know her, right? You never knew her. She's gone now. But you *never* knew her."

I say softly, "I feel like I know her. I *want* to."

Althea drops the cigarette and grinds it with her shoe.

She's about to go back in.

"Althea—"

She's already turned away, but she looks back at me. "I *almost* get it. I am sorry for your loss. Such as it is. But she was my *best friend*. I was *just* beginning to feel like life could maybe happen without her. And now you turn up and you didn't even know her. I shouldn't have said I'd see you. I didn't know. Please don't come here again."

"Althea, please—"

"If you try to come in this way, or into the kitchen, I'll call security. And then I'll call her dad."

She vanishes inside. The fire door slams shut.

I stare at the sky. It's the color of pencil lead, blank with clouds. No moon. No stars.

I'm standing behind O'Neill's, alone. *What now?* A minute passes.

A rush up my spine. The fire door's opening.

Althea steps out, her face drawn. "It's a shock, okay? To see you."

I nod quickly.

"If you want to talk, I've got a few minutes." She rubs her eyes.

While Althea reaches again for her cigarettes, I watch her. The smell of her last cigarette—or maybe just of the stubs in the bucket—lingers in the air. I feel sick, and while it's not directly to do with the smoke, it isn't helping.

She takes a drag. "Maybe you could put that wig back on?" she says, and all the aggression that was in her voice before is gone. "Why are you even wearing it?"

I shake it to help me find the front. "I didn't want to come here and freak everyone out."

"Only me."

"Yeah . . . I'm sorry." And I do mean it. And not just for upsetting her.

I guess she'll contact Sylvia's parents after this. But her dad did come after me in the park. He broke the terms of the agreement.

I twist my hair back and slip the wig on. I'm still raking it through with my fingers to straighten it when she says, "So, what do you want to know?"

"Anything," I tell her. "I've seen her memorial book in the library. But all I've heard is she sang, and she was talented and smart."

Another drag. Her hand's trembling. She sits on the edge of the step below the door and places her feet apart, her elbows on her knees. I stay where I am. If I move, I might throw up.

"She got decent grades," she says. "Mostly she was smart about people. She had this plan to move to New York. She knew someone whose cousin's a producer on *The Voice*, and he was going to try to set her up with a coach."

There are so many questions I could ask. What type of music did Sylvia love most? Which was her favorite band? Where in New York did she think she might live? Could she really sing like Elle King? But Althea said she has only a few minutes, and I'm worried she'll stick to it. So, with my list in my mind, I ask her, "What else did she like, apart from singing? What did she hate?"

"Hate? I don't know . . . humidity. Algebra. People who were fakes. S'mores. She wasn't that into dancing."

"Really?"

Althea exhales with a little shrug. "She wasn't that *great* at dancing. She had rhythm. Somehow she was just kind of uncoordinated." A faint smile . . . then the memory fades, or she blocks it, because the smile vanishes.

"But she liked playing Frisbee?"

"That was her *mom*. She wanted Sylvia to do some type of physical exercise. She said she'd do Frisbee because it didn't sound like exercise. Only it was. And you *had* to be kind of coordinated. I did it for a while. Mostly because I liked hanging out with Sylvia . . . I think they kept her on the team mostly because *everyone* liked being around her, and just once in a while she'd make these totally fluky catches, and no one could work out if she actually was brilliant or it was just her luck . . ." She stops and sighs in the direction of the shadows behind me. The wind in the leaves sounds like someone approaching, retreating, approaching.

It makes me think of that picture of Sylvia and Althea with water bottles, in a glade. "But she liked being outdoors? She went kayaking and fishing?"

Althea looks a little surprised. "Who told you that?" She goes on before I can answer. "We went kayaking a few times. But that's because there was this boy . . ." She stops. "Her dad took her fishing sometimes. But if she caught anything, she always put it back. She said she couldn't watch something die." She waves her cigarette. "She couldn't *see* life and watch it go. My dad, when he was a resident in the ER, he saw people die. He said it takes a few minutes after someone's technically dead for them to go. There's a presence that stays. And then it's gone. The soul, maybe . . ."

The soul? No, I don't want to think about that. In fact, right now I don't want to think about *anything* Althea's telling me. And there's something else I have to ask her: "Were you at the party?"

She doesn't look as though she's understood. Then she does.

I whisper, "Were you at the reservoir?"

Althea doesn't move. Even the glow from the tip of her

cigarette hangs in the air. The throb of bass from the stage a million miles away inside the bar only accentuates how still and silent we are. Then she says softly, "Yeah, I was there."

"What happened?"

". . . What happened? The ice cracked."

"What was wrong with her friend? Was it something to do with Sylvia—the reason she went out on the ice?"

Althea frowns. "*Sylvia?* It had nothing to do with Sylvia. She wasn't even that good friends with Amber. But Sylvia was Sylvia . . ." She squeezes her eyes shut. "If I hadn't been making out with Michael Chan, it could've been me who went after Amber, and I—" She stops. Looks directly at me. "I did all kinds of sports. I was one of the best athletes in school. I could swim when I was *two*. If it'd been *me* on the ice . . ."

A tear rolls down each of her cheeks. It hurts to see Althea cry. She takes a heaving breath. Regains control and roughly wipes her face with her sleeve. She tosses the half-smoked cigarette into the bucket. "So you're twins. Can you dance?"

Can you dance?

I think I was as okay at ballet as any little girl can be. When I used to dance, mostly it was on my own. I haven't danced since the surgery. For all these reasons, I don't answer.

"Are you sporty?" she asks. The softness is gone.

I shake my head.

"But you can sing?"

I shrug.

Althea sighs. She brings her knees together. I know she's ready to get up and go, and I'm not sure how to stop her. My brain feels numb. But then she says, "There was this song she said her mom used to sing to her when she was small, when she was upset or couldn't sleep or she was sick. 'Over the Rainbow.' You know it, right? I tried to sing it to her when she was in the hospital." Her voice starts to break. She takes a deep breath. "I can't even sing, but I thought *maybe* it might help. Then I got to that part about how the dreams that you dare to dream come true, and I couldn't sing those words. Apart from making it as a singer, her dream would have been to have a sister. That's why I had to talk to you. But not again. Okay?"

She isn't crying now but my tears roll. I try not to let them, but there's nothing I can do.

With a heavy sigh, she gets up. "Good luck, Sylvia's sister."

Althea is gone.

I am standing, staring up at the jagged outline of trees against dark clouds, feeling the beat of the music in my chest.

I'm in Lexington, in Sylvia's body, outside a bar that she

sang in . . . and her presence isn't around me, but *inside* me. We are indivisible. I *am* her. She *is* me.

I walk back into O'Neill's through the front entrance with that sensation still lifting me. I glide through the lobby, past leather armchairs and a wall clock, and down the steps. My gaze sweeps the room. It takes in the table I was sitting at with Joe. He's not there.

So it moves on to the other tables in the restaurant area, and the bachelorette party, past the other people dancing, up to the stage.

A redheaded girl in jeans and cowboy boots is belting out a pop song. I know it. It's by Adele. I slip down past the dartboard and the plates of burgers and shepherd's pie, through the bittersweet scents of beer and perfume, the girl's pure voice luring me in.

She hits the song's crescendo. People clap. Hands are raised. Faces are smiling, showing white teeth. I glimpse them in freeze-frames. The world's breaking up. As the girl jumps from the stage with a lasso twirl of her arm, the singer returns to the microphone.

"Okay, guys," she calls. "Last one before we get back to the rest of our set. Any volunteers, come on up here. Only one rule: You'd better be good!"

And I have no choice. It *has* to be me.

If other people make a move, I don't notice them. Already I'm up on the stage and I'm taking the singer's hand. Her red lips are smiling as she says in my ear, "What's the song?"

"Elle King?" I say.

"Okay. 'Ex's & Oh's'?"

I nod.

She calls the title to the guitarist, who salutes. Then she grins out over the crowd. "So here we have . . ." To me: "Tell everyone your name, honey."

I shake my head. She raises a penciled-in eyebrow.

"So here we have 'Ex's & Oh's'!"

As my hands close around the microphone, the drums and guitar start up together in an insistent beat. I stand there, blinking at the crowd. I see a tall older man in fatigues. A girl wearing purple eye shadow and a knitted yellow beret. The bachelorette party, their eye makeup smudged, their arms draped around one another's shoulders. A pretty, short-haired girl blowing a kiss to another girl. A sweaty-faced boy, his hands on the hips of a girl in a plunging top. I hold the microphone, and I see everything, and I feel Sylvia here, alive inside me.

I hear the guitar and the drums.

The whole world is faces.

I hear the guitar and the drums.

Someone's touching my back. A voice in my ear says: "Any time you like, okay?"

I hear the guitar . . . and the drums.

The girl in the beret puts a hand to her mouth. The girl in the plunging top calls, "Come on, girl, what're you waiting for?"

I *know* the words. I heard the song so many times in the rehab gym at the hospital. And on Joe's phone, after learning that Sylvia could sing like Elle King.

I open my mouth. It's dry.

"Okay," says a voice in my ear. "It's okay. I'll take it from here."

The microphone's in my right hand. I want to grip it tight but I can't. The singer pulls it easily from me. And now she's stepping in front of me, spreading her arms to the crowd.

It takes everything I have to jump rather than fall from that stage. My head is ringing, my ears buzzing. There's a deep, heavy pounding in my stomach that I think is my heart. I half push my way into the crowd, with no intention other than to escape the music. But the farther away I am, the louder it seems to get.

I sense eyes on me, but I don't return the glances. A broad hand reaches for my back. I twist to avoid it, which makes me collide with a man in a sports jersey carrying glasses of beer. Dark drops patter onto my arm and shoulder. The smell of it makes me gag.

I try to keep moving, but the stench of beer and men is

making deep strides into my brain. I'm pressed against people as I move forward. I hear Althea: *She was my best friend.* What did she hate? *People who are fakes.* The caffeine from the Diet Coke makes my heart race and skip. If it is the caffeine . . . if it is my heart . . . because I'm feeling suddenly disassociated from my body. The pulse in my neck throbs and leaps, like it's trying to escape.

The guitar chords are so loud now they crash into my skull. The singer's voice waxes and wanes, the music a tide that sucks at me so hard I'm about to go under, but somehow I keep my balance.

I sense a blur of green. A face emerges from the haze. Green eyes, longish blond hair—*Adam?* No.

My foot skids and my right leg buckles. I put out my hands. They hit something, but I can't tell what. My vision bleaches. My pulse scares itself into a roar. I try to move but I can't. I'm freezing cold. And I'm suspended in a terrifying fraction of a second—the fraction before Sylvia fell through the ice, immediately before the end of everything she knew.

"Rosa?"

The voice is deep within my head.

"Rosa."

There's an explosion of light in what someone else might call my soul.

29.

WHEN I RETURN to consciousness, I see Joe's face.

The first thing I hear is a woman's voice.

It's muffled, in the distance. He is close. He's holding me up. Or propping me up. Because I'm on the floor, on coarse, green-and-beige, spiral-patterned carpet, sitting with his arm around my back.

"Rosa?"

I squeeze my eyes shut. Open them. Look at him. I'm able to focus.

"You okay?"

I nod. He lets out a quick breath.

"I was about to call 911."

He glances around. I'm half aware of a couple of waitresses watching. "She's okay," he calls.

"You sure?" one asks.

I force myself to nod. "I faint sometimes," I tell her.

"You haven't had any alcohol tonight?"

"No," I say. "You can check with our waitress. She—" I try to remember her face so I can describe her.

"I guess you're not talking like you're drunk," she says. "You want a glass of water or something?"

I shake my head. Which makes my head spin. I think my eyes are closed when I say, "Can I just sit here for a few minutes?"

"No problem at all." To Joe: "Come find me if she needs help."

The waitresses leave and I lean forward a little, so I can sit up on my own. I rub my eyes. Open them.

Joe says, "Maybe I should call 911."

Ice water to the face couldn't shock me faster to full consciousness. "*No.*"

"No?"

"*You can't.*"

"I should get you back to the hospital."

"*No.* I'm okay."

He frowns. "Did you find Althea?"

I take in my surroundings. Judging by the carpet, and the chairs upturned on tables, and the thud of bass through the wall, we're in a room somewhere behind the bar.

"Rosa, what happened?"

Did he see me onstage? I whisper, "Yeah, I found her."

"No, what *just* happened? You were on the floor. I had to carry you in here."

"I told the waitress. I must have fainted."

He says, "Have you been taking whatever medication—"

"*Yes.*"

He lets go of me. "What did she tell you?"

I close my eyes.

"Why don't you want me to call 911? I mean, if you're not totally well—"

I hold my breath. "I'm okay. It's just all . . . incredibly . . . *complicated.*"

"Yeah, and?"

He's done this before. Again, it startles me. "And so—I—" I don't know how to finish.

He sighs. Shakes his head.

"If you knew—" The air falls still. "I told you: If you knew all the truths about me, you would get in your car and drive away and never come back."

I'm focusing on my hands, my fingers white where they interlock; I'm holding on so tight to all the strength that I have left.

Then an idea comes to me. It might make everything right.

"We could go away—New York, maybe we could—"

But already I can see the answer in his eyes, and it kills my sentence. Kills me.

"Let's get out of here," he says.

30.

WE WALK OUT of O'Neill's together, but only in the literal sense.

I don't know if he saw me onstage, but it doesn't really matter. As we stand at the top of the steps that lead down to the parking lot, I call on the shattered remains of my courage. "You should go back to Boston," I tell him. "I can call a cab."

"To take you where?" he asks.

I don't answer. The wind blows, and it goes right through me. Joe's holding my jacket. He must have collected it from my chair. He passes it to me, and I shrug it back on. I watch him watch me, and see his expression stumble, and for one freezing moment I'm worried he's seen Brandon's number on my arm.

"I'm not going back to Boston," he says. "I told you I'm not going anywhere."

He must see my confusion. All he says is, "Come on."

He heads down the steps. I follow and quickly realize he isn't going to his car, but on toward the main road. We walk in silence, the wind blowing leaves down all around us, the weak moon glowing faintly through thinning clouds. When we reach the road, the whizz of a car makes me stagger back, and I think it's at that moment that we both see it: a plain wooden bench beneath an oak.

My whirling mind pivots to the hospital.

In spite of everything, she loved this bench. Denise. Forever.

It feels like months since I met Joe. Years' worth of regular feeling and experience have been compressed into a few days. I've heard that emotion makes memory and memory makes life. I guess it's true.

All kinds of emotions shift kaleidoscopically inside me as we sit down.

A few inches of gray-brown wood separate our legs.

It's quiet out here—at least, there's no one walking, and only an occasional car. I have no idea what time it is, but most people must be home or wherever else they want to be for the evening. At last, I realize, I can't hear the music from O'Neill's anymore.

His eyes on the asphalt, Joe says, "You've probably forgotten, but you once asked me who was the most interesting person I've ever interviewed."

"The man from North Korea," I say quickly, because of course I haven't forgotten. "The girl."

"That *girl* was me." He twists to look right at me. "I thought, if I tell her, and she says that girl was evil, well, then I'll know."

Althea, the surgery, the hospital, the stage; right now, they all drop off the cliff of my mind. *"You?"*

My brain races as I try to recall exactly what he told me. But he's talking, interrupting my thoughts.

"She had leukemia. We knew she was going to die. She decided to stop the treatment and we flew from San Francisco to Boston. We hired a car and made it to Cambridge. She wanted to see the house she was born in. Now it's this neighborhood store. Afterward, she felt hot. She had a fever. We checked into a hotel on Harvard Square. We got her in bed but it hurt her to breathe. Dad called 911. They took her to Dixon-Dudley and the doctor said she had pneumonia. After four days, she started to get better from the pneumonia. I was there in the room, the monitors bleeping, all this sleet smothering everything outside, and she said to Dad, 'I want to die here. I don't want to go back.' Dad couldn't handle it. He left the room."

I stare at him. His moment in his mother's room. Mine on the transplant table. Ours in the park when I asked him if I'm pretty. And now here, on the bench, in Lexington. All these moments feel inextricably connected, as though strung together from the start.

He says, "I thought, one of us has to help her. It's not going to be Dad. So."

"You went to the emergency drug tray."

"The doctors weren't satisfied. They ordered an autopsy."

"They found you in the park?"

He shakes his head. "Dad said it was him. They arrested him. When I tried to say it was me, they weren't interested. Dad insisted it was him. There was no video surveillance. No witnesses. His word against mine."

"What happened?"

"He got four years. He's in the Northeastern Correctional Center."

I stare at Joe. I have no idea what to say.

"I can't get away from it. I'm stuck. At the hospital. In Boston. With killing my own mother. My dad in jail. Maybe I should leave, but I can't."

Stuck in Boston. Unable to go back, or move on. He's like me, I think. Or how I felt. Mesmerized.

I try to think of something helpful to tell him, but it all

sounds trite. *You did the right thing. It was what she wanted. You did try to tell the police* . . . I don't say any of these things *because* they're trite. How do you reassure someone when it comes to something like this? Not with words, surely. Or not with words like these.

Exhaustion washes over me.

I say, "I wish I could tell you the truth about me. If it was just *my* secret, I would."

Silence. Then he says, "I didn't tell you all that to try to pry your secret out of you."

Shame burns my cheeks. "I didn't mean . . ." My sentence shrivels.

He looks hard at me. "Everyone has secrets. No matter how I look at it, I *took* someone's life. I thought I was strong enough to do it. But when you say *take* a life, that's exactly what it is. *I've* taken it into me, and it'll be inside me *forever*."

"That doesn't change what kind of person you are."

"There's no objective answer, but I should know better than anyone. As far as you're concerned, I'm whatever my accumulated actions lead you to believe me to be. You're whatever I believe you to be. Now you have a different picture of my actions. For you, I've changed."

I try to suppress my analyses and estimations, and my self-doubts. It's with my life-breath that I whisper, "I believe that I feel more *right* around you than I ever have around anyone."

For the first time since I met him, something changes in his eyes. All defenses are down. I don't analyze *anything*. I'm going to rush in. Before I do, he whispers, "Do you? I feel right around you."

31.

JOE GOES INTO the room first. I'm about to close the door with my back, but he's already there, one hand raised, pushing it shut, the other reaching for me.

I kiss him, and fireworks flare through me. He takes his hand from the door, presses it into the small of my back. My back seems to meld to his touch. His hand is inside my top now, on my skin. I kiss him and let the moments happen, one by one.

By one.

By one.

I'm on the bed.

His lips are on mine.

By one.

By one.

My bra is on the floor.

By one.

By one.

His hand is on my thigh.

But these moments aren't crystallized. I'm in a wave of moments.

That kiss by the reservoir. The first time I kissed a boy.

A number on my arm.

A chaste night beside Joe.

A neoprene cap.

A nanoknife.

Back in time, and further back, to before I was even sick, all those moments massing and lifting me here—

I gasp.

I'm part of him now, and he's part of me.

32.

WHEN I WAKE, the first thing I am aware of is warmth. Joe. Asleep.

I realize I'm naked. Traces of last night's pressures remain on my body. Flashes of Joe's face shift through my mind. Then my conscious focus edges deeper, under my skin, through my flesh, burrowing like a worm to my heart. Like a *worm*? I remember a poem by William Blake that Elliot once read aloud over and over, so that in the end we'd both memorized it:

The invisible worm
That flies in the night
In the howling storm
Hath found out thy bed

Of crimson joy

And his dark secret love

Does thy life destroy.

Suddenly, I feel sick. *I'm going to throw up.*

I slip out of the bed and into the bathroom. In a little trash can by the sink is a wrinkled condom. I go over to the toilet, and I retch—but that's it. I'm trembling, my body's like lead, but I'm not going to vomit.

I move to the mirror. I should be used to it by now: looking at Sylvia's face. But this morning, it comes as a shock. For some reason, I'm expecting to see the old me, but it's *her* face, *her* body in the mirror. Her breasts. Her stomach. *Her* arm. With a phone number written on it. If Joe noticed it last night, he didn't comment on it. But it's there.

On a glass shelf above the sink is a bar of soap in a plastic wrapper. I tear the wrapper open. I hold the soap under hot water. I lather my arm and I rub at the ink.

It isn't coming off.

I scrub harder.

The ink is still there.

I rub and I rub. I even scrape with my nails, until the flesh is red and raw.

Again, I hold the soap between my hands. This time, I wash away the tears. My eyes sting, and the tears won't stop falling.

I scrape at my cheeks, wanting them to stop. I make another lather and rub it hard across my chest.

I had sex with Joe.

And he has *no idea* who I am.

He had sex with a dying girl, a plain girl. *Not her.*

Brandon spoke to *Sylvia.* Does that mean I'm dead?

I take a washcloth from the vanity, wet it, and rub my breasts until they are red. Then I go back to my face. What if I'm still down there, beneath the layers? If I scrape hard enough, can I dig myself out?

I glance up. *Her* face catches me in the mirror.

With the heels of my hands, I press my cheekbones to try to force them to recede.

I'm shaking so hard now. My tears won't stop. I'm making so much noise I'm going to wake Joe.

I snatch a towel from a peg and roughly dry myself. I creep back into the bedroom and, without looking at the bed, I gather my clothes from the carpet and put them on.

Silently, I pocket my phone and leave the room.

As I step out into the early morning, a creeping cold begins to flow through my blood. It spreads quickly, conquering my organs and extremities, turning my feet to blocks of ice, so I have to heave them along the path and down to the road.

Despite the weight of my body, I break into a jog. I can't let anyone stop me. So I have to run.

I notice black speckles—birds—soaring in the pale yellow sky. They're free, and it's right to be running. I thought I could live with Sylvia. I thought I could sleep with Joe. But when the news breaks, *Joe will know.* If I run fast enough, I might be able to lose her—

But perhaps I know a surer way to do that.

Trying to force my right leg to keep up, I sprint along sidewalks, across people's driveways. There are no cars on the road. Then there's one. And another. House after house merges in the background, until I find myself on a long, straight road, which starts to curve, and then I see a fence and trees.

A pain is hammering deep in my chest, but it only pushes me on.

I run into the parking lot.

Now I'm on the path. I can see the water ahead.

Joe *trusted* me. I looked Sylvia's best friend in the face and told her I was Sylvia's sister. I told Brandon I was a singer, and I let him write his number on *her* arm. I got up onstage. Joe touched me, but it *wasn't me.* I am whatever my accumulated actions lead him to believe me to be. I am lie after lie after *lie,* and by far the biggest lie about me is her.

I'm at the water's edge. I glance up and see a white cloud,

unevenly massed, like a tumor. It's so cold. Next month, the water will freeze. Kids will strap on skates and play ice hockey. Come Thanksgiving, they'll be racing over the spot where she went through the ice.

I remember the poem by Percy Shelley in Sylvia's memorial book: *Music, when soft voices die, vibrates in the memory* . . .

So many voices are vibrating in my head. Mum's and Dad's, Elliot's and Jane's, Joe's and Brandon's. I thought I knew what to do—or what I could do—and I was wrong. It's *her* voice I need to silence.

I crouch. Tears fall from my cheeks to the pine needles. I want to kick the needles away, into the reservoir, cut down all the trees, and *fill* the reservoir. Suddenly, the cloud mass breaks. Sunlight hits the water, forming a glimmering path.

I take a step. See the water around my ankles, but don't feel it.

Another step. Then another. I'm wading now, pushing fallen leaves into my wake. I'm looking up at the infinity of sky beyond the clouds. I can make all this right. I *can* reconcile the two of us.

I take another step. My tears dry. Her heart calms. She wants this, too.

Another step . . . and the ground is falling away.

Perhaps she could swim, but this is *my* brain.

I pull myself deeper. My arms don't make a splash.

Everything settles. My body relaxes.

And just as I curl up, as I gently hold my breath and allow myself to sink, a lightning strike hits my brain. An image of the night before the surgery. Elliot's face.

Another. Mum is close, her chunky-knuckled hand on my cheek.

Joe: *I'm not going anywhere.*

No.

No.

No.

33.

THE WOMAN WHO answers the door stares at me. I'd stare at me, too, if I was on my doorstep, soaking wet and dripping.

She has warm brown eyes and gray hair in a ponytail. She's dressed for a run. Quickly, she zips up her sports jacket and comes out on the step. "What happened? Are you okay?"

I tremble. I can feel the tears coming. It'd be a tsunami of tears, if I let it.

"You need help?" she says. Her voice is kind. Not soft, but capable. "Let me help you. Come inside."

I can't move.

"Don't worry about the water. Look—it's just the kitchen. Here."

One hand taking my arm, the other on my back, she

maneuvers me inside. I spot movement, and I tense. But it's just a gray-muzzled black Labrador lifting its head from a sofa set against the front wall. The woman lifts a pine chair out from under a family-size dining table. She brings it over to where I'm still standing, on polished floorboards, just inside the door.

"Can you tell me what happened?" she says.

I don't answer. She takes my shoulder, guides me down onto the chair. I'm shaking from the cold, from everything. My body seizes in a shudder.

"I'm going to get you a towel, honey. But tell me who to call—the police? Your mom?"

Mum . . . No, I can't cry yet.

Her sneakers make a soft squeak as she goes to the counter by the fridge and pulls the charger cable out of her phone. "What's the number, honey? Or would you rather do it? Anna?" she calls, in the direction of the open kitchen door. "Anna, can you please bring me a fresh towel?" To me, she says, "It's just my daughter. It's okay. Here." She grabs a tea towel from the handle of the oven door, comes over, gently dries my hands and my face, and kneels in front of me with her phone. "Where were you? The reservoir?"

Her house is across the road from the reservoir. The first one I came to. I nod.

She takes my hand and presses the phone into it.

A pine-rimmed wall clock with roman numerals ticks.

My fingers trembling, I unzip my jacket pocket and pull out my cell phone. It is supposed to be able to withstand half an hour under water. And it looks okay.

"Is it working?" she asks.

I manage to mumble, "I think so." I locate a number and select it.

I hear ringing.

More ringing.

A voice says suspiciously: "Hello?"

My chest heaves.

The woman goes to the kitchen door and shouts again, up the stairs perhaps: "Anna!"

I whisper: "Elliot."

"Rosa? *Rosa?*"

"Yeah."

"Where the *fuck* are you?"

The anger in his voice stuns me.

"Are you okay?" he demands.

I whisper, "Yes."

Which must fully release him: "What the fuck are you thinking? Where are you? You vanish like that—"

"I texted Mum—"

"The police have got an alert out on you. You know what happened three minutes ago? Dad threw up in the corridor."

Silence. I'm shaking so hard now. The tears are running so fast.

"Everyone has been so *fucking* worried about you. You just vanish. And with some journalist?"

Deep silence, frigid as a black hole.

"Where are you?" I whisper.

"Where do you think I am? At the hospital. Where are you?"

I try to answer. Words won't come.

"How could you do this to us?"

"Elliot . . ."

"Mum hasn't slept since you left. Dad walks around like the living dead. I—"

"Elliot."

"All you had to do was tell me. If you wanted to get away, I could have taken you. You could have *told me.*"

"*Elliot.*" I'm sinking into the solid chair. I might just melt onto the floor.

"Are you really okay?"

This time, his tone is a little less harsh. Which releases me.

"No."

He says quickly, "Where are you?"

The woman comes back over to me with a white bath

towel. I ask her, "Could you please tell my brother where I am?"

As I move the phone away from my ear to give it to her, I hear Elliot saying: "Who's that? Is he with you?"

The woman takes my phone. "Hello? Are you coming for your sister?" Pause. "*What* did you say?"

She shoots me the biggest glance of pity so far.

Then, tucking the phone into her neck and reaching out to wrap the towel around my juddering shoulders, she recites an address.

34.

THE CURTAINS AREN'T thick. At least, they don't look it. But they must have a military-grade blackout lining because there's barely a scrap of light in this room.

I'm on my side in a king-size bed, under a duvet, in a hotel robe, feeling the sting of the raw patches where I rubbed at my flesh. And I'm holding Elliot's hand. He's on his back, on top of the duvet, not saying a word, just lying beside me, holding my hand.

After I phoned Elliot, I made one more call: to the Happy Haven Motel, to let Joe know I was okay. But I don't want to think about that right now. I can't.

When Elliot arrived at the house of the woman who helped me into her kitchen, he took one look at my crumpling face and said, "Dark room."

To which she said, "Don't take her into the dark. Look at her; she needs somewhere warm, somewhere light—"

And he said: "You don't have the slightest clue what I'm talking about."

Which shut her up. Which made me sad for her, because she'd been kind, and it was at that moment that I started to cry all over again.

Elliot. How did I let myself get so far away from him?

Now, as we lie here in silence in what I glimpsed, before Elliot drew the curtains, to be a grand room—antique furniture, a brass chandelier, a genuine fireplace, gilt-framed prints—I think, and I cry . . .

Think and cry.

Elliot says nothing, which is unusual for him. He just lies there, holding my hand.

After he came for me and helped me down to the road toward the waiting taxi, I asked what he'd told Mum and Dad. "I said you'd made contact," he said, like I *was* some kind of alien. "And you were safe."

"What did they say?"

"I won't tell you right now."

"But—"

"Seriously, Rosa, you don't want to hear it right now."

He half pushed me into the taxi and asked the driver to take us to the nearest "most opulent hotel."

The driver said, "Where?"

Elliot said, "*Nice.* Somewhere. Nice. To. Stay. With thick curtains."

I saw the driver checking us out in the rearview mirror as he pulled away. Trying to note details of our faces, I guess, if the police asked for witnesses to—what? Something suspicious involving thick curtains in the Lexington region.

The only question Elliot asked me when we got into our room was, "Why Lexington?"

And so I explained—about Sylvia's dad in the hospital park, and Joe and the driver's license, and the newspaper story. I even showed it to him. He shook his head as he read.

"He came after you . . . the father."

"I don't want you to tell Mum," I said.

"Are you *serious*?"

"Just not *now*. Not yet."

I couldn't stop myself from crying, which I guess was one reason he said: "We have to. But okay. Not yet."

Now we're lying here together, and all I can hear is Elliot's breathing and muffled voices and occasional footsteps from other guests on the landing.

When perhaps five hours have passed, I sit up.

In the darkness, Elliot turns to me.

I didn't lose myself in the reservoir.

But I have to accept that I did find myself in a state that, objectively, put me somewhere close.

Elliot hasn't asked why my clothes were wet, and I haven't told him. Still, I need to try to explain because he's the only person who could understand.

I saw her dad in the park and . . . no. There was this boy, and I thought . . . no. I came here and her life seemed . . . no. I slept with Joe and then I felt . . . no.

None of these gets to the heart of my problem. And I think I know what does. My voice low, I say: "I don't know who I am."

Silence.

Then he says: "Imagine a mountain in front of you. Your goal is to get to the summit. But it'll be difficult. There are a few possible routes, but they're steep and icy and you don't have the optimal gear. You pick a route and you set off. It's freezing cold. You don't have any food. Your shoes are wet; your jacket is thin. Your weak muscles are struggling. How do you feel?"

I clear my throat. "Stupid?"

"No."

"Miserable."

"No."

"That's how I would feel."

"And that is where you'd be wrong."

He sits up. "If your goal is to get to the top of that mountain, you *welcome* the cold and the hunger and the pain in your legs. Because if you're feeling it, it means you're getting closer to your goal."

"I don't—"

"Rosa, this wasn't ever going to be easy." He gets up. Pads on thick carpet over to the windows but doesn't part the curtains. "You think you don't know who you are because you have someone else's body and now you know something about her. Maybe you don't know who you are. But it has nothing to do with your body."

"I slept with Joe."

He turns back to me. "Okay. Good."

"*Not* good. Because he thinks I'm like this." I spread my arms wide.

"What did that psychologist talk to you about?"

"Elliot, this is *not me.*"

"Did you *listen* to him?"

"Who? Dr. Bailey?"

"Rosa—Jesus—you don't know who you are? *I* can tell you who you are. I can give you a list. You like *Top Gear.*"

I fall back on the bed.

"You don't think that's something? You like *Top Gear* because you love Dad. Because you love me, you listen to my captions without ever telling me they're crap—"

"I'm sure I did—"

"You're the girl who colored in that banner with daisies stuck all over it that said 'Happy Ninth Birthday Elliot' and when I said there should be a comma before Elliot, you cried. I felt bad about that for weeks. Years. I *still* feel bad about it. You're the girl who used to dance really badly in the kitchen."

"Badly?"

"Who slipped cans of tuna into the shopping trolley so you could feed that feral ginger fleabag and you didn't think Mum knew, and Mum didn't tell you because she wanted you to have happy secrets."

I press my hands to my eyes.

"You're my sister, Rosa. You're *my sister*. You're the girl who is alive because she chose to go through one of the hardest things any person has ever done, because she wanted to live so much, and I was so fucking glad she did, because I can't imagine our lives without you."

"Elliot—"

"You're the girl who, despite knowing how upset and scared and fucking *mad* we'd be, disappeared with some guy."

"But I wasn't thinking about you. And that was bad—"

"No, it was bad for us—but in a way it was good for you. Because you're not just my sister. You're not just Mum's daughter to save. If you don't make your own decisions, you'll never know who you are. And who you are has nothing to do with what you look like. It has nothing to do with the girl who gave you her body."

He comes back over to me. It's so dark, but even so, I make out a seriousness in his eyes that I've never seen before.

"You slept with that boy. *You* did. What he needs to know about you is *Top Gear* and banners and tuna, not what your arse looks like in skinny jeans or what a girl who's *gone* was like. If you'd asked me, I'd have tried to talk you out of coming here, because it couldn't ever have told you anything worth knowing. But you came. And it didn't go exactly right. And not everything will go exactly right. For you or anyone else, including me. So it turns out Aula's got this other boyfriend. A Swedish human rights lawyer. But those decisions I made to do with her weren't wrong."

"How did you—"

"It doesn't matter," he says.

"It does matter."

"Yeah, but not right now."

"I should have told Joe the truth."

"Maybe," he says.

"Really?"

"Maybe. Don't listen to Mum or Dr. Monzales. *You* have to make up your own mind about what you want."

"I'm sorry about Aula."

"In the end, I'm not that sorry. Which tells me something about me."

". . . You didn't love her."

"That maybe I'm clinically narcissistic. I actually think: her loss."

I smile.

I sense him smile back.

"I think it's her loss, too," I tell him.

He takes my hand. "You're not Sylvia Johnson—you know that, right?"

"Tuna. *Top Gear*, banners . . . It doesn't add up to much. Was I really that bad at dancing?"

"You're eighteen years old, Rosa. And you've not exactly had it easy. And tuna, *Top Gear*, and banners—they're just off the top of my head. I can write you an essay if you like."

"I would like."

"Okay . . ."

He squeezes my hand.

"But Joe . . ." I pause. "If I looked like I used to, maybe he'd never have even talked to me."

"Then it would have been his loss."

I want to believe him.

"*You* like pretty girls. Look at Aula. And Catherine Smith.

And I could go on. Since when have you ever gone out with a girl who wasn't objectively attractive? So it matters to you. It's part of who they are."

"And look at me . . . ," he says. "I don't think any girl has gone for me because I look like Bradley Cooper, because I'm well aware that I do not."

"You're a boy. It's different."

"No, it isn't. And out of the girls I've gone out with, which breakup cut me up?"

". . . I don't know. None of them."

"One. Rebecca Stapleton. Remember her?"

"Rebecca?"

"See." A pause. Then he says, "You're not Sylvia, but it's okay for her body to influence how you think and behave. Like it's okay for mine to influence you—and Joe's, and Mum's, and everybody else's. Have you heard of this thing called emotion contagion?"

I lean back against the pillow. "No."

"So, I read about it. It's how you catch other people's emotions just by being around them. There's this ancient pathway in the brain. If someone's happy or afraid, they send out signals in the tone of their voice and the way they're sitting and the expression on their face, and your subconscious brain picks all this up without you even knowing, and it influences how you feel. You can catch fear from someone else. You can catch happiness. Some people naturally do this more than others. But the point is, you're never *just* yourself in isolation. No one is. We're all intertwined with the people we're around."

I find myself thinking of what Joe said about "taking" his mother's life.

Her life is intertwined with his. Mine is intertwined with Sylvia's, but it's also meshed with Elliot's and Mum's and Dad's and Joe's. I guess there are other ways of intersecting identities than with a skull saw and nanoknife. It might even be normal.

Then Elliot says, "But even if I influence you and you influence me, there's still a fundamental me. And a fundamental you. You don't have to deny her existence; just know you're not *her*. And now your job is to do stuff. It's only when you *do stuff* that you get a good idea of who you are. So."

I look at Elliot—or what I can see of him. "The Confucius of Lexington," I say. "How did you get to be so wise?"

I expect him to come back with a jokey answer. I've left the way open, after all.

He says, "That mountain analogy isn't mine. It's basically Nietzsche's. The rest . . . I thought for years I'd watch my

35.

CHOICES . . .

It seems almost crazy that I have them.

For so long, I might not have been trapped entirely by my illness, but I was heavily encumbered. And I was constrained by Mum and Dad. What they wanted for me, and what they wished I would do. Then came the operation and the requirements of post-surgery rehab. After that, I was pushed by what I thought was a need to find out about the girl whose body became mine.

All these forces, acting on me . . .

Now, if I want to be, I'm free.

Which makes me think: plane to Barbados. No, Southeast Asia. I'd love to see Angkor Wat. And Thailand. I think:

backpacking. Diving lessons. Beaches. Hammocks. But first, a trip on my own, or with Elliot, into Boston for cocktails and clam chowder. Elliot even offered to hand over the credit card he said Dad gave him when he left the hospital to meet me. I could go anywhere.

But what do I really want?

What do I *really* want?

If freedom—as Elliot insists—is the ability to make choices, I have some substantial choices to make. And though part of me wants to run away, a bigger part wants to make things right. (Mental note: Even wanting to make things right is a clue to who I am.)

I stand in front of an antique mahogany-framed mirror, below the chandelier in the grand room of this hotel in Lexington, and I look at myself in a new light.

Elliot is right: Just like him, and Mum and Dad, Sylvia will always be part of me—but not the deciding part.

While I'm thinking this, something else in the reflection catches my eye.

On the spindle-legged desk, by a black Bakelite phone, are a pad and a pen.

This time, I know for sure what my list should say. I take the pad and pen back to the bed. Propped up on my elbows on the quilted bedspread, I write:

1. Mum and Dad

2. Sylvia

3. Joe

4. Me

36.

1. MUM AND DAD.

The taxi pulls onto the road that leads to the front of the hospital, to the main entrance, with its polished concrete columns. It's a cloudless day. The sun through the windshield is hot.

I blink, searching for Mum and Dad in the people milling about. I see paramedics in their jumpsuits; patients hunched over and being helped. Then there they are: Mum in her white hospital coat, Dad in brown cords and a gray sweater.

They run toward us even before the wheels have stopped. There's a tragicomic moment when I try to open my door from the inside at the same time as Mum tries from the outside, which causes the mechanism to jam. She's still tugging on the handle while Dad runs around to the other side. Elliot jumps out. Then Dad's half in the car, grasping my hands, saying, "Rosa, my God, *Rosa.*"

He pulls me from the cab and into his arms. Then Mum's there, too, and the three of us hug on the sidewalk. Mum's clean-skin scent and the smell of coffee and Dad's sweater triggers a memory of being seven, on my way to see a neurologist for the first time, not feeling afraid but kind of excited because I had both Dad *and* Mum in the car.

Holding me tight, Mum says, "We need to talk, but Dr. Monzales is waiting in the scanning suite." Her hand drops to mine, and Dad backs off slightly so we can walk toward the doors. Elliot is with us now, beside Dad.

I say in a tone that I think is gentle, "No."

I guess I must have been emphatic, because Mum stops in her tracks.

"I mean, I will," I tell her. "But the scans can wait a little."

"Wait for *what?*" Mum says, eyes wide.

"For me to feel ready. It'll be soon—I promise."

"I don't know what you mean." Her voice is suddenly brittle.

"I know," I tell her. "But that's okay."

She and Dad exchange a glance.

He looks so slight, standing there in the sunshine in his

baggy sweater, the wool almost the same hue as his beard. Surely he's not old enough to be quite this gray. There's so much I wish I could change, and not just for me. All I can do now is try to make the future right.

"I just wish you'd told us where you were going," Dad says. "You could have said, I need to go after the donor—"

"Yeah," I say, "I'm sorry."

"Not now," Mum says to Dad.

"No, *now*. Because I want her to know that's all I wish. But Rosa, there was no reason for you to go there."

Here's a gap, I think, that I can expand myself into.

I take a literal step back, so I'm still close to them but not quite so enmeshed. All around us, people are moving through their own lives. A woman's yelling. A kid with undone laces and an Elmo helium balloon is crying. I block all of that out. I have to focus on what is mine.

"I *had* to do it," I tell them. "But it's okay. It's part of my mountain."

Mum's expression says she'd like to rush me to the scanning suite *right now*.

"Ask Elliot," I say. "He can explain."

Mum turns to him. He nods deeply.

"I hope you haven't been listening too much to Elliot," she says to me.

"Not too much," I reassure her. "Exactly enough."

Once we're inside and up in my room—which feels like some place I *used* to know—we talk it all over; namely, how I even knew to go to Lexington.

Elliot has told them what I told him. He did it on the phone before we left Lexington. Mum's voice was so loud that I could hear her talking about the police. So I took the phone and said, "Please, just wait. Just till I'm back."

Now I drop my bag and jacket and sit down on my bed. Dad comes to sit beside me. Mum takes the chair at the desk. Elliot's standing by the window. I look from him to Mum to Dad to him.

I ask them what they told the police after I left the hospital.

"What do you think?" Mum says. "That a highly vulnerable patient was missing! We had no idea where you'd gone. *No idea.* Rosa. Can you imagine what that was like?"

Dad squeezes my shoulder. "Why don't you tell us what happened? From the start."

And I do—I tell them everything. About the park, the woman with the leaflets, Joe.

"None of this was his fault," I say, as firmly as I can. "I told him I was fine to leave the hospital. He doesn't know anything about the surgery. I asked him to help."

I expect Mum to ask more about Joe. But she's looking at

Dad. "I knew they wouldn't be able to stay away." She says, "They wanted anonymity, too. There's an agreement."

He says, "And would that really stop you? If Rosa's body was out there? If it was the other way around?"

"Rosa's body is not *her*," Mum says, one eye on me.

"Good thing," I say, "seeing as my body's been incinerated."

Evidently, this worries her. "Maybe Dr. Bailey—"

But I interrupt her: "Mum, I don't think I want to see Dr. Bailey again."

"I'm not sure you can avoid it," she says, not unkindly.

"I'm not sure anyone can make me do it," I say. "I'll see someone—but not him. I'll find someone."

Dad frowns. Mum pales. Elliot, who's out of her sight line, gives me a fist pump, which a stranger might assume to be ironic, but I know is not.

I go over to Mum. I crouch in front of her and I take her hands. They're thin. Stiff. She might have made mistakes, but I can't question the engine of her actions: a motivation to do what she truly believed was best for me. The worried expression in her eyes cuts to my heart.

"Mum, I'm *okay*."

She interlocks her fingers with mine, grips me tight.

"Everything you planned for—it worked," I tell her.

"Let's see," Dad says, making me look around at him. "You disobeyed your parents' wishes. You frightened the hell out of us. You went off in a car with some guy and didn't tell us where you were going . . . We wanted you to have a chance at being a typical teenager." He looks at Mum. "We've got everything we wanted."

His eyes have filled with tears. My own tears roll down my cheeks as I look up at Mum. She squeezes my hands tight.

"Some teenagers like staying at home," she says, her voice trembling, "and, I don't know, sewing and—"

"Collecting stamps?" Elliot interrupts. "Knitting little dolls?"

"Maybe some do!" Mum says.

"I could learn to knit," I tell her, and I mean it.

"Dad really could do with at least a few sweaters that date from the current millennium," Elliot puts in.

Mum opens her mouth to protest, I guess, but Elliot stops her by saying, "Didn't someone say something about pizza?"

"I don't think so," Mum says stiffly.

"Then it's a very good thing I am," he says. "Rosa? You hungry?"

I nod.

Dad says, "I think pizza is an excellent idea."

Elliot smiles.

Dad pulls his car keys from his pocket. "You know what *is* a very good thing? That you asked to be on the insurance, Elliot. It'll be quicker if you go for it. I'll have a margherita. Thank you."

Over pizzas that Elliot brings back from Figs, I tell them what I did in Lexington (or most of it), and the little that I discovered about Sylvia.

"Crispy calamari," Elliot says, and hands Mum a box. "The calzone for you, Rosa. Margherita for you, Dad. Spicy chicken sausage for me."

There's a grin on my face that's spreading from deep in my chest. Ever since I can remember, Elliot has made a point of ordering the most unusual topping, whatever the menu, whatever the topping. Some things change. Some don't.

Mum and Dad reveal that they knew a little more about Sylvia than they'd let on to me. Which is no real surprise. I mean, they didn't know that Sylvia sang at O'Neill's, or that she wasn't a great dancer, or that she hated s'mores, or that there are two dogs in Lexington who go crazy at the sight and smell of her.

They *did* know Sylvia was a student at a high school in Massachusetts and she'd fallen through ice. And they had met Sylvia's parents.

The meeting happened at the hospital, Mum said. They exchanged only first names and the kinds of personal details that could not allow each set of parents to identify the other.

"I wouldn't have thought you would've *wanted* to meet them," I say.

"Mostly, I think, it was intended for their benefit," Mum says. "So they could see we were decent, loving people. And I wanted to be reassured that they could handle the donation, and they weren't doing it because they thought their daughter could live on in some way . . ." She sighs. "Her mother had a stroke after the accident, but there was nothing wrong with her cognitively. Not when we met or when they signed the paperwork. Then I heard she had another stroke. Worse that time . . . *They* wanted anonymity, too."

"In fact, they stipulated it," Dad puts in. "We'll have to talk to Dr. Monzales about how to handle this. The police will have to be involved."

"No—"

"No?" Mum says.

"I don't want to press any charges," I tell them.

Dad says quietly, "Rosa, he came after you in the park."

"I don't want the police involved." And I don't. Because I have my own plan for what to do about this.

Dad glances at Mum and says, "If it's possible not to involve the police, we won't. I think that's the best we can give you right now."

"You could have told me what you knew about them," I say. "I could have handled that kind of knowledge."

Mum puts her half-eaten slice of pizza in its box. "Dr. Bailey advised us. You know he did."

"And in the end he was wrong," I tell her.

She shakes her head. "Look what happened when you found out who she was. You vanished off on her trail."

"It was the right thing to do. And I'm back now."

Mum nods. She wipes her hands on a napkin. "And you're not the same as when you left."

"*Mum.*" This is from Elliot, who otherwise has been unusually quiet during the conversation.

Impatiently, I say to her, "How exactly am I different?"

Looking directly at me, she says softly, "Only in the way you should be. The kind that means I know I'll have to learn to let you go a little."

Which makes me cry all over again. As she hugs me, and I feel the slick of my tears between our cheeks and inhale the scent of her, but breathe in her love even more deeply, I think: *a heartfelt truth.* Not from me, yet. But still . . .

Later, after Elliot's taken the pizza boxes off to the trash, I tell Mum I'm ready to be scanned.

They all come with me. As the elevator door opens and we step out into the corridor that leads to the scanning suite, I realize I'm nervous.

Because I'm thinking of the episode in the park, by the woods, and the one by the reservoir, and of what happened in O'Neill's, when I collapsed.

Dr. Monzales is waiting. "Rosa!" He's smiling. I'm sure Mum and Dad have told him everything. But he doesn't look angry. As always, his white shirt is immaculately pressed.

He leads me in, and when I'm settled in one of the black leather armchairs, he slips an EEG cap over my scalp. Next, I'm taken to another room for an MRI scan. I lie there, very still, trying to hold on to the happiness I just felt in my room, and not to listen to the throb of the machine.

When, an hour later, I'm told everything's normal, at first I feel more anxious.

Because all those faints, those visions—they weren't normal. Were they?

But then I think, *Perhaps Elliot isn't entirely right.*

Perhaps a part of Sylvia really does remain with me.

37.

THE DAY OF my return to the hospital is a Monday.

For the rest of the week, I decide to do whatever Mum and Dad and Dr. Monzales want.

So I eat "re-nutritive" meals on a schedule drawn up by the dietitian. I rest in my room with trashy websites and photos posted on Instagram by AikaA, my friend in Tokyo (*What are cats reallllly thinking in these clothes?*), and on beanbags in the rec room. I don't complain when Dmitri spits out a piece of half-eaten chocolate over Super Big Boggle.

"What the fuck is that?" he demands of Jess, who just gave it to him.

"Chili chocolate!" she says. "I don't appreciate the reaction!"

"I don't appreciate being given something that tastes like a snake has ejaculated into it!"

I only smile.

I even accept an apology from Jared.

He finds me in my room. Hovering in the doorway, he says, "I knew that guy from the park. I thought maybe he'd talked you into going off with him for some kind of story, or something. That's why I told the doctors, when they asked. Sorry if that just made more trouble."

"Yeah. It's okay," I tell him.

"I was trying to look out for you."

"Thank you."

"So, he took you—what? Like, for a weekend away?"

"Not really. Look, I'm kind of in the middle of something—"

"Oh. Sure." Halfway through turning to go, he stops. "*Me Before You*'s showing at movie night tomorrow . . ."

"*Me Before You*? I wouldn't have thought you'd want to see something like that."

He shrugs. Looking a little embarrassed, he says, "Yeah, actually, there are sides to me I don't show everyone."

Maybe I've been too harsh on Jared. If anyone knows what it's like to have sides . . . "A friendly night out? And by *out* I mean *in*? Not a date?"

He hesitates. Nods.

"I'll bring the M&M's," I tell him, and he smiles.

I have more scans. All are normal.

On Wednesday, I meet Dr. Monzales in his office. My discharge date will have to be delayed perhaps by another month, he tells me. There is "some red tape, some necessary discussions with the head of public relations—that kind of thing."

True or not true? I don't know. Perhaps this has more to do with Sylvia's father finding me in the park than PR discussions.

"Now," Dr. Monzales says, "before you go, Rosa, I have something for you."

He spins his chair so he's facing the shelves behind his desk. From a cardboard box nestled between a framed American Medical Association certificate and a metal brain on a little stand, which I guess is some kind of trophy, he takes a much smaller, dark blue box.

He passes it to me. I open it. Resting on blue velvet is a pea-size chunk of gray rock encapsulated in an acrylic sphere, on a chain.

"Thank you," I say, uncertain.

"It's a piece of the Moon," he explains. "Your own piece of the Moon. For my pioneer. Let me help you."

He gets up, comes over, lifts it from the box, and carefully secures it around my neck.

A piece of the Moon . . . I don't believe in amulets, but maybe this is something like one.

"Thank you," I repeat. This time, it's an awed kind of whisper.

He nods.

Then, when I'm at the door, my fingers on the smooth, cool sphere, he says, "Oh, there's something else I need to ask you."

My heart sinks. I think, *Please don't ask me more about Sylvia or Lexington.*

"The anti-epileptic you are on is a relatively new drug," he says. "As occasionally happens, even after extensive trials, reports have been coming in of some rare side effects. A very small proportion of recipients are reporting hallucinations. And there have been blackouts. Have you experienced anything unusual?"

". . . Maybe," I say. "Yeah."

"*Yes?* Okay—I will change it. Immediately. We have an excellent alternative. You know, Rosa, you can always tell me—in fact you should always tell me of any problems, *any* at all. If you are willing, can you describe to me what you felt?"

"I've just felt faint sometimes," I say, because I don't want to tell him about the freezing, or the blackouts. He'd wonder, quite reasonably, why I hadn't already informed him. "Yeah, I'd like another drug."

He nods. "Of course."

I should be glad, I guess, that those fainting episodes were due to my drug. But I'm not.

I'm not sure, though, that I'm quite ready to think about why not. And in any case, my mind is jumping. Dr. Monzales's mention of side effects is triggering something else: a recollection of a time with Joe.

Side effects of hanging out with you . . .

I'm trying very hard not to think about Joe.

But every moment my brain idles, Joe's there. Every night, as I fall asleep, his voice is in my head, his hands are on my body, and I relive in slow motion every moment of our conversation outside O'Neill's.

I need to see him, to talk in person.

But I promised myself I'd sort things out with Mum and Dad first. They deserve that.

I do need to see him.

But there's someone else I really need to see first.

38.

I SEND A letter to his home address, because I don't know how else to reach him. I think, *Keep it simple; save the theoretical discussion for the theoretical meeting.*

I write:

Dear Mr. Johnson,

My parents and doctors don't know I'm contacting you.

I think we should meet, and talk. I don't know what you're thinking but this is what I'm thinking: I'm not your daughter, and I think I need to focus on my life, but it must be so hard for you to know her body is out there. I'm sure that's why you came to the hospital, and I'm sorry how that turned out.

I know there's a legal agreement, but it's far more important to me to try to sort out the situation between us than to stick to something

we both signed before the surgery even happened. I am so truly grate-
ful that you consented to the surgery. If you think it might be possible
to meet, text a time and place to:

And I give Elliot's number.

Elliot promised not to tell Mum and Dad on one condition: that if I do meet Sylvia's father, he'll go with me. But if her dad does agree, I wouldn't want to go alone, in any case. I'd want Elliot there.

Two days after I mail the letter, Elliot finds me in the rec room exchanging messages with AikaA about Mum and Dad's plan to relocate us to Scotland. (So—though I don't tell her this—I can build a new life away from people who knew me as I was). Since AikaA lives in Tokyo, I wouldn't have expected her to know much about the place, but she writes: *I LOVE Scotland so much!!*

Elliot passes me his phone.

I could come. Or could you possibly get to the Trinity Hospice, in Hartford? My wife is unfortunately unable to leave. Do you feel you could meet her, too? We'll be there. Any day, any time.

Elliot calls Dad to ask if he can borrow the car to drive to New York to visit Aula (he hasn't told them, apparently, about Aula's other boyfriend, or their breakup). He also tells Dad that he wants to take me. He guarantees that I'll be safe. Mum would argue, of course, but does she really need to know?

We'll drive, I'll meet Aula, we'll come straight back . . . Dad, to my surprise, agrees.

Less than twenty minutes after showing me the message, Elliot leaves to pick up the car. Only half an hour after that, my phone vibrates. I dash out through the gym and the park, and around to where the ambulances pull in, through a rainstorm, to join him.

It's the first time I've been in this car—Mum and Dad's American car. Given his dress sense, and yes, his beard, Dad might look like the least likely purchaser of a Dodge Charger, but that's what they have. It's deep red with black leather seats.

Another car-related surprise: Elliot drives excessively cautiously. Maybe it's because of the rain, which is falling even harder as we clear Boston. Cars stream past us on the highway, one after the other. The windshield wipers sweep back and forth like a hypnotist's watch. When I wake, we are passing through a little town, and the rain is still falling. The homes and stores are faint in the murky gray. Nature might be attempting to obliterate the work of people, but it's failing. If I were a god, I'd blow the rainclouds away. But all I can do is suffer them, stifled in the car, subjected to Elliot's random song list from his phone. (Only once do I object: "Not Elle King," I tell him.)

In fact, for virtually the entire two-hour journey, we don't talk. The only significant question he asks me is this: "Where did you get that necklace?"

I explain.

"Are you *sure* it's a piece of the Moon? It looks like a bit of that gravel by the gym door."

"It does not."

"You *are* kind of gullible sometimes, Rosa. Has anyone told you that?"

Gullible? I think: *What about Aula and the fact that you didn't know about her other boyfriend?* Nothing in the world would ever make me say it.

"Put it in your essay," I say instead.

At last, I spot HARTFORD on a road sign.

The GPS guides us through the darkness, around a cluster of skyscrapers, into a suburb of huge colonial-style homes, and ultimately to a modern, sprawling, white building that reminds me of the American country clubs I've seen on TV. It has a long, immaculate drive and an oversize porch, with TRINITY HOSPICE glowing in electric blue above the glass doors. As we drive past, we both see a sign: ALL VISITORS PARK AT REAR.

So Elliot drives on and into a near-empty parking lot. The rain has stopped, I realize. The sky is black. Cloudy. No stars.

I get out, into the damp. As Elliot locks the car, I make for a path that looks like it'll take us back to the entrance. I can't see any doors here, but there is a floor-to-ceiling window. Through it, I make out a darkened room: white pendant lights, switched off; pale marble walls; wood tables.

Elliot joins me. He pulls his jacket on over one of his apparently endless collection of obscurely worded T-shirts (this one might be in Icelandic, judging by the rune-type characters). "You sure about this?" he says.

Which makes me remember asking Joe if he'd take me to the reservoir, and him asking if I was sure. . . Joe. I can't think about him right now.

"Yeah," I tell him.

He says, "You do realize this has the potential to go very badly . . . and you don't *have* to do this."

I'm a little surprised. "You agreed to bring me."

He nods.

"You showed me the message."

"I wouldn't lie to you," he says. "And not showing you that message would have been a kind of lie."

"A big lie."

He nods.

"We've come all this way," I tell him.

"And you realize there's such a thing as the sunk cost fallacy?"

I can't wish Elliot were any different, because I love being with him more than practically anybody else, but there are times . . . "I guess I don't. And I *have* to see him."

He shakes his head. "I thought maybe halfway here you'd change your mind."

"Why?"

He rubs a hand through his patchy beard. "Because I would've. I'd have thought: fuck them; they signed the paperwork—it's my body now."

"This isn't really about them."

"If you're after absolution . . ."

"I don't want absolution."

"What do you want?"

Silence. Except for a siren in the distance and the drip of water from a gutter somewhere. The breeze is chilling me down to my bones. I want to break this moment, and I think: *heartfelt truth.* "I don't know. I want what anyone wants. For things to be okay . . . to find peace."

He says softly, "I hate to break this to you, Rosa, but I'm not so sure there's such a thing." He doesn't sound like he's trying to be coolly cynical. He sounds earnest.

"I hope there is," I tell him.

I continue along the path and around to the front of the hospice. Elliot follows. As the double-height glass doors part before me, I know that this is absolutely what I have to do, and I sense a strength in my core. Confidence, I guess. Which I've never felt before, at least not deep down.

Maybe Elliot's right about something he told me: If you just begin *acting* like the kind of person you'd like to be, you start to become her.

"It is a little late for visitors," the nurse says when we give Mrs. Johnson's name.

She's stationed behind a glass-front waterfall-effect desk in the reception area, peering up at me through black-rimmed glasses and exuding about the same aura of welcome as an MRI machine.

"We've come from Boston," Elliot tells her, in a pseudo-professional voice I hardly ever hear him turn on. "Her husband said he'd meet us here."

"Are you family?"

I nod, cautiously. This is Hartford. There's no reason for her to recognize Sylvia. Unless she's seen a photograph. "My name's Rosa Marchant."

She sighs. One of those people who gets frustrated when she actually has to do her job. But I'll take frustration. It strongly suggests she doesn't recognize my face.

"Okay. You can take a seat. I'll see what I can do."

"Maybe you could find Mr. Johnson?" Elliot says, dropping the voice already. "Is that something you could do?"

With a weary expression, she points toward a line of blue molded plastic chairs.

Elliot bristles, but I don't want an argument. Not here.

He lets me pull him over to sit down. I wonder if the turquoise blue color is designed to fit with what appears to be a water theme. There's the desk, and one wall is filled with a blown-up photograph of a lake with birds—maybe herons—flying away over it. I'm not entirely sure what it's meant to represent. Hope? The future? A joyful journey to a final horizon?

At last, the nurse gets up from whatever she was doing or pretending to be doing and heads off down a corridor that runs back behind her desk. I wouldn't have known unless I was watching. Whatever the soles of her shoes are made of, they're soundless on the polished floor.

"We can still decide to go back," Elliot offers.

I shake my head.

"Stubborn, too," he says. "I'll put that in my essay."

I elbow him.

"And *violent.*"

"And incredibly thorough," I say, "when it comes to retribution for insults."

He smiles.

"Thank you for waiting."

We both jump. Neither of us heard her. But the nurse is standing back by her desk.

"If you could come with me, I'll take you to the family room. Mr. Johnson will join you there."

"Excellent," Elliot says, in a return to the voice.

She leads the way.

I follow, Elliot right beside me.

I try not to think.

I try not to feel.

39.

THE FAMILY ROOM is windowless. Blue chairs are arranged along the walls, which are decorated with framed prints of deserted beaches. There's a low coffee table neatly piled with home decor and food magazines. A few plastic toys in a wicker basket. A vending machine stocked with bags of Hershey's kisses, Snickers bars, and a whole assortment of sweets—including Nerds.

Elliot and I are alone. The LED lights are stark, shameless. I feel exposed. Because I am.

The door opens—

My heart rocks.

He's in jeans and a plain navy sweatshirt. He has shaved. Cut his hair. But his cheekbones are the same, and his eyes are still haunted. And I know absolutely that Sylvia lives on in him, not me.

We stare at each other.

And stare.

The last time I saw him, he was in shadows, in the woods. In the revelation of light, I realize we have the same slightly upturned nose and narrow lips. His eyes are blue, his skin fair. Sylvia's coloring—her dark eyes, olive skin, and brown-black hair—must have come from her mother.

My gaze is still fixed intently on his face. His seems ready to flinch, but doesn't. The way he looks at me, it's as though he's afraid that if he moves, I will vanish, like—to borrow from the theme—a reflection threatened by wind over water.

The nurse says from behind him, "If you need anything, I'll be at the front desk."

It's Elliot who closes the door. He says, "This is my sister, Rosa."

". . . Rosa." Her father's voice is deep, breaking.

He doesn't move. I can tell he wants to touch me, but knows he can't. He looks stunned. If I don't move or speak, perhaps for him I *am* his daughter.

And I am not. So before we talk about anything, he has to know exactly who I am.

"I'm Rosa Marchant," I tell him. "I'm eighteen. I got my

first symptoms at seven. This is my brother, Elliot. I grew up in London. I've never been fishing. I'm not really talented at anything. I never risked my life to save someone else. I didn't deserve this." I spread my arms. "She didn't deserve it. I'm sorry."

I can feel Elliot's gaze hard on my face. But this concerns Sylvia's dad—and me.

Her father hunches over a little. He backs up, so he's supported by the wall. Rubs a hand over his face. Tries to compose himself, I guess, to the extent that it's possible. His arms drop and he looks at me with tears in his eyes.

"You're eighteen," he says, his voice low. "You got symptoms at seven. You deserved another chance. You look . . ."

"I know," I whisper. "It must be so weird for you."

"You came to the hospital," Elliot puts in, accusingly.

Sylvia's dad's gaze flickers. "Yeah . . ." He shakes his head. "I'm sorry. I shouldn't have done it. A friend, she reached out to a nurse who was at the meeting when we signed. She was going to look after Sylvia. When we heard you'd moved into the rehab facility, my friend offered to wait in the park, in case you came out with the other patients. When she saw you . . ." He hesitates. "I shouldn't have gone. I wasn't going to. I only wanted to see you. Just for a minute. I didn't even mean for you to see me."

"It's okay."

"I don't think it's okay. And coming after you . . . If it were my daughter, I don't know—I probably would have had me arrested. The doctors told me it was you who didn't want to involve the police."

He blinks suddenly at the lights, the walls, and the chairs, as though realizing for the first time that he's physically inside a room rather than suspended somewhere, isolated in our conversation.

Then he rubs his face again. "The doctor told me you picked up my wallet from the park. He said you said I dropped it when I ran . . . So I guess the guy in the hoodie was you?" He glances at Elliot.

"Not me."

He nods slowly. To me: "But you do *want* to meet us . . . ?"

So many whys. I think: *Focus on the most important.* "I want everything to be okay. I don't want to live anymore thinking you're out there and not knowing what you're thinking and wondering if you're wishing you'd never said yes."

He swallows. "You know, I look at you and it's a miracle. For you. I know: Sylvia is gone. There was nothing we could do to bring her back. But we could save someone else. Two lives. When she went out on the ice, she saved *two* lives. How many people get to do that?"

Tears spark at my eyes. I don't even try to stop them.

"She'd have wanted this," he says intently. "At first, truthfully, *I* wasn't sure. It was my wife who persuaded me. Sylvia would've wanted it. And if we couldn't bring her back, we could honor who she was."

"You could have donated her organs," I hear myself saying. "And still buried your daughter."

He looks a little surprised. "Yeah, we could have donated her organs. We thought about that. The truth is . . ." He pauses. "I have a nephew. He's seven now. The only reason he's still here is because someone did something for him that no one else could. He was four when he got very sick. My sister—none of us could get all the money for the treatment he needed. She did some barbecues and yard sales to try to raise money. Someone, we still don't know who, heard about it. One morning, she got a call from a lawyer, asking if she'd be willing to accept a donation. At first, she thought she was hallucinating it, from all the sleeping pills. When a doctor came to tell us about you, and they told us that surgery like this was your only hope, it was my wife who said, this is what we *have* to do. And we did bury her. We did bury Sylvia. I know rationally, consciously, that if you're going to donate organs, an entire body is not different in kind. I thought, if we don't save you, what are we saying? Let this girl die?"

He wipes his eyes with his hands, dries them on his jeans. "It was the doctors who said it was better to do this essentially anonymously. And we agreed. I know your parents thought it was better, too. Anyway, I read a lot and I thought a lot about how to think of you. I decided maybe I could think of you like her cousin. Now that I've met you, I think maybe I *could* see you that way. Not like you're *my* family. Just that you're like her in some ways, but not her. I mean, you look like her, but I don't look at you now and think: That is Sylvia. You don't move like her. Your voice is similar, but it's not exactly the same. Your eyes: I look in them and, thank God, I see somebody else."

He shakes his head, dismissing inner doubts, perhaps. Then he goes on: "After I got your message, I thought a lot about what to say to you. In the end, it comes down to this: It was a gift of life. I want what's best for you. For all our sakes, I think maybe it's better if we don't see each other again. But you owe us nothing. I'd like you to know that."

I think of the fact of my existence. The breaking of the mesmeric spell. My metamorphosis. My night with Joe. "I owe you everything."

"No, because it was given freely and absolutely. You owe us nothing, and it's very important to me you don't think that you do." He hesitates. "My wife had a second stroke. People say to me: what bad luck. First you lose your daughter. Then you lose your wife. And there's nothing I can say to that. Because it's true. Bad luck—that's what it was. There was no meaning in any of it or any real silver lining for me. But at least we made something out of it for you."

Silence. Except for the lights humming, the hidden electricity animating the room.

"Is there somewhere we can go and get coffee?" I ask him.

It's abrupt, I know, after what he just said. But I feel like ours is a relationship in which we've ditched the pawns and gone straight to the queens.

"Coffee?"

I nod. "If it'd be too weird . . ."

"No, it's okay. Coffee? Yeah, there's a café, sure."

It's totally dark, and uncomfortably close to bitterly cold, but we take our mugs out to the rear parking lot.

Elliot is watching us from inside, from a table by the window. I asked if he'd wait in the car, but he said no, how could he live with himself if Sylvia's father had a breakdown and abducted me—this with her dad standing there with us, in the empty café.

"He doesn't mean it," I said to her dad.

"I absolutely do mean it," Elliot said.

"Is it all closed?" I asked. "I can't see anyone . . ."

"We can go around," her dad said, too emotionally struck, I think, to get into anything unnecessary with Elliot, including any type of conversation. "I'll get it. What kind?"

"Any," I said.

He opened a hatch by the register and flicked a switch, illuminating a couple of white pendant lights. He went over to a machine, grabbed two mugs, pressed buttons, and returned with a couple of half-pints of liquid the same not-quite-black as the sky.

"Did you—" he started to say to Elliot, but I interrupted him.

"Elliot can help himself. He's fine if we go outside and talk. He'll be able to see us through the window."

I watched Elliot closely the entire time I was speaking, willing him to obey like I was some kind of Jedi. And Elliot, as he did back in the gym a lifetime ago, allowed himself to be willed.

So now here we are, Sylvia's father and I, in the cold, under the clouds.

The air was damp earlier, but the wind's picked up. It seems to have swept away all the moisture. Even from my body. My mouth feels as dry as the air.

I sip the scalding coffee, which doesn't help. I watch vapor rise from the surface and vanish. Where we're standing, the glare from the parking lot lampposts is not strong. I can see him and he can see me, but this is much less overwhelming than being in the family room. He looks tired, I decide. But wired. I understand. Since he hasn't had a chance to drink any of the coffee yet, this must be because of me.

Another sip. "I went to Lexington," I tell him, and I see that this is news to him. Althea obviously hasn't called him. "I had a wig. And glasses. And I had this list in my mind."

"A wig?"

"Yeah. I had this list. Kind or unkind? Loves? Hates? Happy or unhappy? Hopes and dreams? I thought if I could get some answers, maybe it would help."

"How?" he asks.

Isn't it obvious? "Help me understand who I am. Because I have her body."

He looks at me with an expression that says there's something crucial I'm failing to understand. "Rosa—she's gone."

I nod. "I know. I just thought—"

"So if I talk to you about who she was, will that influence you?"

"It might influence my ability to make peace with her."

"You are not at war."

"No, I know, but . . ."

"But?"

I squeeze my eyes shut.

He says, "You know, I was the one who thought at first: Are they *insane*? They're asking if our daughter's body could be resurrected? Like, I don't know . . . like a Buddhist reincarnation. Another girl, reincarnated in her. Because that's what this is. A man-made miracle of rebirth."

My eyes open. I stare at him. "Yeah."

"And a part of me *did* think maybe this would be a way to keep her, to hold on to her just a little. That maybe whoever the girl was who got her body, maybe she'd take on something of Sylvia, and Sylvia wouldn't be entirely gone." He shakes his head. "Look, I don't believe in souls. But I know it's not unnatural to think like that. However, what *you* have is a collection of cells, of skin and bone and flesh and nerves, and at some point in time before now they happened to be in a constellation that made up my daughter's body—her physical vehicle, not her."

"You sound like Elliot," I say quietly.

"Your brother? Then he talks a lot of sense. Look, I said before there was one thing I wanted to tell you. Actually, there's also something I'd like to ask you. Not that I have the right to ask you anything."

"You can ask me anything."

Silence. I'm not sure if he's reconsidering or composing himself. He swallows. Clears his throat. Waits until I meet his gaze, his eyes and mine interlocked.

Then he says, "We loved our daughter very much. I hope she knew it. Do whatever you want. Never think of us again, or even Sylvia. Do what you want with this body. But love yourself."

I stare at him.

The world stops spinning.

And in that absence of motion, my remaining confusion stills and falls away. Suddenly, everything seems clear, though not in the way I think I expected it might. *Do what you want.*

Now tears spill out of me, but honestly, I think they're mostly tears of relief.

Sylvia is gone.

Those episodes were side effects of my meds. Hallucinations.

This body is not her.

I have lost whatever I had of her.

And if she is totally gone, it really is up to me what I do.

He takes a sip of coffee. "This really is bad," he says. "You think it's burned?"

He's asking me about coffee. *Sylvia's dad.* I welcome the

normality of this. I really do. But I'm not quite ready to get away from the profound.

"Actually, there's something I think I have to do, and I want to tell you. You won't like it, but you said . . ." I stop, and refocus. "It's a big thing."

A big thing. Ugly and utterly inappropriately everyday words for an atom bomb of an action. But I know it's my actions now, not my words, that will matter.

Astonishingly, a trace of a smile breaks through the exhaustion on his face. "Bigger than the miracle of you standing here in a different body, drinking coffee with me?"

I think for a moment. "Not quite bigger than that," I say.

40.

UNSURPRISINGLY, MUM IS mad when she hears about the trip to Hartford. She's angry with me, with Elliot, with Dad.

"It's all right," I tell Mum. "Her dad and I agreed we wouldn't see each other again."

"*You*," she says, eyeing Elliot as we stand together in my room. "If you weren't going back to London tonight anyway, I'd be hustling you onto a plane."

Elliot's strength is special, I think. To me, he's like a flame that cannot be blown out. It takes an awful lot for him even to flicker. Totally unruffled, he says to me, "Call if you need me, okay? Uni's got kind of used to me asking for time off. I guess I should get around to telling them you're not actually dying anymore, but the leeway it gives me is definitely helpful."

Mum says, "*Elliot!*"

I only smile.

"Doesn't that upset you?" Mum says to me. "Elliot, I know you meant it as some kind of joke, but there is a *line.*"

I shake my head.

"Perhaps I should ask Dr. Bailey to talk to you," Mum says to Elliot.

"I'm sure Dr. Bailey's far too busy writing up his notes about Rosa," Elliot says. "After this is all made public, he won't get out of bed for anyone less than Oprah."

Dr. Bailey, by the way, has not tried to coax me back.

I've seen him twice. Once, in a corridor, he gave me a quick smile. The second time was in Les Baguettes. I pretended to be studying the fruit selection while out of the corner of my eye watching him select a croissant.

He turned to me. "Good choice. I only eat these so when I have a decent one someplace else, I can appreciate just how delicious it is."

"I have had better croissants," I told him, smiling a little.

"I've had better everything," he said, turned away, stopped, looked back. "That could be misconstrued." He frowned. "I meant in food terms, right? I wouldn't want there to be even the chance of a misunderstanding. You were a wonderful patient. I wish you everything you deserve out of life."

I had to swallow to stop myself from crying. He wasn't visibly affected. But then, he is more emotionally controlled than I am.

Things that *I am* . . .

The fact is—and I realize this might sound strange—I've been making a list. So far, I've noticed, a lot of the items are in the negative.

I am not regretful about going to Hartford to meet Sylvia's father and to sit down by the bed of her unconscious—but not entirely unresponsive—mother, though my own mother seems to think I should be.

I do not want to live in Scotland. Nothing against Scotland as a place—I can totally understand why most people would love it—but it has no meaning for me.

I am not the kind of person who will be pushed into a decision.

I am the kind of person who can make important decisions and stick to them.

I've been thinking a lot about that conversation with Sylvia's dad over the hospice coffee, and also about something Elliot said in our dark room: *Don't listen to Mum or Dr. Monzales. You have to make up your own mind about what you want.*

When I think about what I want to do now, I jump to the second half of my second list—that one that went *Mum and*

Dad and then *Sylvia*. There are two remaining items: *Joe* and then *Me*.

No matter how much I worry about and, yes, even dread the decision I've made—and what it'll do to my family—I *have* to do what's right for me. I guess loving yourself doesn't always necessarily involve making the people you love happy, though it would be nice if the two were aligned.

This decision of mine is what brings me to now: walking out into a somber, gray afternoon in the park.

41.

THE PHONE CALL I made to the Happy Haven Motel ranks very high on the list of memories that make me shrivel up inside.

Others on the list: making up stories about myself—pretending to be this girl who wasn't sick. Telling Brandon I was a singer. Allowing him to write his number on my arm. Lying to Sylvia's best friend.

But I'm not sure any of that *quite* reaches the same low as the deception I practiced with Joe.

When I phoned him, I was slumped on that pine chair in the kitchen of the woman who helped me. My head was a mess. But I had to let him know I was okay.

". . . Hello?"

He sounded as though I'd woken him.

"Joe?"

"Rosa?"

There was a pause. Maybe he was trying to make sense of my voice on the line. The last time he saw me, I was beside him in bed.

"Where are you?" he said.

"I just called Elliot. My brother. I'm in this house."

"What house? *Where?*"

I was sobbing again. I pressed at my eyes with the towel. "Joe, I'm sorry, I—"

"What house? Are you okay?"

"Yeah. I called Elliot. He's coming to get me."

Silence.

"Joe—"

"Look, Rosa, if you think you made a mistake . . ."

"I've made a *lot* of mistakes." I lowered the phone a little while I tried to regain control of my breathing. I was about to say, *But not you.*

I didn't get a chance to, though, because I paused too long, and he said, his voice very low: "I'm sorry you feel that way. What house? Are you safe?"

"Yeah, but—"

"It's okay, Rosa," he said, though he didn't sound like it was. "Will your brother look after you?"

". . . Yes."

"If you decide you want to talk to me sometime, you know where to find me."

And the line went dead.

I called back. He didn't answer.

Why didn't I have his cell phone number?

I slept with him. And then I walked out. That's what I did. I might have had my reasons. But he doesn't know what they are.

I was focusing not on him, but on me.

And I thought I was strong.

But the girl who inspected herself in the window of her pre-op room that snowy late afternoon last spring has changed so much, in ways that go deep below the flesh.

I check the time on my phone. Ten minutes to go till Joe's due. The park is empty. The colors have faded; winter is on its way. I can't even see any tourist boats out today. Or nurses with noodle boxes. Or orderlies on break. Or Joe.

But there are nine minutes yet until he agreed to meet.

I sit on the bench inscribed in memory of Denise, and check my phone. I have a signal. I must be far enough away from the ER to be clear of the blockers.

I'm not thinking about what I'll say to Joe, because I've

already decided that whatever I think I'll say will probably change in the moment. My only rule for myself is heartfelt truth.

After that, if there is an "after that" for us, I'll ask for his help with what I have to do next.

My phone vibrates. I'm in such a scramble to check it that I almost drop it.

A text message from Elliot: *Eating a Greggs vanilla slice. What you up to?*

I reply: *Wishing I was eating one.*

He texts: *Their custardy goodness isn't as good as you remember.*

Which might make me wish for one even more . . . but doesn't.

Again, my phone vibrates. This time, when I look at the screen, my heart seizes.

It's not from Elliot.

Caught up at office. Can't make it. Sorry.

Worst-case scenario?

I'm not going there.

I think, *Joe is thoughtful, determined, vulnerable . . . hurt.*

Back inside the gym, I find Vinnie and ask to borrow forty dollars. Raising an eyebrow, he says, "You've got a hospital account, right?"

I nod. "But this is for something I can't put on it. Please. Just this once. I won't tell anyone you lent me the money."

"It's not for anyone to buy alcohol or anything illegal, right?"

"It's not for *anything* illegal. I promise."

"I guess I shouldn't," he says. But he takes his wallet from a zip pocket in his track pants and hands over two twenties.

I look up the address for Bostonstream on my phone while hurrying to the cab stand by the main entrance. I don't know if anyone sees me, but I don't really care. After jumping in the back of the first cab in line, I read the address out, twice, to be sure the driver's got it, and the car pulls away.

I'm aware of—but I don't focus on—the fact that I'm out in the world, alone.

At this time of day, the traffic's light. We speed past the old naval yard buildings and on into the city. Just over fifteen minutes after leaving the hospital, we pull up outside a narrow office building only a few doors down from the burger place I went to with Joe.

There's nothing on the wall to advertise that Bostonstream's based here. I double-check my phone. This is the street number on the website.

As I walk in, I realize I have only ever once before felt more nervous.

The entrance area is decorated in faded tones of gray. There's a slightly musty smell. No desk. But on the wall by the front window, I spot a plastic sign listing the occupants of the six floors. A2 ACCOUNTANCY . . . JOHN L. BURROUGHS, ATTORNEY-AT-LAW . . . BOSTONSTREAM.

I take one of the two elevators to the third floor. As I walk out into a corridor, I'm confronted by poster-size screen grabs from the site. Headlines scream out at me: BOSTON'S SEXIEST BACHELORS! RED SOX TOP ODDS AT WINNING WORLD SERIES!

Over to the right is a frosted glass door with a buzzer and BOSTONSTREAM on a red plaque. Before I can move from my position in the corridor, the display by the second elevator shaft pings. A woman in her twenties—thin, very pretty, purple sweater with black skinny jeans, stiletto ankle boots, bright lipstick—walks out . . . with *Joe*.

She looks at me looking at Joe. And at Joe looking at me. Says to him, "I'll see you in the meeting." Then she strides off, leaving us together.

The last time I saw Joe, we were naked in bed. I knew this was bound to be awkward. I just really didn't want it to be.

He's in a dark gray shirt with sleeves rolled to the elbows and jeans, his satchel slung over his shoulder. He looks paler. Slightly less charged with energy, maybe. But still absolutely capable of freezing me in space and time. I take in the curve of his body, the pulse in his neck, the star tattoo.

"Hi," I say.

He sighs. "Look, Rosa—"

"I know, you're caught up at work. But I really need to talk to you."

Eyes on a spot on the wall beside me, he nods. "And you think I will reliably drop everything to do what you need."

This hurts. I want to say: *That's not true.* He *offered* to take me to Lexington.

"That's not—" I stop myself. How do I get past all of this?

At last, he looks me in the eyes. His gaze is so intense I have to force myself to hold it.

"You told me you'd made a lot of mistakes," he says. "Fair enough."

"But I was finding it hard to explain," I say, taking a step toward him. "And you didn't answer when I rang back. So I didn't get to say, *but not to do with you.*"

"You left while I was asleep."

I take another step so that I'm close enough to touch him. "You remember that conversation outside O'Neill's, when I said I feel right around you?"

"You think I'd forget that conversation? I told you something about me I've never told anyone. Except the police." He shakes his head.

"I said everything was complicated. I want to explain. Please."

"I told you: You don't need to explain anything."

"But I do. *Please.* You did everything for me. And it's really important to me I tell you the truth."

The elevator pings again.

Two men in jeans and hoodies step into the corridor. They nod at Joe. At the very last moment, he reaches back and slips a hand between the closing elevator doors.

He walks in, turns, looks at me. Holds out his hand to keep the doors where they are. "We can't talk in the corridor," he says.

While the elevator descends, we don't speak. He focuses on the numbers on the electronic display. It takes forever to reach two. A lifetime to one.

He's first out of the elevator and first outside. The sidewalk is crowded, just as it was when he brought me here for burgers. We weave between people with briefcases and take-out coffee, in suits, in tights and sneakers, in Lycra shorts and bicycle helmets.

It's starting to rain. English-style drizzle.

Across the street, by Boston Common, I notice a couple of benches. They're separated from a baseball diamond by black iron railings. Joe must see them, too. Without exchanging a word, we slip between slow-moving cars and sit down, me at one end of the bench . . . him at the other.

The world moves around us, subdued in the rain. Women

stop to fit plastic covers onto strollers. A man opening a golf umbrella almost takes out an old lady hobbling past with a terrier and a cane.

There's nothing I can do but sit here and get wet. It doesn't really matter. There is so much I want to tell Joe. But I didn't plan what to say, and I'm not sure where to start.

From behind us—from the baseball diamond, I guess—come yells from a bunch of kids.

I think of what Elliot told me back in that hotel in Lexington about who I am. If I want Joe to know the truth about me, I have to start somewhere.

"When I was a kid," I say, interlocking my fingers, holding my own hands, "I had this hamster called Cheeseball. I used to sew him outfits from my old clothes. When I was nine, I entered a picture of him wearing this cape decorated with sequins into a pet photo competition, and I won. I got a year's supply of this brand of crisps. Elliot said the cape was the lamest thing he'd ever seen. But I didn't care. One of the single happiest moments of my childhood was finding out that I'd won two hundred bags of crisps . . ." I sigh. "I'm sorry. I wanted to tell you the truth. About everything. Just, there were some things I had to do first."

At last, he looks at me. The rain's sticking his hair to his face. He pushes back the lock that falls over his eye. Oh, I want to touch him.

"When I said outside O'Neill's that I feel right with you, I meant it," I tell him. "And I haven't felt right for a really long time. And the problem is, you have no idea what I am."

His eyes narrow. No going back now. Just tell him. *Tell him.*

My voice wavering, I say, "You remember saying you could tell us apart—me and Sylvia Johnson?"

He's watching me very closely now. He nods.

This has the potential to go very badly. But I have no choice. And I don't mean because when the hospital breaks the news of the surgery, he'll realize—because if I follow through with my plan, that announcement won't happen—but because I have no choice but to come clean with him, if I'm the person I want to be.

My hands are clenched so tightly in my lap it almost hurts to separate them. I say, "You heard about that paralyzed man in China—the first human head transplant?"

He nods again, very slowly.

Deep breath. I can't say this if I'm looking at him. So I focus on the solid oak trees ahead of us, almost bare now, and dripping.

"I had a terminal nerve disease. The only way to save my life was to try either a head transplant or—" Tell him. *Tell him.* "So, my doctor had developed this procedure. Instead of transplanting the whole head, you transplant the brain. The recovery period is longer, but if it works, you have something that looks like it's normal."

The drizzle still falls. It's soaking my face, my hands, my hair.

Spell it out, I tell myself. *Don't leave him in any doubt.*

"I have her body. She was in an irreversible coma. Her parents donated it. What you are looking at—who you were with, what you slept with—is Sylvia Johnson's body."

Silence. It stretches. Then, from a thousand miles away, I hear shouts from the baseball diamond. The muffled roar of traffic on the street.

Joe still says nothing.

I glance at him. His expression is blank. Unreadable.

I twist away from him, so I'm sitting with my back flat against the bench. Everything slows. My heart. Time. I wonder if this heart was ever broken before. But it's almost okay. I hoped . . . Whatever I hoped, I also knew, deep down, it wasn't going to happen. Sylvia's dad might think I owe him nothing, but with something as monumental as this, of course there's a price to pay.

There was a time, I realize, when I was used to this feeling: the sinking weight of worst-case expectations confirmed. I guess I allowed myself to hope that time was past.

At last, with effort, I force myself up off the bench.

Joe asks quietly, "Where are you going?"

I swallow, hoping my voice won't break. "Back to the hospital."

Because if he can't accept this, I can't ask for his help.

I take a step away from the bench. A tear rolls down one cheek. Another step. A lot more tears.

Beneath the tears and the disappointment, I search for, and I *do* find, relief. I wanted to be the kind of person who would tell him. And I've told him.

A year ago, I thought no one could *ever* find out, or what would be the advantage of looking "normal"? Now I know better.

Besides, I think: *What did you expect him to say?*

If you lie and lie and lie, someone will catch you in the end, even if that someone is you.

My vision slipping out of focus, I start back across the road. To the sound of screaming horns, I reconnect with the sidewalk. I find myself among all these people heading home from work, or going to meet a friend for coffee, or searching for something nice for dinner. Whatever normal people do. I'm still crying, but it's raining. Everyone has an umbrella up or is hurrying along, neck bent. No one is looking at me.

I walk away from Joe's office, past the burger bar, with a huddle of people lining up outside, until I'm at the corner, and

I'm confronted with the statue of Poe. What would he have made of my life? *The Reincarnation of Rosa M.?* I don't want him. What I really want now is a cab.

I face the traffic, which is blurred by the rain. Taxis streak past, throwing up spray, occupied.

I should have brought an umbrella. The rain really is heavy now, and I'm soaked. I might want Joe but perhaps I don't need him. And he certainly doesn't need me.

That's what I'm telling myself—that we don't need each other—as I turn my back on Poe, thinking I'll walk along the streets in search of a taxi stand. But then someone is in my path, forcing me to look up, mouth open in surprise, but also perfectly ready, it turns out, to be kissed.

Joe's arm is around my back. His mouth is on mine. And it feels so much more intense, so much more vital, than it ever did in Lexington. Maybe because I know he, fully and truly, is kissing no one but *me*.

42.

I KISS JOE BACK.

My arms are around him. My body is pressed against his. Every place he's touching lights up.

He holds me tighter. I let my hand move to the back of his shoulder. Kissing him here on the street feels less like a way of merging identities than of losing identity; and for the moment, that is more than okay.

"You're shaking," he whispers.

"I'm *shivering*," I tell him. "I'm *soaking wet*."

He lets one hand drop to mine. Holds it.

He's so close. His shirt is drenched. Beneath the fabric, I can trace the cut-marble curves of his chest, of his shoulders.

I guess I don't need to tell him that I'm surprised he's here.

And that happiness is pulsing through me with every beat of my heart.

I say, "If you'd stayed away, I wouldn't have thought you were a bad person."

"That's not why I came after you."

He's left the way open. And I'm going there. I have nothing to lose now. "So why did you?"

"A lot of reasons."

His mouth is so close. His body is right here. I want to kiss him again. But I search his face. "Like?"

"Like I didn't want you to think I thought badly about you. You've got more courage than probably anyone I know . . . except maybe me."

There's a trace of a smile in his eyes, but if he's trying to loosen this conversation with a drop of levity, I won't let him—not yet. "I wasn't brave. If I wanted to live, I had no choice."

He squeezes my right hand and it's like he's palpitating my heart. Like resuscitation.

"Partly, I mean, in telling me," he says. "I took a life for what I think was the right reason. But you didn't *take* a life. You took something that would have gone to waste. You did it for the right reasons."

I grip his hand as tightly as I can. "And I didn't tell you. And I slept with you."

His smile cracks open. "Yes, you did."

"So it must seem horrible and really weird to you, because you have no idea what I actually look like?"

"You don't actually look like anything other than this."

"I wasn't pretty," I tell him. "I wasn't pretty at all."

He frowns. "There's nothing I can say to that that's sensible. Anyway, I told you: I don't think *pretty* is the right word. And I remember saying I could tell you and Sylvia apart." He shakes his head. "The only sensible thing is to take you completely as you are. I can't divide you into parts. I have met some very pretty girls. Some have even been interested in me. I didn't feel *anything* about them like I feel about you."

He smiles again—at my expression, I guess. Sunlight on sea. It warms me right through.

"So you are not completely freaked out?" Because I have to be sure.

"I don't think so."

"A lot of people would be completely freaked out."

"Maybe."

"A lot of people would think it's completely immoral and it's playing God, and—"

"I don't care what they'd think. A lot of people would think that about me."

For a few moments, we just stand there together, by Poe, under a sagging awning. Just two enamored kids taking shelter from the rain. Which shows what other people know. I think: *Perhaps he'll change his mind, but for now, absolutely, I will take this.*

Telling Joe the truth was, I think, the second biggest risk of my life.

I think: *I'm the kind of person who will take significant risks.*

We find soft leather armchairs in a café close by. The misted-up windows and stacks of paperbacks and board games on the shelves make it even cozier.

When we've got our drinks, the first thing I ask is if he isn't meant to be at a meeting.

"I should be at a meeting," he says, nodding. "I should also be in jail, or at home with Dad."

I say quietly, "You should be at home with your dad *and* mum. I should never have got sick. But here we are." I push the mint leaves in my mug around with my spoon and take a sip. It's the first time I've had mint tea made with fresh leaves, and it's a minor revelation. "The first time I met you, I thought you knew. I thought, he must be videoing everything and in five minutes I'll be all over the news."

"If you thought that, why didn't you walk away?"

"After I told you about the surgery, why didn't you go back to your office instead of coming after me? You could have taken your editor the story of the year. You still could."

His expression darkens. "Why would you even think I might do that? I wanted to help you, remember."

And I do want him to help me. But Joe's taken in a lot. I can wait another day for the favor I want to ask him. Right now I want to enjoy just being here, with him.

He frowns at my neck. "You weren't wearing that before. It's kind of unusual."

My hand darts up to my necklace. "My doctor gave it to me."

"Your doctor? It's a strange-looking stone."

"Actually, it's a bit of Moon rock."

"Are you serious?" His face softening, he reaches out to touch the acrylic sphere. "It came from the *Moon*," he repeats, his voice so low I can barely hear him. "When Neil Armstrong talked about what it was like to look back at Earth from the Moon, he said, 'I didn't feel like a giant. I felt very, very small.'"

"Your mother told you that?"

"I read it . . . in a book she gave me."

"To the stars." I touch his tattoo. "This is to do with her?"

"We come from the stars," he says. The expression in his eyes like none I've seen before, except for on that bench after O'Neill's. "When our sun ceases to exist, our atoms will be blasted into space. So maybe mine and hers will be together again someday."

"To the stars," I whisper.

He nods.

"What was it?" I ask him. "A hobby? Or was she a cosmologist?"

"Kind of in between. She volunteered at the California Academy of Sciences."

"I'd like to go there," I tell him.

He looks down, takes my hand, gently twists my fingers in his. "I'd like to take you. One day."

I stay sitting there, with Joe, not talking, waiting for him.

"So, I'm wondering something," he says.

I nod.

"Was there supposed to be a moral to the story about the hamster and the chips?"

I smile. I can't help it. I shake my head. "I was just trying to think of something true to tell you about me."

"Did you eat all the chips?"

"A lot of them. And I don't even really like crisps."

"So why did you eat them?"

"I guess . . . Elliot used to win things a lot. Academic things at school, anyway. This was my moment of triumph. So what if it was because of a sparkly hamster cape?"

He smiles. Then he glances away. I follow his gaze to a clock on the wall, by the board games.

"I don't want to go," he says. "But I should get back to the office. Someone's helping me with a story. A real one, about a center for immigrant kids."

I nod. "The beautiful woman from the lift?"

His smile returns. "If that would make you jealous, then yes . . . Actually, it's the editor. You'd better have my cell."

I find my phone, activate it, and enter the number he tells me. I'm halfway up out of the chair when he reaches for my hand. I sink back down.

His expression is intense, and I'm suddenly scared that, though he just gave me his number, he's realized he's actually *not* okay with who I am—or with me asking about his mother.

His face so close, he says, "Other side effects of hanging out with you: insomnia, due to recurrent recollections of a night in a motel in Lexington . . . the sensation of having been pulled up from under ice."

My heart melts, burns, implodes, does all kinds of medically impossible things.

"I guess we must be on the same drug," I whisper.

A smile—the deepest so far—warms the blue of his eyes. "Just so you know, I'd like to take as much as I can for as long as I can."

"Yeah," I say. "Me, too."

43.

THE RADIO'S ON. It's set to a channel in a language I can't understand, and I don't ask the taxi driver to change it because I'm happy tuning in to my thoughts.

As Boston's apartment blocks and stores streak past, blurred by rain on the windows, I'm thinking of Joe—*of course, of Joe*—and also Louise Brown.

The first IVF baby, born in 1978, her life has been devoured by the world's media ever since. Only recently, she revealed that her parents received blood-spattered hate mail after she was born.

If devoutly religious types believe *she's* an abomination . . . Well, I already have an idea of what they'd make of me.

But it makes no difference. I know what I have to do.

Wednesday.

3:24 A.M. I compose a text to Elliot: *Is there anything I could do that would make you not love me?* Then delete it.

I think about what he told me: *Don't listen to Mum or Dr. Monzales.* You *have to make up your own mind about what you want.*

10:30 A.M. There's a room off the gym designated as a break space for the rehab nurses. The door's often left ajar, and I've glimpsed a plain-walled space with a fridge, kettle, vending machine, and half a dozen uncomfortable-looking chairs.

Jane, I know, usually takes a break at ten thirty. Jane, I've also sussed out, is not that popular with the other nurses, so there's a reasonable chance I'll catch her by herself.

I knock, then go in without waiting. The thud of feet on treadmills, the scrape of the gait-training system, relatives' encouragements, and even Vinnie shouting "Move it!" are all silenced as I click the door shut.

There she is, her long brown hair down, entering a code into the vending machine keypad, alone.

She takes a heavy step to face me. "Rosa?"

A bar of something drops into the collection slot.

"I'm on a break. Do you need something?"

"I need to talk to you."

"Patients aren't—"

"I *need* to talk to you."

Whatever she just bought, she leaves it where it fell.

"You want to sit down?" she asks.

I shake my head.

I'm nervous. But I shouldn't be. "I came to tell you I heard you," I say, hoping my voice sounds stronger than it does in my head. "I woke up one night when you were praying over my bed."

She gives me a look that I know is meant to mean: *silly girl.* "Praying for someone is a good thing, Rosa. Prayers have a real power to heal."

"You weren't praying for me."

She looks wary. Folds her arms.

"I heard you. I should have said something, but I didn't." My blood's rushing. I wanted to keep calm, but it's not possible. "I heard what you said, about the disunion of the soul and asking God to bring peace to whatever I have."

"Peace is a wonderful thing, Rosa."

"You were praying that I'd die!"

"No—"

"I heard you."

"You were recovering from the surgery," she says firmly. "With all those meds, you could have imagined anything."

"I *heard* you." *Too shrill. Rein it in.* In a calmer tone, I say,

"And I know you're the nurse who passed on information to Sylvia Johnson's father."

Now she goes very pale.

"If you make a headache go away with a painkiller—isn't that unnatural?" I ask her.

"Rosa—"

"Agriculture—that's unnatural, too, right? Isn't that playing God?"

She shakes her head, as though *I'm* the unreasonable one.

"I know: Whatever I say, you won't get it. You shouldn't work here," I tell her. "You shouldn't be a nurse here."

"Who have you talked to?" Her voice is almost a whisper.

"No one yet. I've thought a lot about it. If I were the only patient you worked with, then maybe I'd keep it that way . . . but I'm not."

My heart's thudding so hard it's hurting.

But as I leave her and go back into the gym, and I'm surrounded by noise and kids and the blues of harbor and sky through the unscreened windows, the unpleasantness of confrontation transitions into a rush of achievement. And I *am* going to tell Dr. Monzales. Partly because while I'm the first of my kind, soon, I'm sure, there'll be others like me.

• • •

Midnight.

I'm lying in bed, staring at the ceiling, wide awake, thinking.

After lunch, I found Dr. Monzales in his office, and I told him about Jane.

"I am . . . stunned," he said. And he looked it. He promised there would be a full investigation, but for now she would be put on immediate suspension.

With that done, I'm ready to ask for Joe's help.

I can't put it off any longer.

I call him.

I hear ringing.

More ringing.

". . . Rosa?"

"Hi. Can you talk?"

There's a muffled shuffling. Maybe he's rolling over. Then a click. Perhaps of a lamp switch.

"What's wrong?" he asks.

His voice is slow. Still sleepy. I wish I were there with him.

"There's something I have to do," I say. "And I need your help. But it'll help you, too." I sit up halfway in the darkness and reach for a pillow from the floor to stuff behind my back.

"You don't need to help me," he says.

"Will you listen?"

". . . Yeah, of course."

For a long time after I outline my decision, Joe's silent. I even start to wonder if he's fallen back asleep. Then he says: "Right now, this might seem like the only way, but it isn't. You *do not* have to do it."

I sigh. "You won't help me?"

"Don't ask me, Rosa. You can't ask me."

"You *won't*?"

"I *can't*. So they might seem twisted sometimes, but I do have principles. I can't upend them for anyone, or I'm not who I am."

That sinking feeling drops right through me.

". . . Okay." I press the red circle on the phone and let it fall onto the duvet.

Twenty seconds later, it rings.

"Joe?"

"You hung up on me."

"Sorry . . . I was thinking. You can't help. I understand."

"I can't help directly. But if this is what you're sure you want to do, I've got a much better way of going about it."

"You do?"

"Believe me—it's the only quarter-sane way."

Thursday.

I leave my tray of porridge, coffee, and orange juice untouched.

I grab my jacket and slip out of my bedroom. As I pass the rec room, I notice Jared in there, on one of the beanbags, asleep.

I continue on, taking the route that's always led me to freedom—through the gym and into the park.

This early morning, it's cold. And murky. So dark, in fact, it's as though the sun hasn't risen. Through thick gloom, I watch the lights of an airplane as it rises up and right across my field of view, which makes me think of my first nights here at the hospital, and how desperate I was to be whisked away.

I remember Jane, and her lie about the mirrors. Jane catching me when I lost my balance in the park. Jane praying over me. Joe by the bench. Joe outside O'Neill's. Joe in my head, in my heart, in my bed.

I zip the jacket right up to my chin and make for the path that skirts the harbor wall.

In my pocket, I have what I need.

I picture Mum, Dad, Elliot—and I reject the *no* in the back of my mind. Because I have to bring resolution to Sylvia and me, and the fact is, I'm convinced there's only one way to do it. No one else, apart from perhaps Joe and Elliot, might understand, but this is *my* life, which Sylvia gave to me, and *I* believe it's the only rational thing to do.

I've experienced so much since I arrived in Boston. So many strange and supernaturally vivid moments. So I shouldn't feel too scared of the next step—and yet, I'm terrified. I think: *I am the kind of person who follows through even when she's terrified.*

• • •

My phone vibrates in my pocket. It's Joe. I accept the call.

"Hey," he says.

"Hey."

"Where are you?"

"In the park."

"It's not too late to change your mind."

"Yeah. It is."

The phone at my ear, the harbor to my left, I walk to the bench marked for Denise. It means something to me, so I'll do it here.

I sit down. Behind me, the hospital looms. I tuck my hair behind my ears. And I look out over the water, at the moored yachts and blocks of offices and apartments containing people who have no idea that *I—the kind of* I *that I am—*exist.

It's time, I think.

"I am a little scared," I confess into the phone.

Silence. Then he says, "So, there's this other quote I remember. Maybe not exactly. Hold on . . ." Twenty seconds later, he's back. "I found it. John Young, when asked if he felt nervous before he made the first space shuttle flight, in 1981, said, 'Anyone who sits on top of the largest hydrogen-oxygen fueled system in the world, knowing they're going to light the bottom, and doesn't get a little worried does not fully understand the situation.'"

"I guess I understand the situation."

"I guess you do."

My plan is to make the telling last as long as feels right.

After I record my story—from first symptoms right through to my new talking, walking self—onto my phone, I'll send the audio file to a list of email addresses that Joe compiled for me. There must be 150 names on it. Editors and deputy editors of news websites and blogs, newspapers and magazines around the world. I'll also send it to Althea Fernando, with a note apologizing for the awful lie I told her about being Sylvia's sister.

Would I have Sylvia's blessing to do this—to tell the world about us?

I don't know.

When I called Joe and woke him up at midnight, I asked *him* to write my story. If he did, he said, he'd be exploiting a personal relationship, which his ethics wouldn't allow. It would also draw the media spotlight to him, and inevitably to his parents, and he didn't want that.

It would make him famous, I said.

"I already told you I don't care about being famous," he said. "I care about being the kind of person I want to be."

I told him I cared, for myself, too—which was why I

couldn't change my mind. And if I didn't do it, I'd always be scared, waiting for the day someone finds out. And I'd *always* be pretending to be something I'm not.

From Denise's bench, I look off to my right, to the patch of now pretty sorry-looking trees, where Sylvia's father found me. I can't see anybody. Not there, or closer to the hospital, or by the harbor wall, or under the cedars. The football-playing doctors and the nurses with their noodle boxes will come later. Or maybe they won't come at all, partly because of the bad weather, but also because of what I'm about to do.

"You still there?" I say into my phone.

"Yeah," Joe says. "I've got the stills we took of you into one file. I'm going to email them to you. When you've finished recording, send everything out to the list. Don't forget to include the time of the video conference."

"I know, I won't."

"This should satisfy the ones who want the immediate story. But you *will* still be hounded. You're absolutely sure you don't want to talk to your doctor first, or your parents?"

"You're sure you don't want the exclusive?"

He doesn't answer. He knows I already know what he'd say.

"Anyway," I say, leaning back on the bench, eyes up on the dim sky, "you'll always have a backup story to sell. If you get desperate."

"Yeah, what's that?"

"My secret sex with Frankenstein's daughter."

Silence.

"That was meant to be a *joke*."

"But there will be nasty headlines," says a voice from behind me—not from my phone.

I twist my head around and slowly lower my phone from my ear.

I get up. *Joe*. He's in gray jeans and a black jacket, collar up, and he's striding from the direction of the main entrance.

I feel a smile spread right across my face.

"Okay?" he says. "I didn't think it was the greatest idea for you to do this alone."

I reach out. He's *here*. Now my arms are around him. His are around me. By Denise's bench, where we met. His warmth and solidity are a still-unfamiliar shock.

"There *will* be nasty headlines," he says again, this time with his lips close to my ear. "You'll have to try not to read them."

I nod into his neck.

"And after you're done, you have to go back inside to your room. You promise you'll stay there till we work out how bad the fallout is?"

I nod again. "I know the plan."

"I know how they work," he says, pulling back a little so

he can see my face. There's so much concern in his eyes that it hurts. "Some of them will be *merciless*. But if you give them everything you can now, it'll help them move on."

"Maybe there'll be a war somewhere," I say, as brightly as I can, hoping he knows I'm not serious.

He nods. "Maybe some celebrity will have a sex change. Maybe there'll be a new diet."

"So eventually, I'll slip into old news and every so often, someone will think: We should do a follow-up on that Frankenstein girl. And I'll be . . ." I look away. Down. At the grass, wet with the night's rain. Then out, past Joe's shoulder, at the harbor and the skyscrapers, which are beginning to take clearer shape through the gloom.

". . . You'll be what?" he says.

"I don't know." Deep breath. "Maybe somewhere with you." Silence.

At last, I let myself look at him. My heart's jumping, but he's smiling. By far the brightest light around is in his eyes.

From behind us, hidden by the hospital, comes the rattle of metal wheels across concrete. A delivery being pushed for unloading. A faint siren grows louder and louder. A gull flying overhead sounds its empty cry. I listen to all of this—the familiar noises of Dixon-Dudley Memorial—and to the throb of my pulse in my head.

"Ready?" Joe says.

I nod.

And so I sit back down on the bench. Joe sits beside me.

I reverse the direction of my phone's camera, so I'm looking at my face in the screen.

Even this dim light is overexposing my features. I don't see the girl in the picture in the article, squinting in the sun. Or the girl in a tight gray dress, microphone in hand, photographed during her *awesome gig*. And I don't see in my eyes who I used to be, either. Which seems right. We've both changed.

I don't know what's going to happen after I send off my story. I have no real idea where I'll be in a week, or a year.

But I'm going to try to become the person I want to be.

I'll also try to do what Sylvia's dad asked—love myself.

More than that, I'm determined to make the most of everything, for us both.

I lean against Joe and take a deep breath. My hand steady, my gaze focused on the screen of my phone, I start to speak.

ACKNOWLEDGMENTS

Thank you—

To Julia Churchill, my agent in the UK—without your help and support, this book wouldn't even exist. To James—your support and belief were crucial. To Allison Hellegers, my agent in the US, for your enthusiasm, and for knowing exactly who to go to with a flawed manuscript. Which brings me to Anne Heltzel. I'm extremely lucky to have you as my editor.

Thank you also to the staff and students at Lexington High School, and to Joe Douglas, my first teenage reader.